DEAR DEE

Sue Uden was born in 1946. She has had a diverse career including spells as a PA, a doctors' receptionist, a journalist for the John Lewis Partnership and teaching assistant in Primary School. Along the way she has published some freelance articles and short stories. *Dear Dee* is her first novel. She is married with two children and four grandchildren.

DEAR DEE

Sue Uden

DEAR DEE

*To Kim
with best wishes
Sue Uden*

Olympia Publishers
London

www.olympiapublishers.com
OLYMPIA PAPERBACK EDITION

Copyright © Sue Uden 2011

The right of Sue Uden to be identified as author of
this work has been asserted in accordance with sections 77 and 78 of
the Copyright, Designs and Patents Act 1988.

All Rights Reserved

No reproduction, copy or transmission of this publication
may be made without written permission.
No paragraph of this publication may be reproduced,
copied or transmitted save with the written permission of the publisher,
or in accordance with the provisions
of the Copyright Act 1956 (as amended).

Any person who commits any unauthorised act in relation to
this publication may be liable to criminal
prosecution and civil claims for damage.

A CIP catalogue record for this title is
available from the British Library.

ISBN: 978-1-84897-147-9

This is a work of fiction.
Names, characters, places and incidents originate from the writer's
imagination. Any resemblance to actual persons, living or dead, is
purely coincidental.

First Published in 2011

Olympia Publishers
60 Cannon Street
London
EC4N 6NP

Printed in Great Britain

For all my family

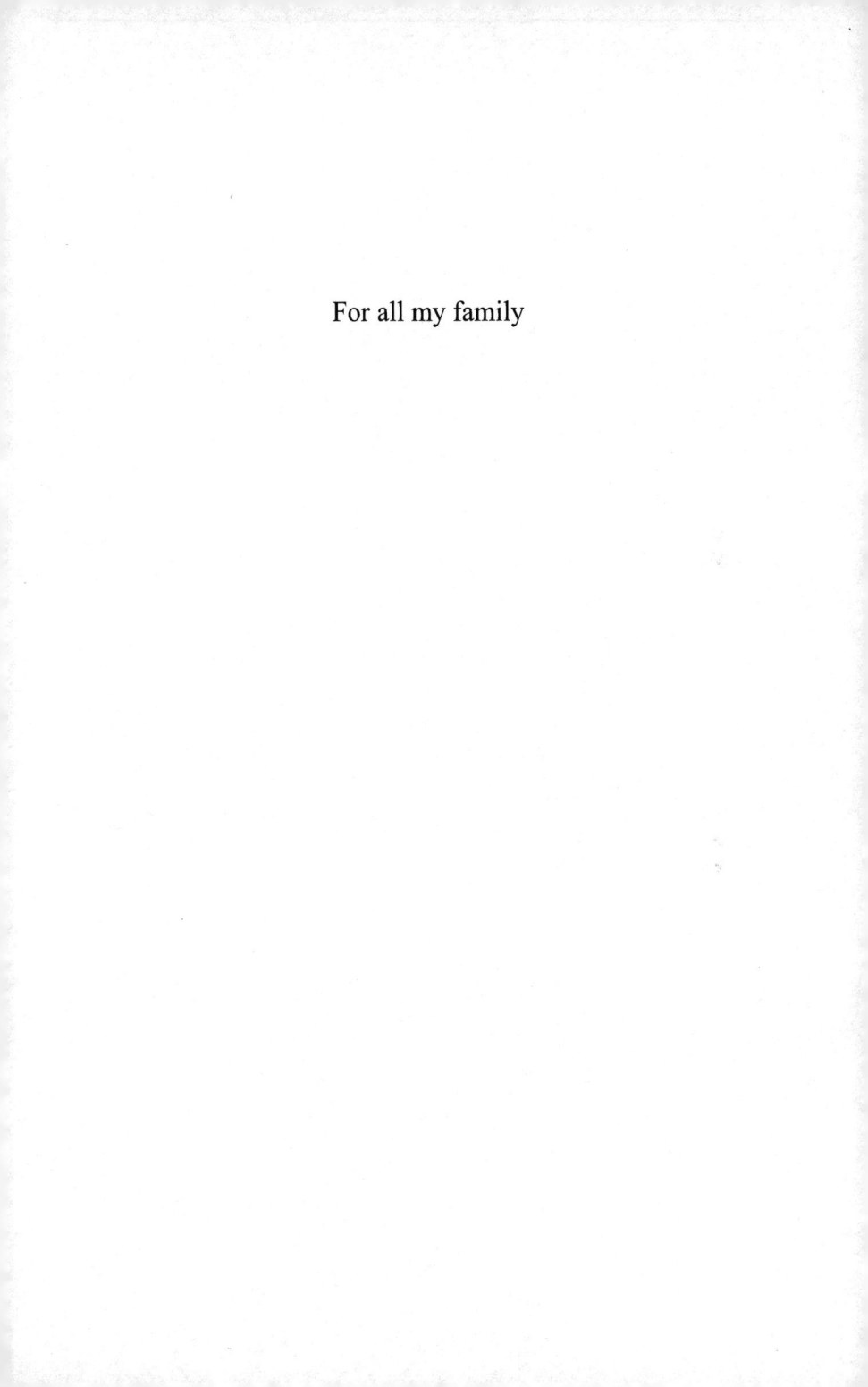

CHAPTER ONE

Born at Dorking Maternity Hospital on 25 July 1950, to John and Nickii Tolley, a girl, Jacqueline Ann, weighing 9lb 3ozs. Mother and baby doing well...

John Tolley looked up from his scribble on the back of a used envelope. He chewed his pen thoughtfully. Perhaps he should buy a paper to remind himself how other people do it. Let's see – time, date, place. Of course, time? He put an arrow before the *25* and wrote *0.15 am* above it. Looks? Ah yes, he put another arrow after the *3 ozs* and squeezed in *with a mop of dark hair*. What else? What else did he notice about that swaddled little bundle with a screwed up scarlet face and a squashed boxer's nose? Eyes? Colour of eyes? Well she didn't open her eyes; or did she? Perhaps he should ring the hospital and find out. A tug at his sleeve interrupted and a small voice wanted to know whether *she* could see the baby before she went to Grandma's. Quickly he scribbled, *A sister for Claire,* on the bottom of the envelope and put down his pen.

Scooping up his eldest daughter, he sat her on his knee. She looked up at him with her round eyes, the colour of deep Mediterranean Sea.

"Well *can* I?" she begged.

He put a finger under her chin and rubbed her nose with his. She giggled. An Eskimo kiss. But he told her that she must be patient. Little girls can't see very new babies. She would have to wait until she had been to Grandma's, and Nickii and the baby came home.

"How old is the baby?" she muttered pointing her head at his toes.

"She's, let me see. Nearly six hours old."

"So she'll never be four years like me?"

John rested his chin on her soft, ash blonde curls. When she was born, these curls had come out in a thick black fuzz too.

"Yes she will," he said, "She'll be four years one day, but then you'll be twice as old, because you'll be an enormous eight!"

And then, to avoid any complicated explanation of why she wouldn't always be twice as old as the new baby, he quickly took Claire into her bedroom to choose toys for her to take to Nickii's mother's. He sat on the edge of her small bed. The wicker crib that she used to sleep in was standing against the wall. Nickii had decked it out with white lacy frills; all clean and fresh and ready for its new occupant. That won't last long, he thought. The months and years would race by, and before they knew it, the girls *would* be four and eight. Where would they be? Would they still be here in this tiny bungalow? Or would they have been able to move on. Onward and upward, what would happen to his two daughters? What kind of lives would they have? Could he make them happy? Could he make them rich? Could he keep them healthy? *Que sera, sera*, he thought, and went in search of a bag to pack Claire's toys.

***

Thirty-seven years and two months later, Jacqueline Ann Hildegaard was sitting on the cold stone step of the back porch of her mother-in-law's cottage. Naturally, she could remember nothing of the day that she was born. All she knew was that she had wished, over and over again, that it had never happened. Leaning against the door, a small tiled roof protected her head and shoulders, but her painfully thin legs were stuck out in front of her into the drizzle. Her hair, the colour of dark rich peat, hacked short with kitchen scissors, was stuck to the shape of her skull by the damp. Her mottled blue eyes, amid dark circles, over prominent cheekbones, were staring ahead of her. She watched raindrops trickle over an aborted rose bud. Fading red petals, tinged with rotting brown that never made it to the sunlight. Its stem was spindly, tall and wild, devoid of leaves and brushed by the tips of grasses in the wind.

There was something about the rose that Jackie liked. It was free, not tethered or pruned. So much more beautiful gently swaying there in the wet drizzle, than being sprayed and fussed over and then put in a twee vase to die. Just like the flowers that her mother had strategically placed around the house. And Claire was the same. Wilting petals dropped on well-dusted furniture, waiting to be whisked away, changed and titivated. Flowers in vases; beds all made and tidy and neat food in the fridge. Jackie had been like that too, once; toddler bathed and ready for bed; laughing in the playpen and smelling of Johnson's baby powder. Supper in the oven and cats munching from bowls in a tidy kitchen. But that was two more children and a marriage ago. When you hide from the milkman week after week because you can't pay the bill, you forget about putting flowers in vases. You just hide under the stairs and pray silently that he will leave the milk because you need it for the children.

Still, even then, Jackie remembered, when she used to hide from the milkman, she had some good days. Days when she felt positive and in control, days when she went to the employment agencies, looking for part-time work while the children were at school. Then, after she picked them up from the school gates, they would go up onto the common to look for dead wood for the fire. The wood collecting contests had been fun. The children running about, laughing and giggling and struggling with logs that were far too big for them. But now there was no fun. Jackie could only recall those days as though staring at a picture of some other family. She couldn't live the memory, feel the warmth and hear the children laughing. She was just numb. And her children, where were they? Off and away, that's where. It might just as well have been on the other side of the world. And being brought up by a woman who bore no blood relation to them whatsoever. That was why Jackie had just had to get out of that house, to get away from the numbness.

Suddenly she began to shiver uncontrollably. She had not noticed the cold at all until now. But it had been a long walk from the station and the shoulders and back of her trench coat were wet through to her skimpy sweater. She couldn't imagine where her mother-in-law had got to. Being a Saturday Jackie expected her to be there. But when she had arrived, the car was missing and there was no cacophony of barking coming from inside the house. She had assumed that Selena had taken the dog for an early morning walk, so she came round to the back door. It was locked, which was strange because Selena never locked her back door. But Jackie just sat down there to wait for Selena to come back. She had been feeling very tired. It was a relief to lean her back against the door, and quite peaceful watching the silent drizzle descend over Selena's rampant garden. But now she was feeling rather sick and would have liked a cup of tea or coffee. Perhaps she needed some food too. She could not remember when, or what, she had last eaten? Food didn't bother her most of the time. She ate like a robot. Somewhere inside her, there was a subconscious instruction that said sometimes you eat or else you die. The same instruction that had stopped her from dying at times when that was all she wanted in the world. Eat and stay alive, it said. Why?

Wearily she put a hand down on the cold stone doorstep and bent one knee. Nobody takes this long to walk the dog, she thought, and heaved herself to standing. Leaving her fraying nylon weekend bag under the porch, she walked slowly, but purposefully, around the side of the cottage. She knew the neighbour where Selena usually left her key. She lifted the doorknocker and gave it one sharp tap.

"I've come for Selena's key!"

Mrs Jarvis looked at her blankly at first, and then with eyebrows raised in surprise. Jackie just stood squarely and rigidly on the doorstep.

"The key. I've come for Selena's key."

"But, I don't remember her saying... perhaps she did. Perhaps I've just forgotten. You're Jackie, aren't you? Selena's daughter-in-law? Well the key's here," she said, taking a key from the window ledge by the door. "Funny, I don't remember her saying you were coming; I didn't expect her back for... are you alright? You look very white! Would you like a cup of tea before you go back?"

"No thank you. I'll be fine." Jackie said, without looking at Mrs Jarvis at all.

"Oh well. ... Well let me know if you want anything won't you dear!"

Mrs Jarvis called after her as she walked back down the path.

Inside the cottage now, Jackie closed the front door behind her and leant against it for a second. The small sitting room felt cold and smelt musty. There was an unearthly stillness crawling over the house. Turning round, she reached up and slipped the bolt on the top of the door. Then bending down, she slid the bottom one across too. She walked slowly into the kitchen and turned the key in the back door. Opening it just wide enough, she grabbed her bag from the porch and closed the door again quickly. There were bolts at the top and bottom of this door too. Jackie slid them across. She dropped the bag on the kitchen floor and went back to the tiny sitting room. Moving a pile of books and magazines, she sank into a deep armchair. She sat there staring at the bolted front door. She had not even bothered to take off her wet coat.

***

Claire held no recollection of the day that her sister was born either. But she had always had a notion of a memory of walking into her old bedroom and peeping over the edge of the cot. Of talking in whispers and touching the tiny hand of the sleeping baby that was her sister, and was very precious. And with that picture, came the sensation that her life had somehow changed from that moment. She also didn't remember the time that she had spent alone with her father in those two days. How she had to tell him to cut her toast into soldiers at breakfast, and how she had chattered all the way to her Grandma's in the car. It just seemed to Claire that she had spent very little time alone with him over the years. She wondered if that was why she had this feeling of nervous excitement at spending a day alone with him now.

The wipers battled to keep the windscreen clear and cars swished past them in the outside lane. Her father had been driving sedately, knowing that Claire had been a neurotically nervous passenger ever since a previous car accident. Sitting side by side, they looked like father and daughter; both with the same olive skin, the sort that tans at the first flash of the sun. Both with the same bushy eyebrows, except that Claire's were tamed through years of plucking, and with the same little flare to the ends of their noses.

They had been driving for several miles now behind an ageing Austin Allegro at a painfully slow speed, even for Claire. The driver appeared only to be as tall as the height of his steering wheel. John Tolley glanced in his mirror and flicked his indicator, which wasn't really necessary since there was nothing at all behind him. Giving Claire an apologetic grin, he nipped neatly around the grubby, mustard coloured obstacle. The speedometer flickered back up to 70 then 75 and 80mph.

"We'll be late if we carry on at that rate." he said, reaching behind Claire's seat with his left hand for the map, "Why don't you have a look for where we turn off. I know it's before Worthing but I'm not sure exactly where. See if you can work it out from the map they sent us."

Claire stretched down to the floor beside her for the leaflet giving the programme for their day and then leafed through his ring-binder map for the right page.

"Well according to the leaflet it's a small road called Titmore Lane and according to the map I think it will be signposted Durrington. It's a turning to the right about five miles after Arundel."

"Oh yes, I think I know." John replied, "but we'll have to keep our eyes skinned because I think it's a dual carriageway along that bit and it might be easy to miss the turning. Mummy was stationed at Durrington for a while during the war you know. I remember going to see her there several times."

Claire remembered a photograph of her mother in the family album, sitting in the sun and playing with a Labrador dog. She was wearing a pair of fairly voluminous shorts, which would be highly fashionable again now. She could remember being told that that was taken at Durrington during the war. All before her parents were married and when Claire was nothing but a vague possibility. Driving along in comfortable silence, they came to the ring road around the castle town of Arundel. Tucked inside the leaflet on Claire's lap was the note her father sent her back in August.

Dear Claire and Michael,
Quick note. Just to send the enclosed programme for the writing day at Worthing. I've booked in with sessions as marked. If you decide to come and do different sessions, we could swop notes....

Her father had dabbled with bits of writing since he was a boy and had many files of typed pages in varying degrees of yellowness, and copies of old company magazines for which he had written articles years ago. Claire first developed the same interest when she was about ten years old, long before she knew that her father had it too. She had started writing 'The Twins'. It was her secret. Kept hidden in her bedroom drawer and worked on whilst lying on her bed with the door closed. It was written in a shorthand notebook with a ring top that she had bought from Woolworths with her pocket money. After about thirty odd pages, she showed them to her mother. Nickii was very encouraging and said she looked forward to more. But there was no more. The magic seemed to have gone out of it after that. Nearly twenty years had gone by before the desire to turn her mysterious notions and feelings into words on a page arose in Claire again. And then, only very recently, had her relationship with her father become enriched by this shared hobby. For some time now, they had each been going to different evening classes; and sending their 'homework' to each other for mutual criticism and comment. Various manuscripts had travelled backwards and forwards in the post in the same dog-eared envelope. The envelope had become a standing joke. Claire sent it to him first. Pristine. Crisp and new, a brown A4 envelope, containing a short story she had written. Then the envelope came back, with her address written by the side and his crossed out, containing his comments on her story and some notes and jokes for a TV sitcom from him. No point in wasting money on a new envelope every time, he had teased. The process had continued until the envelope was covered with black felt tip arrows and used stamps and held together by bits of yellowing cellotape. When Claire had received this note, she had been tickled by his suggestion that they should do different sessions and swap notes, so that they could get the best possible value out of their fees. He had chosen 'The Craft of the Short Story' for the morning and 'Writing for TV Sitcom' in the afternoon. Claire chose 'Planning Your Novel' for the morning and 'Short Stories; putting ideas into Action' for the afternoon, thinking they would be both useful for her, and for note swapping with him.

.... Oct 3rd is a Saturday and it's an early start so you could stop over Friday night and Saturday night. We're off to putting. Tennis and beach later. It was tennis and swimming yesterday! With love from us both. Dee.

Glancing over those last sentences, Claire's mind was jolted back to Jackie. This note must have been written when her parents were looking after Jackie's children during the summer holidays. Had Jackie been in or out of hospital then? And where was she now? She was about to speak the question out loud, for the umpteenth time, but she thought better of it and kept quiet. There was just a chance that her father had managed to forget it all for a moment.

"I think we're nearly there," he said, looking in his mirror and moving into the outside lane, "we'd better keep our eyes skinned for this – what is it Lane?"

"Titmore," Claire said.

Titmore Lane turned out to be a narrow country road that would have been very picturesque on a summer's day. Winding around the lanes and past some cottages that looked as though they had come straight from the cover of a chocolate box, they were suddenly confronted by a roundabout. With no time for looking at the map, John drove smoothly around it and went straight on. If in doubt, go straight on, was always his motto. But it didn't work this time. Quickly realizing that they had gone wrong, they came to a small railway station, the forecourt of which made a very handy turning point, and soon they were approaching the same roundabout from the opposite direction. Although they had, by now, worked out that they should turn right, John took one complete turn around the roundabout before turning off. Claire looked at him. He was wearing his cheeky grin; the one that said 'this is a bit of fun isn't it!' He was enjoying himself. She was glad she hadn't mentioned Jackie.

As they pulled into the car park, she glanced at her watch. Ten minutes to nine. Time for a quick cigarette before we go in, she thought. She didn't smoke in his car anymore because he had given up smoking his pipe years before and now he hated the smell. Years ago though, when she was at secretarial college, and her father sometimes gave her lifts into town, he used to keep packets of Rothmans in the glove compartment and offer them to her as they drove. He gave her her first driving lesson in that car. That was quality time, she thought, now that she looked back. He was so patient and calm; especially when she drove all over the pavement on her first attempt.

"I'm just going to walk about for five minutes and have a cigarette before we go in."

She said, picking up her handbag and reaching for the door handle.

"Oh go on, have it in here," he said, pulling out the ashtray, "It's cold out there and we can open the windows. We've got plenty of time; I don't think they actually start until 9.30."

Claire wound down her window several inches and held the cigarette so that the smoke curled out into the chilly air. Little splatters of rain fought their way in onto her skirt. Sitting there in the car with her father in this affectionate mood while the rain splattered on the roof above was like being wrapped in a soft cosy towel after a cold swim.

He was looking at the programme now.

"It's the speech after lunch that I'm looking forward to," he said, "the one by the literary agent fellow *How to be Published Successfully*. I wonder if the fact that he is here means he's looking for new talent. I'm keen to see what he has to say and it would be interesting to find out what sort of books he specialises in, if any. Perhaps I'll be able to have a word with him afterwards."

Claire was half watching another arrival making extremely heavy weather of parking his car.

"Um, Yes," she said thoughtfully, "Well, I suppose it would help to have met someone in the flesh, rather than sending a faceless letter with the manuscript. But presumably you'll have to wait until you get some reaction. You've already got someone reading it, haven't you? I thought you could only submit to one at a time. Isn't that the submission protocol?"

"Well. I'm not sure about that. But anyway I've had it back from the two I sent it to actually. So I'm looking for number three now. Third time lucky perhaps!"

He glanced at his watch.

"Shall we make a move? I expect we'll have to register and get name tags, like a couple of school kids – and speaking of which – I need to go to the loo!"

As they walked through the car park towards the reception door, Claire was thinking about the day when her father first told her he was writing that novel. It was the first time she had seen his top lip curl under and grow thin with emotion. He and Nickii had come to visit them some months before, and the four of them, Claire and Michael and her parents, went for a pub lunch by the river. Claire had asked how Jackie was, and her father had been almost snappy. He said he didn't want to talk about it. But then he had looked at her, with that thin top lip, and told her that he was, however, three quarters the way through a novel about the whole thing, and he would ask her to read it soon. Claire remembered how her heart sank with instant foreboding. Her immediate reaction was that it was a terrible mistake. She had talked to Nickii later; asked her if he couldn't be persuaded out of it. But her mother had said he was passionate about it and there was nothing she could do; and that anyway, in some ways she was pleased because she thought it was having a cathartic affect and helping him to relieve the tension.

CHAPTER TWO

Nickii Tolley was grateful for anything that would relieve the tension for John. She worried about him constantly. After his heart by-pass the year before, he had started to look a bit better. But nowadays most of the time she could see that look of strain that he had had before the operation. While Claire and her father were on their way to the Writers' Workshop, Nickii was stomping around the garden of their cottage in his wellington boots. When he was not using them, she quite often did, as they were much easier to slip on and shake off. She was wearing his old gardening anorak too, because it was baggy and cosy and kept off more rain than her own. And she was irritated that her soft grey hair was being whipped and flurried by the wind, having spent a lot of time washing and taming it with the curling tongs at six o'clock that morning. They always seemed to be awake at the crack of dawn.

It was a large garden – well over half an acre. They both thought it was too big now, but they had loved the cottage and the garden, obviously, had come with it. They had underestimated the amount of their time that the garden would swallow up. Having spent two years' of regular house hunting trips looking for the 'right' house, finally there had been something about this one, nestled in an enclave of attractive cottages all grouped around the village church. They fell in love with its scruffy thatch, like an oversized straw hat on a scarecrow. When they had moved, they had hoped to say goodbye, not only to suburbia, but also to all the problems that had dogged them there during the last few years. First there had been Claire's divorce. Then both their respective parents had been ill and then died. John had become ill and needed the heart by-pass. And then there was Jackie. Nickii trudged over the wet lawn from flowerbed to flowerbed, snipping at bits of greenery from the shrubs, the secateurs wet and slippery in her hands. Jackie was missing, but it was still Nickii's turn to do the church flowers.

Going into the passage that they had nicknamed "the walk-through" which linked the kitchen of the cottage with her art studio, she shook the muddy boots off her feet. Having doors onto both front and back gardens, it was a very handy place for depositing boots and shoes – and dumping wet cut flowers. Without taking off the soggy anorak, she went into her studio to find one of her green plastic sheets. These were most practical inventions, flat heavy plastic sheets with handles on all four sides, which she used to carry the flowers into the church. She was annoyed with herself for forgetting to pick the flowers the day before. She would normally have soaked everything overnight to make it last longer. She had been going to do it when they came back from shopping yesterday, but that was before the start of the latest episode on their emotional rollercoaster.

They had been relaxed and happy then. They had driven into Chichester with a Beethoven piano concerto playing in the car. They were looking forward to having Claire and Michael for the weekend, and had been planning to fetch Jackie on Sunday for the day. The shopping had all gone quite smoothly and Nickii teased John in Waitrose about his way with the checkout girls. If she made him go in front, they always got their bags packed for them with smiling friendly service. It never failed. Just one glance to take in the tanned olive skin, tall straight back, distinguished grey hair and cheerful grin, and they were bending over backwards to help. He was jolly lucky, for a man of sixty-four, to be getting reactions like that, Nickii said. John said it was a load of old phooey and just coincidence.

That was only twenty-four hours ago, she thought; as she hung the anorak on a window catch. And now here they were in the teeth of another crisis. Just as they were putting the shopping away and were about to sit down for some coffee, the phone had rung. It was Marjorie, the social worker who was keeping an eye on Jackie. Marjorie said that they hadn't seen Jackie since early Thursday morning and she thought she ought to let them know that it looked as though Jackie had gone missing again. After that Nickii had completely forgotten about cutting the flowers. She wondered now if she should try to 'phone the house again before she went into the church, and whether she should take Michael a cup of tea.

Some girl answered the 'phone. Nickii could picture her face but couldn't remember her name. Nickii asked for Jackie.

"Jackie's out," the girl said blankly.

"Can you tell me if she's been in this morning?" Nickii asked, trying to be friendly and calm.

"I don't think so. Bob's here – do you want to talk to Bob?"

The girl said as blankly as before.

Nickii didn't hold out much hope of Bob knowing any more than anyone else. She just asked the girl to ask Jackie to 'phone her Mum. Then she went back into the kitchen and took the kettle to the sink.

Over the four years that Nickii had known Claire's second husband, Michael, she had learnt that he liked to lie-in at the weekends. There was every chance that he would not stir until she had been into the church, finished the flowers and come back, but she decided to take him up some tea anyway. She wanted to ask him to listen out for the 'phone. Confronted by the closed door of their spare bedroom though, she suddenly felt a bit shy. They hadn't seen much of each other in those four years and now here they were, alone together in the house for a whole day. How would Michael feel about having his mother-in-law walk into his bedroom?

Very pleased of a hot cup of tea, as it turned out.

"Thank you very much," he said with a smile, "the one that Claire left me does seem to have gone a little cold!"

"I'm just going into the church to do the flowers," Nickii said, putting the mug down by the bedside lamp. "I'll probably be about an hour; do you think you could keep an ear out for the phone? Don't worry if you want to have a shower or something, but it's just that...."

"No problem." Michael said, leaning on one elbow and looking at his watch, "I'll have a shower when you get back. In the meantime I can happily spend a bit more time here and if I get fed up with that, I'll seek out some of your art mags. Uh.... there's no news then?"

"No, not yet; and I don't suppose there will be.... but you never know! The art mags are on the table in the sitting room. Shall I get them for you?"

"No, don't be silly," Michael said, sinking back into the pillows, "I'll get them if I get insomnia."

Nickii smiled. Claire had said several times that Michael could make a study of sleeping. He was working up to a degree in it, she said. Well, Nickii thought, if it makes him that much easier to get on with than her first husband, she was all for it.

"What about breakfast?" she said. "Won't you be hungry?"

"If I am, I know where you keep the baked beans. Go and do your flowers – and don't worry about me – or the 'phone!" he said pulling the duvet back up to his chin.

There was still a damp drizzle and a bitter cold wind, as she closed the front gate and went into the churchyard. Her shoes crunched on the gravel path as she walked through the cemetery and up to the church porch. She wondered how Claire and John were getting on. She liked that they had gone off for the day together. He had been looking forward to it; perhaps it would keep his mind off Jackie. Yesterday, after the phone call, his lips had turned quite blue again. Nickii wished the whole thing didn't get to him so much; that he could stand back from it occasionally, rather than letting it gnaw away at him all the time. She laid her secateurs and scissors on the seat of the porch, so that she could turn the big circular iron handle on the church door.

It was empty and silent inside. Usually there would have been a familiar face in there, somebody cleaning the brass or sweeping the floor; but today there was nobody. Nickii was pleased. She would prefer to be alone this morning. She could get done more quickly for one thing, and, although they couldn't possibly have moved into a friendlier village, Nickii would rather not chat today. All of the local residents here knew about Jackie, not about the fact that she was missing now, but about her illness. They couldn't fail to; Jackie had done some very strange things around the village in the last couple of years and news travels fast, even in the kindest of communities. Nickii didn't want anyone to ask her how Jackie was right now. She had a suspicion that one or two of the neighbours were surprised that Jackie didn't live with them anymore. And, as she dismantled the flower arrangements from the previous week, sorting them out on another green plastic sheet on the floor, she was beginning to feel that if they had kept Jackie at home, this would never have happened. But in her heart, she knew it was not true. For nearly four years Jackie had lived with them and been in and out of hospital. For a lot of that time they had the children living with them too; but then, finally, they had gone off to live with their father when he had found himself a new girlfriend. But during that time Jackie had never been really well – or happy. She could just as easily have disappeared from here as there, Nickii told herself, and went to look for some new oasis in the cupboard at the back of the church. The frustration that all their love and support couldn't make Jackie better had become too great. They had needed some rest; and they had hoped that moving into that house might be a beginning for Jackie to build a new life for herself. She was almost 38 years old. She couldn't be expected to enjoy living with her parents; and they needed some time to themselves. Time to do what they wanted to do in the cottage that they had planned to enjoy to the full before they were too old.

However, in spite of all that, Jackie still spent every weekend with John and Nickii, and Nickii tried to remember if anything had happened last weekend. She racked her brains until her head throbbed trying to think of anything that might have upset Jackie. But she couldn't think of anything in particular. Things had been much the same as they always were. She could remember waking up on Saturday night and hearing Jackie moving about downstairs. But that wasn't unusual. Jackie seemed to sleep a lot during the day and then be very restless at night. They had talked about that a lot; during those endless hours of conversations about the what, how and why of Jackie's illness. They could not work out whether her strange sleep patterns were a part of the illness, or due to the drugs that were pumped into her. Standing back from the pedestal to look for the best position for one of the full red rose blooms that she had sacrificed from her garden, Nickii thought that a lot of the time the drugs seemed worse than the illness. For instance right now, wherever she was, she was much, much too thin and with the thinness came irritability and then sullenness, sudden aggression, cunning and total unpredictability. But, some months previously, she had been overweight; fat and virtually comatose. Her bright eyes were dull, her hair long and listless, her pretty angular cheekbones and her neat little chin lost on her swollen face. Drugs are supposed to make people better. Why can't they get it right? Why couldn't they have her back the way she was? An attractive, slim and happy, ordinary young mother.

Sweeping her discarded bits of stem and stalk onto the green plastic, Nickii remembered the Jackie of years ago; when she was a curly-haired, vivacious and affectionate little girl who was always ready for a kiss and a cuddle. How they used to call her Jokey Jackie – and how that got shortened to just Kee! Kee was the daughter they once had. She was the one who was full of fun. Nickii smiled now as she remembered their shopping trips to Selfridges with Kee. She used to run through the hat department, tipping the hats down over the dummies' noses with abandoned glee. But Jackie was the daughter that Nickii had now; sometimes even Jacqueline. The fun and laughter had disappeared along with the affection. Still Nickii would have given anything at all to know where she was.

***

A woman in her fifties, wearing a Laura Ashley print skirt and a carefully matching pale green blouse, appeared beside the table that Claire and her father had chosen for lunch. She asked if she could join them and set her plate down on the table next to John's. He half stood up and muttered a welcome. It was evident to Claire that he could not remember the woman's name. That amused her, but at the same time she felt irritated. They could hardly say 'no bugger off' could they? And Claire had been enjoying having her father to herself.

"This is my daughter, Claire." John said, as the woman settled herself happily next to him.

Claire mustered a hypocritical smile and stretched out her right hand across the table.

"Pleased to meet you!" she said.

"So you're interested in writing too, are you?"

The woman started to make polite conversation.

"Yes she is," her father had said, before Claire had time to reply, "and Claire has the satisfaction of being a published writer, which is more than a lot of us can say!"

"Oh really! How interesting," the woman said, giving Claire what felt like a piercing look. "What was it that you have...."?

Claire winced and wished that she could crawl under the table. The satisfaction that she had once felt had since been smothered under the hundred weights of rejected brown envelopes that had landed on her doormat. She had allowed herself to dream of great things, but all too soon had realised that those few small successes had been a complete fluke. Now she felt such a fraud that she could not look the woman in the eye as she muttered.

"Oh it was just a couple of articles and a short story, but it was a while ago now."

"Well I hope you haven't given up! Lots of people would give their eyeteeth..."

Feeling distinctly uncomfortable now, Claire looked at her father for help and the woman's voice drifted off into the distance. Her father was smiling at her and she could see something in his smile that quite took her by surprise. It was pride. Suddenly she could see that he was proud of her couple of measly articles and a short story and she hadn't realised it. The woman's speech had obviously ended with a question and now she was looking at Claire quizzically.

"No. I haven't given up. I shall keep on scribbling away. Actually I've started working on something longer...."

This set the woman off talking about her own work, and soon she and John were chatting away about their class and their tutor. Claire was able to listen politely, eat her meal and watch them. This woman obviously fancied her father like mad, but was trying to be subtle with her flirting. John was in his sociable and charming mode, which the woman might have taken to be some mark of achievement. Claire wondered, with some glee, whether she would bother if she knew she was wasting her time. Then she remembered how they had teased him about his secretaries in the past. Two of them, who were with him for years, as faithful as Miss Moneypenny, had finally left, reluctantly, and emigrated to get over their disappointment. How nice it was to know that your parents' marriage was as solid as a rock. Something her own children had been denied, she thought, with sadness and guilt. But she had always made sure that they knew when she was pleased. Hadn't she? Suddenly she felt an irrational desire to rush to a telephone to tell her children she was proud of them. When Claire and Jackie were children it was Jackie who always shone. It was Jackie who got the scholarship to the posh school. Jackie who got top marks, Jackie who got to university. Claire seemed to scrape everywhere. Perhaps she was so used to the feeling of failure that she didn't know how to recognise pride when she saw it.

The Laura Ashley woman was still chatting away and Claire had dreamed her way through her meal and was now looking at an empty plate. She manoeuvred her chair back a few inches and leant forward.

"I'm sorry to interrupt," she said, "but that queue for the pudding seems quite long. If you'll excuse me, I'll go and join it. Would you like me to bring something for you?"

Her father said, "yes please," and left the choice of his dessert to Claire. The woman said that she would skip the sweet, thank you, because she was going to join some friends for coffee.

By the time the queue had diminished, and Claire reached the end, what had been a choice between crème brulee and trifle had turned into trifle or trifle. She picked up two glass dishes of those perennial buffet-do-afters, and weaved her way back through the tables. He was alone now and grinned at her as she sat down.

"I couldn't remember her name!" he said.

"I know. I just about spotted that! There was only trifle left I'm afraid. I would have got some coffee at the same time but there were no trays. Still, you managed to cover it up well. Who is she anyway? She obviously fancied her chances!"

"Well she used to go to one of the Chichester evening classes. But I don't know exactly who she is because I didn't admit that I couldn't remember her name. Rather embarrassing really. Faces are easy, but putting the names to them... well, usually I can give Mummy a dig and whisper up some help – but I was floundering a bit there!"

"Oh well. I shouldn't worry about it; it's over – she's gone now. But you could've done with Mummy for defence, I reckon!"

"Oh, don't be daft." he grinned again. "She was just being friendly. And anyway I just talk about Mummy a lot and then they get the message. Aren't you going to eat that pudding?"

"No. I don't really like trifle. I shouldn't have picked it up in the first place. I'll go and get us some coffee shall I?"

"No. I'll get them!"

He pushed back his chair and stood up.

"You sit there for a moment. You haven't finished your wine either! There's an ashtray there – it looks as though you could treat yourself to a cigarette. I'll leave that trifle there though – I might finish it when I come back!"

Claire had a quiet chuckle as he walked away. Waste not; want not, she thought affectionately. She reached down to the floor for her handbag and took out her cigarettes. She had been planning to nip outside before the afternoon session began; but looking around the room, she could see that there were just a few people smoking. The room was clearing a bit now. People were obviously wandering off to take some air and muster themselves for the afternoon. The day had collected a strange and varied group of people and there were far more men than Claire had expected. She had somehow thought that a Writer's Day of this type would have attracted mainly women, but the proportion of men there must have been at least a third, and there was also quite a cross section in age. But all of them were so terribly earnest. Fired with enthusiasm after their morning sessions, they were sitting in clusters around the tables, questioning, supporting and chivvying each other about their current projects and dreams to come. All of which made Claire feel totally depressed about her writing. She felt like a tadpole in a tropical aquarium; that she couldn't ever hope to be 'one of them'. And the morning hadn't inspired her at all. Rather the opposite. The accent had been very much on the writing of romantic fiction; with the implication that before you can get anywhere you need to serve your apprenticeship by writing a romantic novel. Claire was left with the dismal feeling that she stood about as much chance of winning the pools as she did of joining the ranks of published 20th Century novelists.

But, giving herself a mental shake, she decided that she would not let it get to her. Perhaps the afternoon would be more uplifting and she was enjoying her day with her father. Looking at the coffee queue she could see that he was nearly there. She remembered how her mother had smoothed down his rebellious grey hair and straightened his tie before they left that morning. Then, looking away again, she pictured the college dining room on a normal day, buzzing with the hum of student chatter. She was just betting herself that they didn't have white paper tablecloths and fresh flower centrepieces, when she realised that she was watching her father come back with the coffee. His hands were shaking. He was looking down at the cups with a frantic frown of concentration. And his hands were shaking so much that he could hardly carry them. Suddenly she could see only him. It was as though every other being and object had evaporated, and Claire had swallowed an ice cube. Time was suspended. There was a bluey tinge around his lips, and the coffee was lapping over the edge of the cups.

"I seem to have spilt a bit in the saucer on the way! Better tip it back in. We wouldn't want to waste it would we – I had to wait long enough for it! But now I'll eat your pudding as a reward!"

"Oh no, we wouldn't want to waste it." Claire said. And she sorted the coffees out, wiping the bottoms of the cups with her serviette. The blood was creeping back into her veins and she was telling herself that she over-reacted. His hands were just a little wobbly, that's all.

CHAPTER THREE

A squirt of orange juice scored a direct hit into Nickii's eye, scattering droplets down her cheek. She brushed the back of her hand across her face and squinted as she plopped a scalped orange segment into a bubbling saucepan. With Michael's laughter at some afternoon film coming in salvoes from the sitting room, she was making a prawn curry for their evening meal. She made a chicken curry that never failed to leave plates so clean they hardly needed to go in the dishwasher. But Michael didn't eat meat. So she was doing exactly the same as usual, but using a large packet of frozen prawns instead of chicken. She was, however, a just a tad dubious about it. She popped the next orange segment into her mouth, following it by a decidedly crunchy and chilly prawn. She hadn't eaten since the two pieces of toast she had had at breakfast. Any form of lunch had been postponed by mutual agreement with her son-in-law. Nickii was getting to like him more and more, even if it was his fault that she was dubious about the brew that she was creating.

When she had come back from the church this morning, a waft of baked beans had greeted her at the door. The smell immediately made her think of the children. Which immediately made her think of Jackie. But she was already doing that anyway. Michael had been sitting at the kitchen table, crouched over a swilling plate of beans on buried toast with swirls of brown sauce and slices of cheddar cheese on top. Surrounding his plate, on their bare pine kitchen table, was the open packet of sliced bread – leaning perilously like a toppling tower, the HP Sauce bottle, and a slab of cheese, in its supermarket wrap, supporting a waxy knife. When Nickii had asked him if he had found everything he wanted, he had looked up from the sports page of their Daily Telegraph and smiled cheekily.

"Well. Since you ask, for absolute perfection, perhaps the next time we come you could get in some Daddies! This HP is too fruity; doesn't mix well with the beans!"

After she had been racking her throbbing brain as to what she could give him for breakfast! She had made a mental note to get some Daddies sauce for the cupboard, and gone to get her latest art magazines from the sitting room. Then she had sat down with him at the table as he immediately slid the top magazine from the pile and started to leaf through it. When finally he pushed his finished plate to one side, he stood up.

"I fancy a coffee now! Would you like one?"

Nickii had made a move to get up.

"No. No. I'll do it." Michael said, taking the kettle across to the sink.

Nickii had been pleased to just sit there for a moment but she was wishing he would say that the 'phone had rung and Jackie was safely ......well somewhere! But he didn't mention the 'phone, or Jackie. And since it was obvious that if it had, he would, Nickii hadn't asked. A part of surviving was staying calm. And a part of staying calm was not talking about it all the time.

Then they had had a long and inspiring conversation about art. As Michael was an architect, Nickii had just taken it for granted that he was interested in her magazines simply because he was an artistic type. But she hadn't realized that he was so deeply interested in painting too. They had commiserated with each other over the frustration of finding the time to paint. Michael hadn't done any for years, and Nickii found it virtually impossible to use her studio for its actual intended purpose. Finally she had found him a big pile of back issues of The Artist and Artist Monthly so that he could take them home to read.

Wiping bits of onionskin, orange pips and splatters of flour off the mahogany surround to her hob, she begged herself not to forget to turn it off in twenty minutes or so. Then she walked through to the door of the sitting room. The voices from the television and the sound of Michael's giggling grew louder as she pushed open the door.

"You sound as though you're enjoying that – whatever it is! Would you like a sandwich or something now? I don't know what time we'll be eating tonight. I don't think they'll be home till gone seven and I'm a bit peckish myself!"

***

"Hm, the delicious smells that have been wafting in have been working on my stomach too, so, yes please, a sandwich would be very nice."

Glancing away from the screen at Nickii as he spoke, Michael was struck by the resemblance of Claire to her mother. For that instant he saw Claire's tired and worried look.

"What would you like in it?" Nickii asked.

"Oh, er, cheese and tomato? Whatever, shall I come out?"

"No, don't worry. You finish watching your film. I'll bring them in here. Would you like a tea or coffee?"

She had a small dab of flour on one cheek, Michael noticed as she walked out of the door. It had crossed his mind during the day that Nickii may think him rather callous. He had purposely not mentioned Jackie once. And now here he was roaring with laughter at this silly film while he knew exactly what she was suffering inside. He knew because he had been there too. And although it was all behind him now, the memories were still as vivid as limpets on a rock under bare feet. Those hours, endless hours, spent waiting by the telephone. Bleak evenings walking around dark streets, peering into countless crowded cafes looking for a particular face. The suede coat that she wore, the taste of the tears on her face.

When Claire had told him, soon after they had met, that her sister was ill, Michael hadn't been surprised that that insidious sickness could spread its net so wide. He had spent many days, afternoons or evenings visiting in mental hospitals. He had seen the range of its victims. But why, he had asked himself, did the fringes of the net have to come edging towards him again? He had been tempted to run. Did this scourge run in families? Was he just walking into the torture chamber all over again – with his eyes wide open?

But as the months passed, and he and Claire had become closer, Michael told himself it was Claire he loved, not Jackie. Anne had had two sisters and they were both perfectly sane, so why should he think that Claire would change. The bloody disease was everything else but it surely wasn't contagious! And slowly he had talked himself out of his fear and developed enough faith in Claire's stability to ask her to marry him.

As the titles rolled, indicating the end of the film, Michael picked the remote off the sofa beside him and zapped the screen into blackness. If Nickii knew what he had been through, she must understand why he hadn't talked about Jackie. But for Nickii's sake right at the moment, Michael hoped that she didn't. He wondered whether Claire had told her mother that his first wife had committed suicide.

***

There was quite a cluster of people grouped expectantly around the Writer's Agent, clamouring for the chance to speak to him. John was determined to speak to him too, but he thought it better to wait. The way that group were behaving one would have expected them all to have one arm in the air shouting 'Please Sir ... Me, Me.... It's MY turn!'

He spotted his tutor from the evening class standing a few paces away and took Claire's arm.

"Come, I'll introduce you to Tim. I'd like you to meet him."

Tim saw them coming in his direction and spoke before John had a chance.

"Hello John. Well it's been a good day, hasn't it! Quite a long one though! Are you off now? I'll see you at class next week!"

"Well, yes, we will be off shortly; but I just want to see if I can have a word with, oh – what's his name? Any way, the agent chap before we go. First though, I would like you to meet my daughter, Claire. Claire this is Tim."

Tim shook Claire's hand.

"Nice to meet you!" he said, "hm, you look alike. Easy to see you're father and daughter. He talks about you a lot you know. We've heard all about your success! Congratulations!"

John noticed a look of incredulity on Claire's face as she said 'Hello' and 'Thank you'. And then Tim asked her whether she was working on anything now. Looking over Tim's shoulder, John could see that the agent had extricated himself from the gaggle and was at the desk scrabbling around in his briefcase. He excused himself from Tim and Claire and walked over.

"Hello, my name is John Tolley," he said. "I don't want to bother you now; I can see you'll find it difficult to get away! But I wonder, could I take one of your cards? I have a finished novel that I would like to send for your opinion in a few weeks – if that would be alright!"

Tucking the card safely into his wallet, John turned back to look for Claire. She was standing across the hall by the entrance to the 'Ladies.' She spotted him and gesticulated that she was going in there. He mouthed back that he would meet her at the car and walked down the corridor towards the entrance hall. Pausing at the unattended reception desk, he browsed through a scattering of competition leaflets lying there. He had noticed them when they arrived, but there was too much of a production line for registering then to stop. He picked up a couple. He would give them to Claire. Perhaps he could persuade her to have a go; but he probably wouldn't enter any himself, as he was going to be too busy with his novel. The speeches and tutorials that day had confirmed his suspicions that he would need to go through it again. But with another contact to send it to, he was fired with renewed enthusiasm.

He wanted this novel published almost more than he had ever wanted anything. Through all his strivings and successes in business, nothing had been as important to him as this had become. He saw it as a form of retribution, revenge against the man who had turned his very soul inside out. Pulled it, stretched it and twisted it into a capability of hatred that he never, ever would have believed was within him. The man who had taken his money and his goodwill as though it was nothing but his due; the marriage rights that came with Jackie, the man who while taking with his right hand had pointed the finger of contempt at John with his left. Who fostered and nurtured his contempt and fed it into Jackie – slowly but surely like an intravenous drip. Who had to wear silk shirts and travel first class on the train to a job that would earn commission one day, while his wife and children were at home with no food in the fridge. Who insisted that cocaine was harmless, and, since John had no experience of drugs, how could he comment? Too right then, he couldn't comment. But he could comment on how this man worked his satanic spell on his daughter; drove her to the end of her tether and way, way beyond – and then put her on a train and banished her from his life. And in using him as the main character in his novel he wanted to show the world that such a creep existed. This slimy slithering worm that had burrowed its way through their lives, tossed them all up like squirming mounds on the sand and then wriggled away to smoother ground, should be dug out to feel the heat of the sun on its leathery skin.

Reaching the car John patted the pockets of his jacket looking for his keys. His hand shook a little as he aimed the key at the lock and the memory of spilled coffee started to come back to him. He dismissed it quickly, and lowered himself into the driving seat, steadying himself with one hand on the roof. It was a relief to be there in the familiarity of the car and with a few moments quiet. He did feel tired. It must have been the day's concentration, he thought; but nothing that a quick pint wouldn't take care of. Perhaps they would stop off at some nice little pub somewhere. Just him and Claire, after all, it was not often that they spent the day together; a drink on the way home would be a nice way to round it off. He started to think of the pubs he knew between there and home and then he saw Claire come out of the door. She stopped for a moment, as though to get her bearings, and then clutching her coat across her front against the cold, she started to walk towards the car. She was watching her feet as she walked – in the way that Jackie did. And suddenly his thoughts did an about turn. They looked more alike, his daughters, now they were growing older. Jackie's hair was darker and Claire's now had some quite discernible grey streaks. Claire was slightly taller and, if only she wasn't stooping like that, normally walked with a confident gait. But they both had similar skin and eyes, and would have been of similar build if only Jackie hadn't got so thin. They took after his side of the family. Claire was getting closer now. She looked up and smiled at him from a few yards away. Then his mind did another leap. If a soothsayer had told him thirty years ago that one of his children would go crazy, loopy, nuts? There wasn't a word that he could accept, all of them made him shudder, but if such a prediction had been made he would have thought it could only be Claire. It was she who was always more moody and withdrawn, she who they found hard to understand and difficult to reach. Jackie had just been an open, affectionate and fun loving kid. He leant across and pushed open the passenger door as Claire reached the car.

***

It was growing dark in the cottage now. Selena never did turn up. But never mind, Jackie thought, it is better this way. There was a good chance that Selena would have sent her back anyway. She certainly would have insisted, in that quiet calm way of hers, that people were telephoned so that they would know where she was. And, Jackie decided, she didn't want anyone to know where she was. Not yet. The phone had rung earlier. It could have been several times. She couldn't remember. The noise had filled the whole house, bounced off the walls and up the stairs and down again. Jackie just watched it, grey, immobile and noisy. *Brr, brr. Brr, brr. Brr, brr....*

It was probably her mother. Jackie could see her, standing by the telephone table in the dining room back at the cottage, waiting patiently – hoping Jackie would answer. She had stood by the kitchen door of Selena's cottage looking out into the garden. She was going to go out there, but somebody might come along. Better to stay inside. She had seen a dog. Her dog; the beautiful red setter they had once. He was bounding around in the long wet grass, his tongue lolling out of the side of his laughing mouth. Then the phone had stopped ringing and she had turned round to look at the silent object. When she looked back the dog had gone.

Now in the gloom of the sitting room she was watching a spider. It had just scuttled into her circle of vision on the floor; then stopped a few inches from her feet as though her presence had frozen it to the spot. Her father used to pick them up in his hanky and drop them out of the window. They used to giggle and scream hysterically, she and Claire – and her mother too sometimes.

"Daddy, Daddy, Dad-dee... there's a spider in the bath!"

Now she watched it. She watched it watching her, as it slowly grew darker in the room and she could hardly see it anymore in the red and black pattern on the rug. Then suddenly it darted away from her. She lifted her head and watched it scuttle under the skirting board opposite.

Intsy wintsy spider, climb the water spout
Down came the rain and washed the spider out
Out came the sun and dried up all the rain
Intsy wintsy spider climb the spout again...

Poor spider. Up. Down. Up Down. That was exactly why Jackie wanted to stay there. If she was alone, she didn't have to climb the spout. Out there everybody wanted her to climb. Climb and clamber, reach and stretch, struggle and heave to get better. But they didn't catch her when she was falling did they?

She had tried to tell them she was falling. She told the doctor. She told Claire. She remembered that now. It was such a long time ago, before she had Flavvy. But she could see the day clearly. Sometimes that happened. Pictures of the past came as sharp and clear as a sunny morning after a thick fog. It had been raining. She took the children on the train, and then waited at the station for Claire to come home from work. They all walked back to Claire's house in the rain. Claire made tea. Inside Jackie was screaming, 'Help me. Help me. I'm falling. DO SOMETHING. PLEASE do something.' But the words wouldn't come. The children were running everywhere. Claire was tired. They weren't used to talking to each other. They had sat at Claire's kitchen table and Jackie told her that Lytton said she was going mad and he wanted her to go away. He wanted to lock her up in hospital. She tried to tell Claire that she didn't think she was going mad, but she was frightened. Frightened that she might. She told her how she had sat by the river with the children. How she stared and stared at the water and just wanted to fall in; but there was something, somewhere that said she couldn't do that. And then Claire had started to make up beds for the children so that they could stay the night, but the phone rang, and Claire told Lytton that they were there. He came to fetch them and they all went home on the train in the dark. Lytton said that if she ran away one more time she would have to go into hospital. And she did.

It had been like being on a slide. One of those shiny polished slides in a children's playground. Where you sit at the top and know that while you hold on you are safe. But if you are frightened, your hands begin to sweat and they lose their grip. You start to slide and the weight of your body carries you down. The wind whips in your hair and you slither faster and faster down through the pit in your stomach. No time now to reach out – too fast – too late. You are at the bottom.

And then the bottom is safe again. There is no further to fall. All alone there in Selena's dark cottage, Jackie could sit safely at the bottom of her glassy slide. Out there they wanted her to grip on to the sides and haul herself back up. Struggle up and then slip back, struggle and slip, struggle and slip. They just didn't know how tired she was.

CHAPTER FOUR

John noticed that the needle of his petrol gauge was flickering downwards, ominously near empty. We will stop at the Tangmere garage and get some, he thought. If he had to go anywhere suddenly and in a hurry, he wouldn't want to worry about petrol. He had given up on the drink idea. Or rather he had decided that they had better get straight home. There might be some news. They might need to go out and pick up Jackie tonight. But then again, of course, his common sense told him, as he switched on his headlights into the half light, if they *had* heard anything Michael could have driven with Nickii to fetch Jackie. So she could even be there when they got home. He turned for a second to look at Claire sitting quietly beside him.

"I did think we might have a quick drink on the way home. I'm quite thirsty for a beer and I expect you'd enjoy a rum and coke; but at the same time I wonder if we ought to get straight back?"

Just having had the idea, he now felt a twinge of guilt at changing his mind; as though he were breaking a promise to Claire. He wished his emotions weren't so raw. It was as though he had to question and ratify every thought these days. And all the time he was thinking about going, or not going, to the pub with Claire, he realised that whilst he longed for Jackie to be there when they got home, he also really hoped that she was not.

"Well, it would have been a nice idea; but I think you're right. I expect they'll be looking out for us by now and Mummy's probably cooking. I am looking forward to a drink, but we can have one at home can't we! I wonder how they've got on all day; what they talked to each other about!"

Claire's reply was a relief. She was happy to go straight home and at least she knew that the thought had been there. Suddenly he felt more cheerful again. Thinking about how Michael and Nickii might have been spending their day aroused the possibility that, if they could forget Jackie just for a few hours, the four of them could spend a pleasant evening together.

"Oh I expect they'll have managed to keep each other company – or they might have just done their own things all day. Mummy was going to show Michael some of her paintings I think."

Which reminded him that he was going to tell Claire about one of his ideas. He made a mental note to bring it up in a moment, as Claire turned to him, he could half see her smile out of the corner of his eye.

"There's quite a possibility that Michael didn't get up till lunchtime; and he could have watched television all afternoon – so they may not have seen each other at all!"

There was teasing tone to her voice, not bitterness, he noticed; and thought, once again, about the huge difference in her choice of husbands. She had grown up a lot while she lived on her own.

"Oh go on with you!" he said. "You wouldn't have him any other way! But while I remember, I have been dreaming up one of my little schemes that you might suggest to Michael; a way for you to make some extra cash!"

"Oh you and your schemes!" she said, her eyes back on the road now, but with the same teasing tone. "So what is it then?"

"Well; do you remember the cards that you used for your change of address when you moved, the one with Michael's sketch of your house? Well, Mummy was very impressed with that; she's still got it somewhere; and every time it crops up she says how good the sketch is. So, I thought, it would be a very nice little sideline. You could advertise in the local paper, show a couple of examples. Michael could knock off the sketches and you could get the cards printed for people and make a tidy little profit. You would only have the printing costs and I reckon they'd go like hot cakes. Just a few evenings a month and you'd have some holiday money – or whatever!"

"Well – it sounds like a good idea, but...."

"Oh, just a moment!"

They had reached the garage sooner than he expected.

"We need to get some petrol, and I like to do it here because they're a penny cheaper than anywhere else!"

As he switched off the ignition, Claire went to unfasten her seat belt.

"Let me do it for you," she said.

Whatever for! John thought. I always do it!

"No. Don't be silly!" he said as he opened the car door, "you just relax – it won't take a moment."

Claire watched him in the wing mirror as he aimed the nozzle into the tank. She had seen his hand shake again when he switched off the ignition and was struck by that same fleeting shiver of fear that she felt at lunchtime. This was not the first time that she has seen through his confident and capable exterior to the vulnerable person underneath. And each time it cast a little tremor through the ground beneath her. It was completely on impulse that she had wanted to jump out of the car and do the petrol for him. Then there had been embarrassment in the air. He was obviously quite astounded by her offer. But not offended, she hoped, as she watched him walk through the door of the garage on his way to pay the bill. Actually, of course, it had been a totally selfish impulse. She had wanted him to rest so that she wouldn't have to feel frightened. But his fiercely independent spirit was definitely not ready to be mothered by his own daughter.

"Well that was a good job jobbed;" he said, clicking himself back into the seat belt, "now we can get home to that drink! So – what were we talking about?"

"Your idea for the moving cards...."

Claire really appreciated the fact that he had spent time dreaming up a scheme for her and Michael to make more money. They could certainly use some of that. But she knew that Michael would never pick up on it. Michael simply did not have the same entrepreneurial belief in himself that her father did. Still she didn't want to appear ungrateful, so she simply said,

"...it's a very good one and I'll mention it to Michael. I just wish our brains bubbled with ideas the way yours does! You're the same with your writing; fed with one thought from your class for 'homework' and you come up with half a dozen different angles. I sit there and chew my pencil and can't think of a bloody thing!"

He looked away from the road for a second and grinned at her.

"Oh ideas have never been my problem, but getting them accepted is altogether different. And don't forget that all my years in advertising were good training for getting thoughts down quickly."

Claire was just mulling that over and realising that it was probably very true. Being forced to come up with ideas, slogans and catch phrases on a daily, or even hourly, basis must help you to lose the inhibitions of trusting your first thoughts. And then into her brain appeared a childhood image of a television advertisement. There was a guard in a busby by a sentry box, the gold strap under his chin wobbling around while he sucked at a lump inside his cheek. She tried to remember the ditty that went with it; was about to ask him and remind him of how they used to avidly watch out for it as kids because they knew he had had something to do with the making of it, but he was too quick for her and his mind was still firmly in the present.

"Actually one of my favourite ideas at the moment is my 'Round and About' one for a television documentary. Have I told you about that?"

"I seem to remember the title vaguely, from one of your selections you sent me in the envelope; but I can't...."

"Well, the idea is for a running documentary based on regional competitiveness. You know how our village always has something going on? There's the Harvest Festival and the Summer Fete, then there's the Christmas pantomime in the village hall and the Nativity Play. Virtually every month there's something going on. So it occurred to me that the same sort of things are going on all over the country and it would be interesting for them all to see something of what the others are doing. And for those that are not doing anything to be enlightened as to what goes on elsewhere. One could invite comments and new ideas from viewers; not necessarily as a competitive thing, so that any particular region wins, but more to show how much energy and enthusiasm these people put into their lives. They're having fun and enjoying themselves but at the same time, in most cases, they're also raising money for genuine causes. Seems to me that would make cheerful, positive and fascinating viewing!"

Claire admired his enthusiasm, not only in his ability to seize what was going on around him and turn it into a creative idea, but also for his seemingly total confidence that it could work. Now he was explaining to her that he thought it would work best with the independent television companies, because it if went out in different areas across the country, their field crews could work competitively against each other and keep the programme content fresh and alive.

"Sounds good to me!" she said, "The more light-hearted living and the less blood and gore the better as far as I'm concerned. So where do you go from here? How on earth do you get something like that from your head to people's living rooms?"

"Ah well – you see – that's what I mean! Getting them accepted is altogether different. But in any case I'm saving it on the back burner for some light relief later. First of all I am going to get the novel re-drafted and sent off."

Claire couldn't help thinking that was a shame. The very tone of his voice had changed from light to heavy when the novel had come back to his mind.

Turning off the A27 now they were driving along the country road towards home. With dipped headlights lighting the surface of the road ahead, her father slid the car around the bends with the skill of one who knows every inch of the road. There was a silence in the car, a comfortable silence, but a silence nonetheless. Claire knew that he was thinking about Jackie. After his last words about the novel, and the fact that they were nearly home, he couldn't be thinking about anything else. She wanted to say,

'Before we get back, I want you to know that I've enjoyed my day. It was lovely having you all to myself. Thank you for asking me to come with you.'

But the silence and the furrows in his forehead over the bushy eyebrows acted like a clamp on her jaw and she did not speak. She felt as shy of him again now as she had done when they first set out that morning.

Nipping smartly off the main road and down the lane, they pulled up in the church car park in front of the cottage.

"I'll put the car away tomorrow," he said, putting on the handbrake, "they'll have to park around me if I'm not up before the 8 o'clock service. Let's go and get that drink!"

***

Thinking that this time she really did hear the crunch of car tyres on the gravel outside, Nickii went to open the front door. With a tea towel scrunched under her arm, she peered down the path in the porch light. Then recognising their voices behind the hedge, she left the door open and went back to the kitchen with a feeling of relief. Quickly putting water in a saucepan, she was putting it on the hob as John called out.

"Coo-eee," from the door.

"Hello."

She called back, going through to the hall to greet them.

"Did you have a good day? Was it inspiring and useful?"

He bent his head to give her kiss and then started to pull at the knot of his tie. He doesn't look too bad; she thought, a bit tired but quite relaxed. At least his lips are not tinged with that bluey colour.

"Yes, we had a good day; we'll tell you all about it. I found it very inspiring, but I don't know about Claire. And what about you? What have you two been up to all day long?"

She could hear Claire and Michael talking and laughing in the sitting room as John started to take some glasses from the cupboard in the old fireplace and put them on the table.

"Oh well, we've had a pretty good day too I suppose. I'm sure you'll hear all about it later."

He turned to her from the doorway into the dining room on his way to the drinks cupboard.

"What would you like to drink?" he said, "I bet you haven't had one yet! I hope Michael's helped himself though! Uh – there's... no news, I suppose!"

"No. No news. I'll have a gin and tonic, please; and I did offer Michael a beer, but he said he'd wait for you to come home."

He went to ask Claire and Michael what they would like to drink and Nickii opened the cupboard next to the hob to look for a packet of rice. There had been no need for him to ask. They had both known that Jackie's disappearance would be the first thing on their minds as they greeted each other. There's no news then! No, nothing, not a word. Voicing it was just a formality. And when he came back to pour the drinks, going through to the walk-through for ice from the freezer, while she sliced open the avocadoes for their starter, it was all done with the same silent communication. So, what do we do next? Well, I don't know, just wait I suppose. He put her glass down on the worktop beside her and gave her a peck on the cheek.

"I'm going to take my beer and sit down with Michael for a bit," he said.

He and Claire crossed each other at the kitchen door.

"I've left your drink on the table for you!" he said in passing, "you must be gasping for it by now!"

Claire had changed into her jeans and a bright pink floppy sweater. That colour suits her, Nickii thought, as she looked round.

"Hello;" she said, "was it a good day. Have you come back fired with enthusiasm?"

"I'm sorry, here you are slaving over a hot stove as usual and I haven't even been out to say hello yet. Is there anything I can do?"

Claire replied apologetically.

"Well, you could make some vinaigrette for these for me – or lay the table. Shall we eat out here do you think; or will they want it in front of the television?"

"Oh, let's eat out here; it's less hassle than carrying everything backwards and forwards – and we're more likely to talk to each other then!"

She was looking along the shelves of the dresser laden with crockery and picked up a jug.

"I'll make the vinaigrette first, can I use this?"

Nickii nodded and stood with her back to the work top, watching Claire as she went over to the spice racks, peering along them looking for what she needed.

"Daddy looks a bit more relaxed – as though he's enjoyed himself!"

Claire put a selection of jars on the table next to the jug and looked up at her. She seemed to hesitate before replying.

"Yes, I think he did enjoy it;" she said eventually, "we had one or two good laughs. You must ask him about the woman who chatted him up at lunchtime! Have you got any wine vinegar?"

Nickii put down her glass and bent down to her sauces cupboard in search of oil and vinegar. It was quite a production, this dressing of Claire's, but she often asked her to do it when she was here because the end result was well worth it. As she passed the bottles up to her, Claire drew in a breath and then said.

"I suppose you've tried Selena's?"

"Yes, that's always one of the first places we think of. I've tried to telephone several times today and there's no reply. I think Selena must be away. We would have to phone Lytton to find out if she is; but I don't want to get him involved yet because Daddy gets so upset – even at the mention of his name!"

"Well, I wonder if that's another possibility. She may have gone there. Perhaps she wanted to see the children!"

"No. I know for sure that if she had arrived there, they would have rung us immediately and sent her straight back."

As her words echoed on the air, Nickii winced mentally at the thought that one of her children, for whom she had dreamed of health, wealth and happiness like any other mother, could be treated like a pariah. And, even worse, that they had at times been driven to feel the same way themselves.

CHAPTER FIVE

Jackie was growing more aware of an empty hollow feeling in her stomach. It had been dark for a long time now. Many times she had told herself that she should get up. Just stand up, switch on the lamp on the sideboard, pull the curtains and go into the kitchen to see what there was there that she could eat. She had gone over the actions one by one in her mind as though, if she rehearsed them often enough, she would be able to carry them out. But still the actual trigger to turn them into reality would not come. It was as though her body were made of stone and cemented to the chair she was sitting in. It would be nice if someone would just put something in front of her. Something tasty that she could just nibble and pick at. Just put it there and then go away and leave her alone. But of course it wouldn't be like that. They would watch over her and fuss.

She remembered the day room of the first hospital she was in in London. It had been years ago now but she could still picture everything, in it. She could feel herself sitting in the chair at the end of that room as though it were only yesterday. Day after day, evening after evening she sat there, as the time for meals grew steadily closer. Cold grey lino covered the floor; yard upon square yard buffed by a fat and lethargic cleaner wielding an enormous polisher, right over the top of the stains and cigarette burns. Sometimes she used to wonder who seemed the more spaced out, the staff or the patients. She remembered the plastic covered chairs of hideous colours spaced around the grubby cream walls. In the middle of the room red formica-topped tables would be ready laid for the meal; with regulation spoons and forks and flimsy plastic knives. Proper knives not allowed – just in case. Cheap coffee tables with splayed out metal legs carried ancient tatty magazines and overflowing foil ashtrays. There was a large busted woman in a green overall who used to shuffle from table to table, plonking a pale blue plastic salt and pepper pot on each. At the far end of the room, near the door to the corridor, there was a battered table tennis table. And there was a girl, Jackie couldn't remember her name, who always wore a feather stole around her neck and gripped her table tennis bat with long, scarlet finger nails. She used to play with a sad little man in brown slippers. They played to pass the time. No scoring, winning or losing. They just batted the ball backwards and forwards. Pat. Pat. Pat. Pat... like the slow ticking of a clock.

The dull smell of institution food used to grow stronger and stronger, filling Jackie's nostrils and turning her stomach. And she knew that very soon it would start all over again.

"Come along Jackie, you must come and sit at the table and you must eat something!"

But they refused to understand that she couldn't just eat willy-nilly. She needed to monitor and test what she was eating in relation to the way she felt. There was no denying then that something was wrong in her head. But what and why? No doctor had said to her – this is what's wrong with you and if you take this pill and do this you will be better in two weeks or two months or two years. Oh no, there was nothing as logically sensible or helpful. They just seemed to ask her what she thought was wrong with herself. Why did she feel unable to speak for days on end? Why did she think she felt compelled to wander off alone and walk the streets in the middle of the night? What was she thinking about when she took the basket of things out of Boots without paying?

Their questions had made her so angry she felt she would explode. How was she supposed to know? If she knew, she wouldn't do it would she! She was losing her husband. She was losing her children. And it was cold and lonely on the streets at night.

She used to sit in that chair and think about it all. And out of the muddle the only thing that made any sense to her was that it must be something she was eating. She must be allergic to something. And so she had experimented in every way she could think of with what she allowed into her body, from not eating anything at all, to cutting out starch, or sugar, or protein, to eating only fruit or only vegetables. In the end, try as she might, she couldn't form any pattern out of it all; and nothing seemed to make any difference to the confusion in her mind. So she just gave up. She stopped fighting the system and the staff in the hospital. She stopped arguing with Lytton when he came to visit and told her she was mad. She just accepted it and allowed her mind to do as it wished.

Looking back now it seemed rather pathetic to Jackie that she could ever have believed that she could change the events of the last few years simply by changing what she ate. And now out there, beyond the night fallen outside the window, all over the country, people were eating; stuffing their faces, mouthful after mouthful, from heaped plates of food, without a thought of what it may be doing to them. And then they would get up from their tables and get on with their normal and sane lives.

Last weekend, on Saturday night, she had sat with her mother and father in the kitchen at the cottage. They had had what they called 'home-made' fish and chips; frozen plaice fillets cooked together with oven baked chips and eaten with big juicy pickled onions. And then ice cream covered with chocolate strands for afters. Was it Saturday or was it Sunday? Oh whichever – what did it matter now! But she remembered how pleased they were that she ate well that night. And even that made her feel uncomfortable. As though at the slightest glimmer of progress, so much more would be expected. She had thanked them for the meal and gone into the sitting room, while they started loading the plates into the dishwasher. Sinking into the sofa and listening to them chatting quietly in the kitchen, she had been pleased to be alone and away from the pressure of knowing that they wished she would not only eat but talk to them as well. She wondered if she would ever be able to explain to anybody how it is. About those ghastly pregnant silences, which you know you are expected to fill with an answer to a question. But there may be two or three or twenty answers swilling around in your brain and you simply cannot choose one quickly enough. Or there may be no answers at all. And so you just say yes, no, or I don't know, and watch the faces of frustration.

Then her father had come in with the coffee. He put the tray down on the step in front of the inglenook fireplace and sat down in his chair. But he hadn't switched on the television, or asked her if there was anything she wanted to watch – which he usually always did, even though she always said, no she didn't think so. Instead, he had cleared his throat and asked her whether she had thought any more about divorcing Lytton. The same old arguments; push, push, push. They hadn't lived together for four years. He would pay the legal fees. And if she was divorced he could think again about buying her a small house to live in. Then the children could come to stay – and maybe, one day, if she felt up to it, she could have them living with her again, permanently. Then Jackie had become deafeningly mute completely on purpose. It was quite simple. She was not prepared to discuss the subject and that was that. She had stood up and left the room without a word.

Suddenly, standing in the full glare of the kitchen light, she realised that she had carried out all the actions that she had rehearsed so many times, without giving them a second thought. She yanked open the door to Selena's fridge and stood back to look inside. Without bothering to bend down she could see that it was pretty well empty. There were some eggs and a couple of very red tomatoes with slightly wrinkly skins; a dish containing the ends of some butter and a few slices of bread in a polythene wrapper. With no great feeling of disappointment, since there had been nothing in particular she was hoping to find there anyway, she gave the door a push and it closed onto its rubber seal with a little suck. She was angry now. Now that she had so vividly remembered her father's softly spoken words. It was all very well him being so horribly gentle and considerate but it was her life he was talking about. Her marriage. She didn't want a bloody divorce. And she didn't want any bloody food either. She would rather have a drink.

She turned on her heel and went back into the sitting room. There she bent down in front of the sideboard where Lytton's mother kept her limited supplies of booze. She used to watch Lytton do this in the days when they stayed there together. She didn't want a divorce because a part of her still hoped she would be able to retrieve those days. Opening the small oak door she found this cupboard fairly empty too. Chinking the bottles against the silence she discovered several half full bottles of various sherries, one whole bottle of red wine and a selection of nearly empty sticky liqueur bottles. Taking out the fullest bottle of sherry, she straightened up and walked briskly back to the kitchen in search of a glass. Somewhere, way back in the depths of her mind there was a whisper that said 'don't do this!' But it was being drowned by the angry confusion that was drumming at the edges of her skull. Removing the cork with a soft plop she dropped it on the worktop and poured the silky golden liquid from the bottle until it reached about two inches up the pattern on the side of the tumbler. As she tilted the glass to her lips she quelled that whisper once and for all by muttering to the black kitchen window.

"Oh for God's sake, surely I'm entitled to some pleasure and there's nobody here to care in any case!"

***

Michael opened his eyes and squinted at his watch. From the car doors banging and voices he could hear outside, and the ringing of the church bell, he guessed it must be nearly ten thirty. And he was right. His watch told him that it was actually 10.26. Time he made an effort and got up he supposed. Although this was not the first time he had been in the conscious state this morning. It certainly had not been an uninterrupted, premium lie-in; not like yesterday's. But never mind, he thought, waking up and knowing that you're not going to get up is almost as good as not waking up at all. The first time had been at about 6.00 am when he had heard John and Nickii talking in muted voices in their bedroom next door. Their whispers wouldn't have woken him, but one of them had probably been down to make tea. It must have been the creaking of their bedroom door that did it. And, of course, Claire had slept right through that, with her legs forming a triangle across the bed and squashing him against the wall. For someone who said he had a degree in sleeping, she could sleep pretty deeply when she tried. *And* she would never admit to taking two thirds of the bed. He had once threatened to take a photograph to prove it, but she had just laughed, probably knowing that he would never bother to carry it out. He had got up to have a pee then; scrambling across Claire's splayed out legs and into the crafty little loo that John and Nickii had had put under the eaves adjoining their spare bedroom. At least when he came back Claire had changed to the foetal position, giving him a bit more space in the bed. As though in a token of gratitude he had nestled up to her curled back and drifted back to sleep. Only to be half woken again when she had stretched out and got up; and then fiddled around getting her dressing gown off the hook on the wall. And then again when she came back and announced.

"Tea!" Putting a mug down on the oak blanket box that served as a bedside table.

Remembering this, he stretched out his hand and wrapped it around the outside of the mug. Stone cold, of course, what did he expect! But he sat up and took a swig of it anyway. Cold tea is better than no tea. Then he heaved himself higher up in the bed and pulled aside the curtain to survey the day. The bed being positioned across under the window as it was, was a hazard in terms of cold and draught from the outside wall, against which he was often thrust by Claire's legs, but great for forming plans and decisions for the day regarding the weather, without having to set foot to floor. And, also, if things looked too bleak, one could consequently snuggle down and go straight back to sleep.

Today, there were bits of blue sky and white clouds travelling quite fast across them, which indicated a breezy autumn day. Perhaps he could persuade them all into a walk by the sea. He let the curtain drop and tossed back the duvet, swinging his legs around and setting his feet on the floor. He sat on the edge of the bed and thought how he always felt out of place in this room. Not uncomfortably so really, but a bit like the proverbial bull in a china shop. The walls matched the duvet, which matched the curtains. It was a pretty blue and white print, quite subtle and subdued, but very feminine nonetheless.

Standing up, he picked his jeans off the top of his weekend bag on the floor and slung them behind him onto the bed, then rummaged around inside the bag for clean pants, socks and t-shirt. Initially the place had sounded like the Marie Celeste; as though they may have already gone out and left him. But now he could hear Claire and Nickii chatting down in the kitchen. The sounds crept up around the beams in those old houses. Now he had to decide whether to catch a quick shower or whether, if he wanted to rustle them up for a walk before lunch he should make a more speedy appearance. Telling himself that if he was quick, the time taken wouldn't make that much difference, he grabbed a towel and some shampoo and trotted down the stairs two at a time. He was just lifting the latch of the downstairs loo where the shower was when Claire came through the sitting room.

"I thought I heard you moving around!" she said, standing in the doorway. "We'd given you up as a lost cause. What would you like for breakfast? We've all had ours – long ago!"

He just grinned at her, deciding to ignore the jibe.

"Well I'm going to have a quick shower; but – oh – something easy. I wondered if we might go for a walk – down to Pagham or Selsey or somewhere – or The Witterings – it looks like a nice day. What's everybody doing?"

"Mummy and I are just doing the vegetables for lunch and Daddy's in there!"

She nodded in the direction of John's study. The door was closed, causing a corner of gloom where normally rays of light fell across the hall carpet. "He's been in there since about 8 o'clock. He's started to re-draft his novel on the computer; all fired up and raring to go after yesterday. I'll sound them both out about a walk; it might be a good idea – but we can't be too long if Mummy's cooking lunch!"

She took a few steps in the direction of the study door and looked back over her shoulder.

"If certain people got up earlier, there'd be more time." she said – now that she was well out of reach.

"Well if certain other people didn't keep waking a person up, then they'd manage to get their sleep in wouldn't they?"

He pulled a face in her direction, his hand still on the latch of the shower room door.

"And who was completely sparko when I came up to get dressed?"

He gave up without another word and took quick refuge in the shower. Bolting the door behind him and flopping his towel down on the closed loo seat, he was just reaching for the shower controls when he heard the 'phone ringing. After only a short stab of irritation, he remembered that fortunately it was not his to answer; and turning the water on full blast he allowed his attention to wander to the copious amounts of plastic filler that someone had put around the rim of the shower tray. Whenever he looked at that he felt a great deal of sympathy for their wobbly edges and remembered the frustration of putting that stuff around his kitchen sink.

CHAPTER SIX

By the time they reached the East Beach car park at Selsey, all but the smallest fluffy cumulus clouds had disappeared and strokes of light cirrus were fanning in from the horizon as though an artist had quickly whisked his white brush across pale blue. The sunlight made it almost hot in the car, but the tumbling motion of a discarded polystyrene fast food box across their path indicated quite a breeze coming off the sea. The car park was larger than a couple of football pitches, plus some, with faded markings where the cars might park and patches of weeds and grass breaking through the cracked tarmac. As John drove diagonally across the empty spaces to the far side, Claire spoke up from the back seat.

"This car park always makes me laugh;" she said, "look there's the vast total of four cars over there and two more up there. I don't think I've ever seen more than twenty in here at the most. There's all this space and yet nobody ever comes here. But if you go to Bognor, the place is teeming with people and there are no car parks. Just those few spaces along the front – and once they're filled you've had it!"

"Well I suppose they don't come here because there's nothing much for them to come here for." Michael said, looking in the direction of an empty climbing frame, a children's slide and four rubber tyres dangling forlornly from a wooden beam. A collection that would be more in place on a patch of worn grass somewhere in the East End of London, than as a seaside attraction. All the better for us, John thought, as he pulled up in front of a steep grassy bank that led up to the sea wall. Turning round to smile at Claire and Michael in the back, he said.

"Let the buggers go to Bognor, I say; we like it like this! Shall we go?"

"Actually it does get quite busy in the summer."

Nickii said, as she got out of the car and closed the door.

"We've brought the children down here sometimes and it's been quite packed. It doesn't have the kiosks and the deck chairs, or flowers and fancy lampposts but it does have the beach, the sea and the cafe and loos; and it's the nearest beach to some of the caravan sites so it can get crowded!"

They had parked next to an apple green Datsun Cherry. The front passenger door was wide open and a woman with a dull pink scarf tied in a triangle over a bouffant hairstyle was sitting there staring contentedly at the grassy bank, which completely obscured the sea and anything else of interest. A very dejected Yorkshire terrier lay by the car, tied to the window winder by his lead. When they were well out of earshot of the cars, Claire said quietly to Nickii who was walking beside her.

"Do you think she comes to admire the view!"

"Well she could be waiting for someone! Perhaps her hubby's gone to the loo, or fishing or something."

Nickii whispered back, looking round surreptitiously.

"But it's surprising how often you do see people just sitting there!"

"Must be a few slices short of a loaf, or whatever it is they say!"

Claire said, more loudly now that there was nobody around to hear. But her remark hung on the sound of their footsteps, and the barking of a dog over on the beach. Obviously wishing that she could bite off her tongue and wanting to fill the horrid hush that had fallen amongst them, Claire grabbed at a lump of foliage beside the path. Pulling off a handful of small reddy-brownish flowers she held out her hand in the direction of John and Nickii who had moved together and linked arms.

"You used to say these were dolly apples when we were kids but what is it really?"

Nickii looked at the remains of the stem and leaf in Claire's other hand.

"Oh I don't know!" She said, and then smiled, "that's probably why we called it dolly apples. Is it Ribwort or Knotgrass or something like that? We could look it up – but I don't suppose we will!"

As they came up to the gap in the wall that led on to the sea path, the wind got stronger billowing out Claire's green cotton skirt and flurrying up their hair. Michael took several deep ozone filled breaths.

"So is it right and up to the lifeboat, or left and down to the railway carriages? Or both – up to the lifeboat and back...."

Both directions held a certain appeal for Michael. The lifeboat station, stuck out in the sea like an old garden shed on a miniature pier, inspired his creativity and made him want to have a go at painting it. And, however many times they had walked up there, he could always spot something different to interest him in the row of ramshackle dwellings set almost on the beach itself along towards

Pagham Harbour. Constructed imaginatively out of old railway rolling stock, presumably sometime after the Second World War, each had its own charm and character and never ceased to fascinate.

"Well I vote left and up to the railway carriages. Both would take too long."

Claire said, hugging her jacket in at the waist against the wind and hopping from one foot to the other.

"And I like it that way too."

Nickii said, looking left towards Pagham.

Michael took a few brisk steps in that direction and then turned, waiting expectantly.

"Come on then!", he said, with an enticing shake of the head, "let's be having you. One. Two. One. Two."

They were about fifty yards from a seat. There were several spaced out along the length of the promenade. The seats were like wooden park benches bolted to the concrete slabs of the sea wall. Some of them were dedicated to various dear departed friends and relatives with words and dates carved into the wood or screwed on to the backs on brass plates. Presumably these people had found much pleasure and contentment along this quiet stretch of the South Coast. Whether the next seat 'belonged' to anyone or not, there was nobody sitting there for which John felt truly grateful. He had been searching around in his mind for the best way of telling them that he just felt too weary to walk on. He didn't want to worry Nickii, but he just could not face walking any further. As they reached the seat, he said.

"I think I'll just sit here and contemplate the waves for a while and wait for you to come back. I'm not really in the mood for walking. Perhaps I'll stroll up the other way in a bit and get some ice creams for when you get back."

As Michael, Claire and Nickii strolled on together, heads down and shoulders rounded in conversation, he turned around briefly to see if in fact he was sitting on anybody's seaside memorial. But no the thick wooden planks were quite bare, save for the christening of green bleached stains from the sea gulls. Nickii hadn't been at all convinced. She had wanted to stay here with him. But he had managed to persuade her that he wanted to sit alone to think about the novel. But that wasn't strictly true. He actually did feel very, very tired. His head was throbbing and his eyes smarting. Both were probably a result of staring at the computer; but he felt depressed about that too. Yesterday he had felt buoyant and cheerful about the book, but after working on it this morning he felt completely pessimistic. The revisions and editing were going to take him weeks.

Unexpectedly, he was aware of the sound of childish laughter against the noise of the wind and the waves breaking on the shingle. He turned his gaze to follow the sound. There was a young couple walking along the beach with a toddler between them. The child was wearing one of those brightly coloured, padded romper suits and tiny wellington boots. The parents were holding one hand each. Six steps and then a swing, another six steps and again, the toddler giggled as it flew and they laughed as they ran and then the child landed; already crying out for more. The tinge of a smile quivered at the corners of John's lips. But even their happiness turned to sadness in his mind. He and Nickii did that once. All young parents do it. Probably Jackie and Lytton did it too.

The sound of Lytton's voice hadn't helped him this morning. Whether it was irrational or not, just that husky baritone drawl of his was enough to wind John into a coil inside. He should have waited and let Nickii answer the 'phone. But it had been an instant reflex to pick it up immediately when it lay right next to him on his desk. Lytton had been perfectly polite, even almost sympathetic. He had wanted to know if there was any news. The social workers had rung him too and Jackie wasn't there. And he had confirmed that his mother was away for a few days.

So, where the hell was Jackie? Has she got on a train and gone to London? She had done that before. If so whereabouts in London? And where would she be sleeping? Or, worse, who would she be sleeping with? His mind threw up a picture of the dropouts, druggies and homeless under the arches at Waterloo. He closed his eyes and shook his head to try to clear it. Opening them again he saw that the couple with the child were way up the beach now throwing stones in the sea. He thought, as he had many times in the past few hours, of the conversation he had had with Jackie last weekend. Yet again he felt pangs of guilt because he hadn't told Nickii about it. And anger. A fierce anger mixed with the guilt and increased the throbbing over his eyes. He had only wanted to help for God's sake. He only wanted to make it all better. In the same way as when the girls were small and they fell over and grazed their knees. Lots of kisses to the injured knee, some Savlon, a sticky plaster and a cuddle and that was it. No more tears and on with life and laughter. Jackie needed a life. Whatever it cost, however hard he had to work to achieve it, it wouldn't matter, if only he could make it better. That was all he had been trying to do. She needed a home. Somewhere where she could rebuild her life; instead of living in that half-way house where all of the occupants feed of each other's madness. A small house or a flat somewhere close by, so that they could still offer Jackie support, but without suffocating her. He had already seen several quite suitable little houses. The finance wouldn't be too difficult. He could easily raise the loan. Then, when she was ready, she could get the children back. Maybe just Jodie and Flavvy to start with; being girls and the youngest they would be less trouble to cope with. And later on why not Dane too? But not Lytton. Definitely, absolutely and one hundred per cent not Lytton. John had had enough of trying to make things better for Lytton.

Nickii didn't need to be told about John's conversation with Jackie last weekend. She had guessed it; or something like it. While she had been racking her brains yesterday, she had remembered how she had come in from the kitchen on Saturday night to find that Jackie had already gone to bed. At the time she had thought nothing of it, since it was a fairly regular occurrence, but yesterday she remembered how quiet John had been for the rest of that evening and realised that something had probably been said. She didn't blame him though, anymore than she did herself. How many hundreds of times had they both tried to talk to Jackie only to find that they'd said the wrong thing and upset her?

The three of them had reached the end of the sea path now. Michael asked if they should carry on and made for the steps that would carry them down from the sea and along the track to the railway cottages. Claire hesitated and looked at Nickii, who said she thought they ought to be getting back. The lunch will be getting crispy around the edges by now, she thought, and she wanted to get back to John. They turned back into the wind and started back at a faster pace than they had strolled along. Half way along there was a SOLD board outside one of the bungalows on their right. Seeing Claire looking in that direction, Nickii said,

"We sent for the details of that. It's bigger than it looks and quite nice inside. Daddy was thinking of it for Jackie."

"What, of buying it for her?"

Claire said, looking back at the house with more interest.

"Well yes; but it was only a vague idea. We thought that perhaps if she had a home of her own and the children living with her things might fall into place. If her life was normal maybe she would become so too."

"But do you really think it would work?" Claire asked doubtfully. "Do you think she could cope with the children now? And what about Lytton? Wouldn't they all just end up back together and it would start all over again?"

Nickii suppressed what she knew to be an irrational irritation. Claire had only voiced all of the same questions that they had asked themselves. But she still felt an instinctive pang of annoyance that Claire should question Jackie's ability to cope.

"Well yes, you're right;" she said, "especially about Lytton. And that's why we haven't taken it any further. Daddy wants her to divorce Lytton but she simply won't discuss it. Actually, I doubt whether he would come back. After all, he banished her in the first place and now he has a new life. A new place to live, with his children all around him when he wants them and a new woman to look after them."

Claire's answer was lost on the wind and then they walked on in silence. Nickii could see John now about one hundred yards ahead. He had his legs crossed and his arms folded. He was staring straight ahead of himself at the horizon. As they approached, he turned and leant forward. Nickii noticed the dark circles around his eyes and the vertical furrows in his forehead between his eyebrows.

"That was quick!" he said, with a half smile, "I haven't got those ice creams have I!"

Nickii put her arm through his and gave it a squeeze.

"We don't need ice creams. We're just going to have lunch!" she said.

***

Jackie was eating cornflakes; old and stale cornflakes; nibbling at them one by one from the bottom of the packet. She leant against the wall, once more staring out into Selena's garden through the back door. It was sunny out there now and the trees were swaying gently in the wind. Jackie liked the wind. Or she used to like the wind; the feel of it on her face and the tugging at her hair; like flying. She could be out there. All she needed to do was slide the bolts, open the door and step out; get some fresh air; blow away the cobwebs. But her body and her brain were made of lead again and there was no point anyway. Her cobwebs had grown and multiplied, then fused themselves into a thick black shroud that no wind would ever blow away. The time since she had arrived there had been an eternity and eternity seemed to stretch before her.

Last night was different; better for a while after the sherry. She had seen a glimmer of light ahead; a dream of a new life with Lytton and the children. For a moment it had all seemed so simple. As the sherry eased the pain her mind became clearer, the anger slipped away. It was easy. All she had to do was to tell her father that she loved Lytton. That you don't choose who you love; you just love them. And none of it was Lytton's fault. He would understand if she explained it properly. Then he would buy the house, and ...

But the pain crept back and the doubts grew. Lytton wouldn't stay with her unless she could stay well. She would need to earn money, look after the children properly and the house. She had remembered the scenes of shouting and despair. She had tried more sherry, and then more again, to get back the glimmer of light but it had already been snuffed out by a blanket of hopelessness.

When she had woken the room was utterly dark and she was very, very cold. She had felt sick and then faint as she bumped into strange objects trying to find the stairs. She scrambled up them on all fours in the dark. And at the edges of her weakness were shades of fear. A voice inside her had called out for her mother, but no sound came. The cottage was as silent as the night. Half an hour ago, when she woke up, she couldn't remember how she got onto the bed and under the quilt. She couldn't remember anything after lying in the dark at the top of the stairs and feeling so ill and alone. And now suddenly her mind seemed starkly lucid. Thoughts and memories were tumbling through her brain so fast that she could not catch them as they fell. The face of her doctor as he told her on no account to drink alcohol with her tablets. Pictures of the children, playing and laughing; Flavvy being dressed by Lytton's new girlfriend. Where was Selena? What would she say when she got back. Her fingers scrabbled at the cornflakes in the depths of the box. The greaseproof paper rustled against the silence of the kitchen. She had forgotten the tablets anyway. Claire and Michael were with her parents for the weekend. She wondered what they were doing; what they were talking about. Bob and Melanie back at the house. Bob with his underpants draped over every radiator. Melanie, forever and always washing her hands and twitching, twitching and more twitching. Her room. Her photograph of Lytton. Lytton, The bottle of tablets. How would she get back? Would she go back? She didn't want to go back. And with it all came a rising, pent up panic; building up from her feet on the floor, through her stomach, making her hold her breath. She couldn't breathe. She needed a hole in her skull for the panic to escape, like a rush of steam from a pressure cooker. But there was no escape. She turned from the door, dropped the cornflake packet on to the worktop. It missed and fell. Cornflakes spilled out all over the floor as she paced into the sitting room. She stood in the middle of the room. She wanted to pick up the chair and fling it far through the window. Hear the sound of shattering glass; follow it with the cushions, bottles, and books. But where her head was exploding, her body felt weak again. She sat down in the chair instead. Trembling now, she put her hands over her ears and her head on her knees and waited.

CHAPTER SEVEN

During the drive home from Sussex on Sunday afternoon, Claire had been making the transition between a weekend off and reality, and by the time they had got to Kingston Bridge she had been fully conscious of all the undone things she had left behind. But now after four days of rushing around she had finished all her typing, for a couple of days at least, caught up on the washing and ironing and managed to drag the hoover around the house. This morning she went into Twickenham to get the weekly shopping; and bought a couple of bunches of white chrysanths so that she could change the flowers that had been wilting in their vases and irritating her every time she looked at them.

Now, having even found time to rake up the leaves on the lawn that had also been bugging her all week, she was snipping off some runner beans to go with the fresh plaice she had bought for their dinner. It was a bumper crop this year. The line of plants, stretching just above her head, were still smothered in scarlet flowers and everywhere she looked she saw hanging yet another near perfect specimen. Long straight beans, shining in the late afternoon sun snapped clean in half at the touch of a finger. The satisfaction of picking her own homegrown veg always cheered Claire up, no matter what her mood; the marvel of nature and the fact that she herself had planted the small seed that produced the lush plant and then the fresh, healthy and free food for them to enjoy. It had become her own private cliché that she found herself involuntarily humming.

'*We plow the fields and scatter the good seed on the land, but it is fed and watered by God's almighty hand...*

Then, when she got to the second line, she saw it as a reminder that, whilst she may have dug and raked and popped the seeds into the soft earth, she still couldn't take all the credit. If God or nature, or whoever, had decided that the seed wouldn't grow, then it wouldn't grow and there was nowt she could do about it; as indeed some of them quite often didn't. But then again, she had put in hours of hard work and given God, nature or whoever, a jolly good helping hand. It was quite ridiculous how the same old sequence of thoughts went through her mind; all on her own there at the end of her long garden. She had already gathered more than enough beans for tonight's dinner, but they needed to be picked to leave room for their baby siblings to swell and stretch to their own good size. She would either give some away or slice them neatly into polythene bags for the freezer.

She heard a telephone ringing and looked back in the direction of the house, straining her ears to decide whether it was her own or one of the neighbour's. She decided it was her own but turned back defiantly to her beans. She was not going to run all the way down there. She had left the answer phone on. Let it do its work. It was almost certainly one of her customers and she was in no hurry to receive more work. After three years, Claire was becoming disillusioned with her home-run secretarial business. When she and Michael had bought this house, shortly after they were married, Claire had been working full-time as a secretary. She had been in the same job for five years. But everything had induced her to give that up. The train into central London from Twickenham was tedious and boring, not nearly so simple as hopping on a tube or a bus from her old house. Their new four-bedroom Victorian home was a bargain but in a dreadful state of repair. It had needed decorating throughout and the large garden was completely wild and overgrown. It had not taken Claire very long to decide that she was not going to cope with all this as well as her job. But she still had to earn; at least something. So she had formed a plan. She could combine her old dream of writing with earning money at home. Before the floating capital from the sale of their individual houses ran out, they had spent some of it on an electronic typewriter and a dictaphone. Then she had put advertisements in the local papers and gone through the Yellow Pages, sending carefully worded sales pitch letters to all those entrants likely to be in need of extra secretarial services. The work had dribbled in at first, but after a few months she had acquired several regular customers and enough work to keep her frantically busy for many longer hours than she had originally envisaged. It had seemed to be a success. But, predictably enough, the money she had earned from it did not match up to her dream. And she didn't seem to find any time at all to write. To add insult to injury, two of her customers had been aspiring novelists who wanted her to type their novels. One, after asking her on the phone if she did dictaphone work, had turned up with a full 90 minute cassette of the type that you put in a personal stereo and had then come to collect the work, armed only with a £5 note and no cheque book.

Now the two colanders on the path of the vegetable patch were full to overflowing with beans. Balancing the kitchen scissors precariously on the top of one of them, Claire picked one up in each hand. Walking past their yellowing tomato plants she was reminded that they needed demolishing and the remaining green tomatoes should be brought in to ripen. Half way down the garden she could not resist putting down one of her colanders and yanking out a particularly large thistle from one of the flower beds, thinking at the same time that if she could find time to mow the lawns tomorrow, that would hoover up the rest of the leaves. Reaching the conservatory, she balanced the colanders of beans on top of all the papers on Michael's drawing board and kicked off her garden shoes. In the kitchen their two cats were waiting, front paws neatly together and eyes pointing upwards at hers. Taking the hint, she lifted their dirty bowls from the floor and dropped them into the sink; then walked over to the answer phone on the pine dresser and pushed the replay button. She was pleasantly surprised to hear her daughter's voice rather than a customer's; even the cats looked round.

"Hello Mummy, it's Pippa. I suppose you're in the garden. I just rang for a chat and to say I might come home the weekend after next – if you're there. I'll ring you later!"

Almost immediately, as Pippa's voice died away, the phone rang again, its shrill tone scattering the cats through the kitchen door into the hall with a flurry of paws and loose fur. Claire picked up the receiver and uttered an affectionate 'Hello', without bothering with her usual parrot repeat of their number. But her tender greeting was answered by a surprised and gruff male voice; the very last she wanted to hear. The voice belonged to the customer she had christened Doctor Boffin; who was writing a long and painful paper on *The Theory of Powders* and the inexplicable things that powders do in hoppers, of all things; which involved Claire in typing pages and pages of algebraic fractions followed by more of totally incomprehensible prose. But he paid well and on time, and she actually quite liked him with his shiny bald head and gentle intense manner, so now she agreed for him to bring the next dreaded installment tomorrow morning.

While dialling Pippa's number she wondered whether she could get David to come back for that weekend too. It would be nice to have both of her children at home together again. Although they were not very far from each other, with Pippa studying medicine in Cardiff and David doing his degree in Bath, they rarely seemed to meet up which Claire felt was rather a shame. Mother and daughter chatted for a shamefully long time; just over half an hour in fact. During which time the cats had made it up onto the work top and were sitting on either side of the runner beans as though defying Claire to do anything at all with those before she fed them. Putting down the receiver at last, she ran hot water into the sink and glanced across at the clock on the oven. She had wanted to ring her mother too, but it would have to wait until later now. She had tried every day since the weekend but there had always been no reply. Surely they must be in tonight, she thought.

***

Nickii had also been trying to ring Claire for two days. Twice she had got the answer phone, which she had not been at all in the mood for, and so had hung up without leaving a message, and now she had tried twice in succession only to find the line engaged both times. Particularly irritating since now would have been a convenient time to speak to her, as John and Jackie were both out. With a small sigh Nickii replaced her receiver and went back into the kitchen trying at the same time to decide what they might have to eat that night. She was not a bit hungry and was really far too distracted to think about food. But they could be back at any moment, and they would have to eat something tonight. Not for the first time that week, she wished she didn't seem to be the only one clinging to the reins of normality. Various ideas of basic sustenance flashed through her tired brain, but she turned and walked back into the dining room to the telephone again. She would try Claire one more time first.

But again the number was engaged. The wretched *beep, beep, beep* of the tone added exasperation to the befuddled exhaustion she already felt. But that passed quickly enough. Claire was probably talking to Pippa; and why not. Briefly, Nickii wondered how Pippa was and thought what a long time it was since she had seen her eldest granddaughter. Sitting down in the chair beside the telephone table was a mistake. In the quiet of the cottage her body took over from her mind and told her it was time she sat still for a moment. She stared at the dark grey telephone. A part of her was dreading the call anyway. Repeating the events of the past few days was almost more than she could bear. But Claire would still be wondering. Wondering and worrying about whether Jackie had turned up yet. Still a potted version will do, she thought, as she dialled the number yet again. She did not have to repeat all the tiny details.

This time the engaged signal brought her jolting back to the present. John had actually been gone quite a long time now. And looking at her watch she saw that it was nearly three quarters of an hour since he had left to walk up to the village pub. They had been almost sure he would find Jackie there, after they had discovered that she was nowhere to be found again. Getting briskly up from the chair, Nickii's common sense took over once more. Of course he has found her and he is probably having a pint with her and trying to talk, she told herself, quelling the sprouting tinges of anxiety at source; and the most sensible thing to do about eating, in the circumstances, would be to go out for a meal. So instead of going back into the kitchen she went up to their bedroom to change the scruffy trousers she had had on all day. Looking in the bathroom mirror she saw a face that looked even worse than she felt. The eyes seemed to be sunk in dark rings and the grey tinge to the skin of her face was winning over the remains of her healthy summer tan. Reaching for her bottle of make-up her mind repeated, in spite of herself, the picture of John's face as he had sat in the car on Monday and begged her to leave.

"Please let's just go home."

He had pleaded with such despair on his face.

"Please I can't take any more of this, just get in the car and let us go home."

And there Nickii had been again, balancing on the tightrope between husband and daughter.

"But we can't do that," she had pleaded back. "We can't just leave her here. You just sit there and I'll go and have one more try."

Suddenly the phone was ringing in the bedroom. Hurriedly wiping the make-up from her fingers with a tissue Nickii went to answer it, hoping that it might be Claire. But it was a less familiar voice.

"Hello, is that Nickii?"

For a second or two Nickii did not recognise her.

"This is Selena speaking. I am just phoning to ask how Jackie is now?"

"Oh, hello Selena. It's kind of you ring. She's a lot better thank you."

Nickii said, thinking that was rather a white lie, but ploughing on just the same.

"She's out for a walk with John at the moment."

"Oh, so you didn't have to take her back to hospital then, that's good. Such a setback."

"No we decided that she'd be better off here with us for a while."

Which was not exactly true either, since although that would have been the path they would have chosen, there had been no offer of any professional help anyway. When they had called the doctor and the social workers to tell them that they had Jackie back, it was simply assumed that they were going to keep her. Nobody had suggested any visits, consultations or advice of any sort. And when they had discovered that she wasn't taking her tablets, they had had to drive back up to the house to fetch them.

The creak of the front gate outside distracted Nickii from Selena's words of concern. Then while apologising to her again for all the mess and trouble, she heard John speaking downstairs, which at least meant that they must both be home safely. Dashing back into the bathroom to quickly put on some lipstick she was appreciating Selena's quite genuine sympathy. Then she remembered what a job Selena had had climbing through the kitchen window to get back into her own house.

Downstairs again she found John standing in the kitchen staring out through the window into the evening gloom in the garden. He turned as he heard her come in.

"You look nice; you've changed!" he said, as she walked towards him and slipped her hands around his waist.

"You found her then!" Her words were muffled in his chest, "Where is she now?"

"She's gone to the loo, I think. I had a pint with her; tried to talk; the weather, the church, ordinary things. I didn't even say anything about her walking off like that again, but she didn't say anything. Hardly a 'no' or a 'yes', so I suggested it was time to come back; said you would be getting the meal ready...."

"I was, but then I thought maybe it would be good for all of us if we went out somewhere instead?"

The meal, at one of their once favourite bistro places, was dismal and strained. Jackie stared at her plate, pushing the food around it half-heartedly and hardly eating a morsel. Their conversation struggled and their own tense silences seemed deafened by the busy chatter at the other tables. In exasperation, at one stage, John turned to Jackie suddenly and asked her when her next appointment with the doctor was. Jackie, without averting her gaze from the table beneath her eyes, muttered that she didn't know; she didn't think she had got one. When at last they got into the privacy of their bedroom with the door closed, John got into bed and pulled the duvet over him with a huge sigh of relief. Leaning back onto the upholstered deep buttoning of the headboard, he watched Nickii as she sorted through a pile of clothes. And she watched him as he picked up his bedside book and laid it on his lap with a singular lack of interest.

"We're not getting anywhere, are we?" he said.

They were back to the old guarded whispers in their own bedroom in case Jackie heard or they woke her up.

"Perhaps we should phone the doctor. We can't go on like this. We need some help!" John continued, while Nickii stuffed their underwear into the already overflowing wicker basket of washing and pushed the lid down on top.

"I'll phone in the morning and try to make an appointment," she whispered back.

CHAPTER EIGHT

Driving over Richmond Bridge Michael's spirits were quite high; lifted by the fact that not only was it Friday, but he had also had a cheerful chat and a couple of pints in the pub with his partner. He would have liked another half but had exercised great self-control, he thought, in refusing, mainly because he had come in the car, but also because the time was getting on. Slowing down to a stop, he waited for the traffic to open up so that he could turn right his hand tapping on the steering wheel to the beat of a Van Morrison tape. He hoped he was not in the doghouse; like the night he had got home to find Claire tight-lipped and flushed with anger.

"It's my Friday night too!", she had snapped, "and I don't see why I should spend it turning the oven up and down and looking out of the window to see whether you're going to appear or not!"

'Woops,' he thought, and smiled to himself as he turned onto the paved area in front of the house, beside the Renault. Probably because Claire's father had given them both cars, they didn't refer to them as 'my car' or 'your car'. They both just drove whichever they fancied or whichever was convenient. Although, of course, they both fancied the Celica over the Renault 5, which was rusting a bit at the edges and not at all in the same class. Looking at the clock on the dashboard, as he switched off the ignition, Michael noticed that it was not quite eight o'clock. Hopping out and locking the door, he thought that with any luck he might get away without too much of an ear bashing. Dropping his door keys by the pot of geraniums in the porch was not a very good start, but never mind. In the hall he was greeted by a waft of what smelt very much like baked potatoes. Dropping his bag against the sitting room door, he glanced in there and then in the kitchen, but there was no sign of Claire. Guessing that she might be upstairs, he rested his hand on the top of the newel post and inclining his head upwards called out a cheerful,

"Hel-lo...?"

A muffled reply, followed by the sound of her slippers on the stairs, indicated that she was in her office on the top floor. When she appeared around the half landing he was relieved to see that, although she was looking rather strained, she was managing a small smile and did lean forward for a kiss when she reached the bottom stair. Whilst she was, somewhat mechanically, enquiring after his day, she also mechanically, picked up his bag from the hall floor and took it through the dining room to the conservatory. Michael went into the kitchen and saved any reply for when she came back. Happily, his suspicion of baked potatoes was confirmed. There was a film of condensation over the oven door and a small wicker basket lined with kitchen paper on the worktop waiting to receive them. The scrubbed-oak kitchen table was ready laid and sported a green salad and a bowl of their homegrown tomatoes. He pulled out a chair and reached for the newspaper, which was still lying folded on the corner of the table where he had left it that morning. But he hadn't enough time even to read the headlines before Claire was back at the door. The grey section of her fringe was cast askew over her forehead where she had been running her fingers through her hair.

"Well, how was your day? I'm sorry I *was* listening!"

She said, but just as mechanically as before; so mechanically that he knew that the question did not really beg a detailed answer; more of an,

"OK, how was yours?"

"Oh, OK too I suppose. There are some baked potatoes in the oven, but I haven't got anything special to go with them. Do you fancy a tin of salmon or just grated cheese or what?"

And there went the fingers through the hair again; which all added up to something which needed to come out, that she was trying hard to keep in.

"Cheese is fine for me. So what have you been up to all day? Are you still working up there, or have you finished for tonight?"

She opened the fridge and stared into it for a moment before remembering what she was looking for.

"I will probably go back up for a bit after supper; just a couple of pages. Dr Boffin came this morning; more fractions and hieroglyphics. As usual, he said there was no particular hurry, but perhaps he would come on Tuesday; and then he patiently pointed out that I'd got some of his pis and squares and cubes on the wrong lines last time!"

A piece of farmhouse cheddar and the remains of some roquefort found their way on to a plate and then the plate to the table. Dr Boffin is not the real nitty gritty, Michael thought, and sat quietly waiting for more.

"I spoke to David this evening. We had a nice chat and he seemed cheerful, but he said he thought he and Pippa were meant to be at Andrew and Paula's next weekend, no the one after next, oh you know what I mean, so there's the usual mix up there."

Getting warmer but not quite hot. Michael knew that the rusty rivalry between Claire and her ex-husband usually produced a tired anger, not quiet anxiety mode, which is what she was in at the moment. The bakkies were coming out of the oven now; sliced in half with crispy golden brown tops they were almost enough to take his mind off whatever lay in the shadows behind Claire's tussled fringe. But, better out than in, and he would rather have it well and truly out and dusted before 9.30 when a new thriller started on television.

"Well those mix-ups usually get sorted in the end, perhaps they can both come here the following weekend. What about your Mum? Did you finally get to speak to her?"

Bulls-eye. White hot. A "Yes", engulfed by a long sigh; a sitting back in the chair and no attempt to get down to the business of eating.

"Well. What's the story? Have they got Jackie back? Where was she?"

She leant forward and half-heartedly took the smallest potato and dropped it onto her plate; then she stared abstractedly at the rest of the food on the table.

"Oh, do you really want to know?" she said, with another sigh, "you know what will happen."

"Yes I know; and I know I don't like dwelling on things and talking about it endlessly. But I would like to know if she's safe, and how your Mum and Dad are! And you evidently need to talk about it right now. So, is she back?"

"Yes. She was at Selena's. You know, Lytton's mother. Apparently she rang them on Monday morning. She had been away for the weekend and had come home to put the dog into the house before she went off to work. Then she couldn't open her front door. So she went round to her neighbour to see if she'd been in there for any reason and maybe done something to the lock. It turned out that Jackie had called round to the neighbour to collect the key. Then it dawned on Selena that Jackie was in there and she had put the bolt across on the door. She went round the back and that was the same."

"Well didn't she call out or bang on the windows or something?"

"Well I suppose she did, but presumably she didn't get any response. Anyway she rang Mummy and Daddy from the neighbours and said she didn't know what to do, and she really did need to go to work. So they said they would drive straight up there."

Michael pushed the salad bowl and the cheese in Claire's direction.

"Come along, you've got to eat something! So what happened when they got there?"

"Well they knocked on the doors and looked through all the downstairs windows and tapped on them calling out for Jackie to let them in, but she didn't respond to them either. Then they sat outside for a bit trying to decide what to do. It must have been ghastly. They must have been frantic with worry. Then I think Mummy said they borrowed a ladder from somewhere, I suppose to see if they could get in through an upstairs window, I don't know. But that didn't work either. Apparently, Daddy got really fed up at that stage and wanted to just go back home and leave her. He said he'd had enough, but of course, Mummy felt they couldn't possibly do that, so she left him sitting in the car and went back to have one last try. And luckily just then Selena came back. "

"So did they have to break in then or what?"

Michael asked. Having given up on persuading Claire to eat, he helped himself to another potato and began to grate some cheese over the top.

"No I think Mummy said that Selena managed to climb through a kitchen window. Perhaps there was a loose catch or something."

"So where was Jackie when they got in then?"

"She'd been hiding from them all the time and was in a terrible state, I think, but I didn't get all the details. Though Mummy did say it took quite a while to calm her down and persuade her to go home."

"Well how did Selena...? Look will you, please, eat something. Here take some salad at least before I am forced to finish it! How did Selena take all this, wasn't she rather angry?"

Claire, at last, took a token spoonful of salad onto her plate beside her lone potato; which she cut in half and topped with a knob of butter. The potato was so cold now that the butter refused to melt; making Claire feel even less like eating it. She mashed the butter around in the open potato with her fork.

"No, apparently Selena wasn't angry at all. Mummy said she was quite calm about the whole thing really and even very sympathetic. I've only met her once but she's that sort of person, I think, very serene and level-headed; takes everything in her stride. Anyway, they didn't think Jackie was well enough to go back to the house with the others, so they asked her if she would like to stay with them for a few days. But things sound terribly strained. Mummy seemed really flat and tired and I got the impression she's worried about Daddy. Not that she said anything very much; just muttered something about him being depressed and irritable."

"Oh, I'm sure they're alright. You worry too much; how many times do I have to tell you? They're bound to sound rather tired, but they've been coping with it for so long now, they're used to it. They're much stronger than you give them credit for. But in any case it sounds as though Jackie should see her doctor."

"Well, that's just it!" Claire snapped, with a long and tetchy sigh, which immediately cast a hairline crack in Michael's caring, listening mood. When she snapped and sighed like that he could never stop himself feeling that she was blaming him for everything.

"They tried to make an appointment to see the doctor, consultant, specialist, call it what you will, I don't know, but they can't see him until next Tuesday! It's always been the same and it's gone on for such a long time now. They need help as well as Jackie; nobody's ever really told them what they think is wrong, let alone give them any advice on the best way to cope."

"Well I can tell you why that is," Michael pushed back his chair and stood up, "it's because the stupid bastards don't know what's wrong, that's why. Listen, do you mind if I start clearing up while you eat that? There's a new thriller starting in twenty minutes and it would be nice if we both sat down to watch it."

Claire picked up her fork once more and it hovered for a moment over her plate, only to be dropped across the uneaten remains. Her chair grated across the floor as she stood up sharply and took the plate towards the rubbish bin.

"Perhaps we should do more to help. Perhaps we should offer for Jackie to come and stay here for a while!"

"Oh come on Claire!"

Michael was already clanking dishes in the sink with the tap still running. "You know that just isn't practical. Not that I would mind if you wanted to, but you wouldn't be able to get on with your work and Jackie would be miles away from all her support systems. Are you coming to watch the thriller?"

"What support systems! That's exactly what I've just been saying! And no I'm not. I told you I've got more of Dr Boffin's bloody fractions to finish upstairs."

"Well why don't you go and get on with it then, and I'll finish this off. That way you might get down before the end."

But no, as usual she carried on fiddling and farting about, folding up the tablemats, emptying the rubbish bin into the dustbin outside and putting away crockery. All things he could have done perfectly well himself. And all in complete silence. And then finally when he got in to the sitting room ten minutes after the thriller had started, she went trudging back upstairs with that 'all the cares of the world on my shoulders' look. Effectively it meant that he missed another ten minutes because he was too distracted and cross to concentrate. Why the hell she couldn't leave the typing until tomorrow or whenever, he could not fathom. Or was it because she just didn't want to go and sit down with him? But then, by just sitting there sipping his coffee and watching the screen without really taking anything in, he began to calm down. She was actually right about a couple of things, he thought; how he hated being reminded of all this for one! And she was dead right about the support. Maybe if there was more of that.... Of one thing there was certainly no doubt, and that was that the suffering from this illness spreads like ripples on a pond, from the sufferer to the carer to the carer's relatives to the carer's relatives relatives and their friends.

***

Jackie looked around Dr Bulstrode's waiting room with a feeling of resigned familiarity. It was just the same as it ever had been each and every time she had been summoned here from the ward to come and wait for her appointment. The same four chairs with the chipped varnish on the arms and the springing and upholstery worn. The sort of chairs you would expect to see on a skip, or thrown down askew and dejected on the mound of the local tip. The same melamine coffee table, with the ugly table lamp and orange hessian shade, even the same old dog eared copies of 'The Lady,' at least five years old, a couple of Auto Car and two or three Country Life, probably even older; Jackie had never bothered to look. The window with the security bars, painted once, but now with measly spots of chipped white and the rest blackened and pitted with rust. And beyond them, the fire escape from the ward opposite going down into the well of the dingy courtyard below.

What was different was to be sitting here with her mother and father. Their presence seemed to accentuate the cheerless atmosphere.

They all sat in silence; each trying to avoid looking at the other in spite of the confined space. Her mother started to flip through the magazines, but quickly gave up and stared out of the window as though there were something to look at. Her father gazed dejectedly at the floor. They didn't belong here. They were out of place and out of depth; and at this moment Jackie felt sorry for them. Because in spite of the gloom and despondency that this building, these corridors and this room cast over them, her parents still had some hope. They still believed that this visit might achieve something. That the wise old wizard, Dr Bulstrode, would wave his magic wand and come up with some answers at last.

The door opened and Jackie recognised the face of Paul, one of the dippier ward nurses, standing there with the same white jacket that was far too big for him.

"Jacqueline Hildegaard!"

He muttered, barely audibly, and was gone with the door closing behind him. Jackie stood up. Her mother, who had stood up when the door opened and seemed to take a breath as if to speak, gave her a weak smile and sat down again.

"We'll be waiting here for you," she said quietly as Jackie caught the closing door.

The wise old wizard's office was just the same too. Hardly larger than his waiting room with desk, chairs and filing cabinet of the same vintage as himself. If anything had changed, he appeared even older, his cheeks more sunken, his jowls more droopy and his hair more white.

"Please sit down."

Even his voice sounded more tremulous. But the same gnarled fingers scrabbled frantically slowly through the pile of buff files on the side of his desk.

"Err, Mrs...?"

He looked up at Jackie under his bushy white eyebrows.

"Hildegaard."

Jackie said, looking him back in the eye and thinking. "No, nothing's changed!"

"Sorry, what's that you say?"

"Hildegaard." she said again with the same tone. He needed an ear trumpet to add to the picture. She was resigned to it now. But she remembered the despair she had felt on her first appointment. When she too had believed that somewhere there might actually be a wise old wizard. But then she had realised that this one couldn't really even hear her, let alone listen. Eventually his fingers found the file. They opened it and flipped through the pages, while his tired eyes scanned their surface.

"Well, coming along alright are we? Keeping up with the medication?"

He spoke to the file and not to Jackie; who didn't even feel it necessary to give the compulsory nod, since he was not looking anyway. But the voice in her mind said.

"No, on both counts, actually!"

"Good, good."

Now, at last, he looked up in her direction, but then away at the filing cabinet and back down to the desk.

"And doing alright living out? Finding things to do? Muddling along with your colleagues alright?"

With the last question he looked up again, his glazed eyes not quite meeting hers. But, nevertheless, time for the expected nod, which she gave, robot fashion, while he thumbed through the file again. And her mind said.

"No again. Oh, the house is alright; quite a nice house really and I like my bedroom with the familiar curtains and the duvet cover and the chair; having my own space and my own things and being able to shut the door. But no, I'm not finding things to do. What do you mean finding things to do? Getting a job, I suppose. Well my father suggests that too. Nothing complicated, he says, just something to give me some satisfaction and independence. He says it would build up my confidence again. Well tell me, Mr Wizard, how can I build up my confidence when I haven't got the confidence to get the job. Who's going to give *me* a job anyway, tell me that Dr Bulstrode!"

She was aware of a pain in her fingers and looked down at her hands in her lap. She had been squeezing the four fingers of her left hand so tightly together with her right that her wedding ring was cutting into her little finger. She released them and folded her arms. He looked up at her again.

"Well, is there anything you'd like to tell me?"

"Yes, Yes!" she screamed silently and looked away.

"I'd like to tell you that I feel ghastly; that I've been having a dreadful time; that I'm falling again and I can't seem to stop; that sometimes I know that I'm a constant source of pain and hurt to my parents and I hate it, but I can't help it; that I'm not taking the wretched tablets and I don't know whether to start again. What should I do? I stopped taking them because they make me feel sick, they make me fat, they make me tremble. But now I feel worse than I did when I was taking them. Why can't you give me something different? Why can't you just give me something that will make me better?"

Looking back down at her lap, she said.

"No, I don't think so."

CHAPTER NINE

As the waiting room door closed behind Jackie, John stood up and walked over to the window.

"It's terribly stuffy in here!" he sighed, searching all round it for a catch.

But the sash cords had long since been removed and the windows lashed together with layers of paint. For some reason he suddenly thought of being in the submarine during the war, the unearthly silence and the heat; but he couldn't remember ever feeling as claustrophobic down there as he did in that stuffy room.

"Why don't you go for a walk and we'll meet you at the car?" Nickii said.

"Well I would, but I thought we wanted to talk to Dr Bulstrode!"

"Yes, I know, but I'll stay and see if I can have a word with him. Go on, you go, I don't mind."

Standing on the steps outside in the cooler air, he thought about going back up. It wasn't fair to leave Nickii to try to get some sense out of that stubborn old goat. He remembered the numerous other occasions when they'd tried to do exactly that.

"I'm afraid, that's a question, I can't answer, Mr Tolley, because you see my first loyalty is to my patient;" he had said once in that quaky, stammering voice, "and strictly speaking I should only discuss her case fully with her next of kin, which you no longer are."

John remembered his anger and tension at that particular remark, as he had thought, 'oh yes, and we all know who the next of kin is, but where the bloody hell is *he*, one hundred miles away, that's where.' Before he could stop himself he had snapped back.

"Yes, but the patient is actually living with us, isn't she!"

But still they had all felt justified in asking guarded questions about Jackie's past. Her childhood, her disappointments, did they love her, what about his relationship with her as a father? Those questions had hurt, but he had not minded that so much, at least it showed that they were trying. No, it was the interrogators' manners that had raised the bile, those insinuations of accusation, without any invitation for discussion, or proper encouragement for a full answer. Not a glimmer of thought or understanding for the hours and hours that they had actually spent long into the night, night after night, trying to work out where they had gone wrong; the frantic searching through the medical section in the library, trying to make their own diagnosis, so they could at least do something to put it right.

A few yards down the path bordering the patchy grass that spread across to the car park there was a wooden bench. John walked towards it thinking he would sit there for five minutes and then go back up before Jackie came out. Sitting down, it crossed his mind that nowadays he was spending his life sitting on seats to rest; like some old boy with not much longer to go. He should pull himself together; rake up some of the old verve. Perhaps it had been a mistake to retire early after all. If he had carried on after the by-pass, he might have been feeling fitter now. But still what's done was done. It probably was better to get some young blood into the company anyway; might bring better returns on their shares in the end. And once he had collected the new glasses which the doctor suggested yesterday to stop the strange headaches, and the things that were dropping in front of his eyes, he would get on faster with the book. Thinking that perhaps he should make a move to go back to Nickii, he looked back towards the door and was surprised to see Jackie coming down the steps. She spotted him and started to walk in his direction.

"That was quick!" he said, as she got closer.

"Yes, I know," she said, with the hint of a sigh, and sat down on the seat beside him.

"Mummy's gone to the loo, and I think she was trying to talk to him – but *she* won't be long either!"

Turning to look at her, John thought that she did look physically much better than this time last week; and she seemed somehow a little more relaxed now than before she went in.

"Did he help at all? Were you able to talk to him?" he asked her.

A wry smile hovered momentarily at the corner of her lips.

"Not really. The silly old fool can hardly hear anyway, and he's not interested. His minions are actually more use than he is, but that's not saying much. Sometimes I wonder...."

Her words tailed off and she stared bleakly out across the grass. This was the closest he had been to a real conversation with Jackie for several weeks. And it brought the old Jackie racing back to the present. But she looked so tired and full of despair. Suddenly all the anger and frustration slipped away and he felt nothing but love and compassion. He reached across the gap between them on the bench and took one of her hands in his.

"Never mind, I'm sure you'll beat it one day," he said quietly, giving her hand a gentle squeeze. For a moment her fingers curled around his and they sat in silence.

***

Jackie was absolutely right about Nickii not being very long. As soon as Jackie had got into the lift, Nickii knocked on Dr Bulstrode's door. After several attempts she finally heard a muffled "Yes?" and she went in.

"I'm Jackie's, hum, Mrs Hildegaard's, mother. I don't know if you remember me?" she had said boldly, "I wonder if I could have a quick word with you?"

There was no invitation to sit down, in fact no reply at all for several seconds. Dr Bulstrode just regarded her blankly from behind his desk. Nickii stood by the door feeling distinctly uncomfortable and rapidly forgetting everything she had wanted to say. However, mustering some determination she walked briskly to the chair and sat down, just as Dr Bulstrode also pulled himself together and asked what he could do for her.

"Well, I would like to know how you found Jackie today. You see she has been having a bad time lately and we feel that she has taken a few steps backwards; which is such a pity because she was...."

Dr Bulstrode looked up at Nickii.

"She seemed to be coming along nicely to me," he said quite sharply. Nickii drew in a breath.

"Did she tell you that she hasn't been taking her tablets regularly?"

Why did she feel such a traitor? As though she was dobbing in her own daughter by going to the headmaster and telling tales out of school. How could she possibly ask him the next question? Did he know she had spent the weekend alone, hungry, drunk and frightened having run away to an empty house?

"No," he said. "She didn't tell me that. She gave me the impression that she was quite happy with her medication!"

Tempting though it was, Nickii would not give up. She also knew that to allow herself to get angry would do no good at all. She had to stay calm if she was going to get anywhere. Which she was already beginning to doubt.

"Well perhaps she didn't quite like to tell you, but she told us, that she sometimes misses taking them because she doesn't like the things they do to her. Isn't it perhaps possible to try something different?"

Now it was Dr Bulstrode's turn to draw in a long breath.

"Mrs .. err, Mrs..." he stammered.

"Tolley!" Nickii prompted.

"Mrs Tolley, if a patient seems reasonably stable on the drugs we have prescribed it is not a good idea to go swopping them around. She has not mentioned any undue side effects to me; however..."

He retrieved Jackie's file from the top of the pile beside him on the desk and flipped it open again.

"I will make a note to discuss the drugs with Mrs Hildegaard further the next time I see her."

"But..."

But it was no good. The fighting spirit subsided within Nickii. That was it. Dismissed. She could not go on.

"Thank you."

She said, as calmly and politely as she could, and stood up, picking her handbag up off the floor beside the chair.

Standing outside the door, she felt quite weak with frustration, as all the questions she had wanted to ask came rushing back into her brain all at once. And going down in the lift she could quite literally have kicked herself because there was one particular thing that she had really wanted to discuss with him. She and John had been wondering whether it would cheer Jackie up if they arranged for the children to come to stay for a few days, or at least a weekend. But the last time they had done that, Jackie had been very quiet while the children were there, and so disturbed when they had gone, that now they couldn't make up their minds whether it was a good idea or not. She had wanted to ask Dr Bulstrode's advice. For a second she was tempted to go back, but just visualising his reaction was enough to put her off.

Stepping out of the lift she just hoped and prayed that both John *and* Jackie would be waiting for her in the car. Then, as she pushed open the heavy outside door of the hospital, she saw them sitting together on the seat a few yards away. She breathed a sigh of relief and enjoyed seeing them sitting side by side as though things might be perfectly normal.

***

The roaring and whistling echo that had been disturbing Michael's sleep for some time finally woke him completely. He opened his eyes, and, as they adjusted to the dark and the shapes of the furniture in the room, his ears became fully conscious of a continuous howl in the air outside; like the baying of a huge sick beast. There was something pretty phenomenal going on out there. He tossed aside the duvet, got briskly off the bed and pattered across the carpet to the bedroom window. Drawing the curtains apart in the middle, he peered out into the night. There must have been some kind of a moon, because it was not completely dark. He could see the black form of the big conifer tree on the left of the garden. It was swaying and clashing with the one that grew next to it in their neighbours' garden; like two exuberant teenagers dancing in a disco, their limbs as pliable as the artist's rubber that he used to twist between his fingers when he was thinking. As the howl stretched out to a piercing whistle and then back to a low moan, the trees seemed to dance in time. Half way down the lawn, he could make out the shape of the bright yellow watering can that had been tucked in neatly beside the conservatory door. And just as he watched it, the baying roar strengthened again and the can lifted in the air, turning and twisting like a piece of waste paper, then landed a few feet further down the garden.

Michael was not only alert now. He was excited. This was not just any old wind; this was history. He turned back to the bed. He wanted to share this with Claire. Her curled up body lay completely still, just her forehead and tousled hair on the pillow showing above the duvet. There was an apocalyptic noise going on outside and Claire was still sleeping like a baby. This is really going to be worth some teasing points, Michael thought, wondering whether to wake her. Deciding against that, he shuffled his feet into his slippers by the side of the bed and went into the bathroom, feeling around for his dressing gown. Just as he was doing that, there was a slight, but definite, ping on their doorbell. He ran lightly down the stairs, pulling his arms into the dressing gown as he went, and switched on the hall light. Through the stained glass of the front door he could see the shape of someone standing there. When he opened it, there was such a rush of air that the door nearly knocked him over and the hall rug lifted several inches off the polished floor. Charles, their next door neighbour, was standing there wide-eyed but smiling, with his pyjama bottoms showing under his hastily pulled on trousers.

"Well this is a bit of a do, isn't it?" he said, with a widening grin.

"Thing is, your fence has blown down against my car. Don't think there's any damage much; but I could do with a hand to lift it off!"

"Of course, of course," Michael said, going to put the latch up on the door, "on second thoughts, though, I'd better find my keys. I don't think this door will stay shut on the latch. I'll be right out!"

Shutting poor Charles back out in the noise, he rushed into the sitting room and turned on the light, but of course the keys were not going to be in there. Through in the kitchen, he retrieved them from the dresser and thrust them into his dressing gown pocket. Outside the street was littered with dustbins, lids and branches as though some huge gang had staged a riot and then disappeared. Then looking to the left, Michael could see that Charles' estimate of the damage looked like a bit of an understatement. Where once they had had a front garden each, they now had only one between them. One section of their fence was indeed leaning perilously against the polished surface of Charles' car and the rest of it flattened by their lilac tree which was lying across the neighbour's garden like a giant discarded weed. Battling to keep his dressing gown even on, let alone together, Michael scrambled over the branches of the tree, causing a few superficial wounds to his legs, and some considerable threat to other bits, he thought, while he was doing so. He was trying to get around to where Charles was standing next to his car. Somehow they managed to lift the piece of fence away from the car and lay it on top of the fallen tree, wedging it under one of the stronger branches. From what they could see the car, which was missed by only a couple of feet by the lilac, didn't seem to be dented by the fence either.

"Well, I'm terribly sorry!" Michael shouted against the howling air.

"I'll come out first thing in the morning to clear this lot up."

"Not your fault, old boy; no harm done; we'll have this all ship shape in no time. Well, I think I'm going to make a cuppa and switch on the news. This really is a bit of a do! Quite good fun really, don't you think?"

Michael did think. He was enjoying himself, in spite of the fact that there would be a lot of sawing and shifting to do in the morning. And then just as he was about to scrabble back over the branches there was a sudden lull in the wind and with an eerie silence the street was plunged into blackness. All the lights had gone off together as though the wind had flipped the switch.

CHAPTER TEN

The wind had flipped the switch in Sussex too; and at 6.30 in the morning Nickii was digging around in the coal cupboard outside. With a torch in one hand, she scrabbled coal into a bucket with the other. She had twisted her body awkwardly so that she could wedge one foot against the door, which kept bashing painfully into her bottom as she bent down. If it was going to be this uncomfortable, she was determined to get the bucket completely full. She did not want to come back out here in a hurry. Finally, she could balance no more on the top and heaved the bucket out on to the brick patio with a clang so that she could close the recalcitrant door and bolt it shut. Back in the walkthrough, she could hear the fire crackling nicely in the sitting room and she staggered through there, hoping that none of the coal would drop off the bucket on the way. I wasn't a Brownie for nothing, she thought to herself, as she dropped extra knobs of coal strategically on to the burning kindling in the fire basket. She and John were bursting for a cup of tea, but having no gas in the house meant that power cuts always rendered them completely helpless in terms of cooking. They too had been listening to the howling noise outside and watching the trees dance in the churchyard. They had been awake for hours and Nickii, fed up with waiting to see if the electricity would come back on, had formed a plan. If she could somehow balance something across the firedogs she could put the grill tray over the fire and boil some water. Dropping her sooty gardening glove on the brick edge of the hearth, she went back to the kitchen with the torch trying to remember where she had put the old camping kettle. Before her ingenious plot produced any wisps of steam, the electricity would probably have come back on and she would have boiled the electric kettle in one minute, she thought, but never mind; it was a challenge.

But the power did not come on and by the time she proudly carried two mugs of steaming tea back up to their bedroom, it was broad daylight. She put one mug down on her bedside table and walked around the bed with the other. John must have dozed back off because he was snuggled nicely down in the bed; but as she moved his book to put down the tea, he opened his eyes and looked up at her.

"Well what took you?" he said, grinning from the warmth of the bed.

"I'll give you what took you!" she retorted, going across to pull the curtains before sitting down on the bed beside him; and thinking how nice it was to be able to talk to each other in normal voices. This was their first morning alone together in the house for some time and not for the first time Nickii wondered how Jackie would be after such a night. But that little house is quite solid, she told herself yet again, and Jackie wouldn't have gone off anywhere in one evening surely! I'll phone her in an hour or so to make sure, she thought, taking a sip of the long awaited tea. John shuffled across the bed and nestled up to her putting his arm around her waist.

"Are you coming back to bed?" he asked, "we could be having a cuddle now that we're on our own again!"

Nickii had been planning to use what might be left of last night's hot water to have a bath and wash her hair. Taking hold of the hand that was tickling her tummy, she gave it a squeeze and said as much to John, reminding him that today was the day that they were going to meet the Lewises for lunch.

"The water in the tank won't get that much colder in half an hour or so, will it?" he pointed out with a smile, "and it is still quite early; we've got plenty of time!"

Nickii was about to tease him and remind him that they never stopped cuddling. But she just smiled, and said.

"Oh, alright then!"

Then standing up she slipped off the slacks and sweater she had put on when she went down to make the tea. Wrapping her arms around his warm body under the duvet, she thought that cuddling for comfort was quite different from actually making love, which was a luxury that, for one reason or another, they seldom allowed themselves these days.

Some time later when he was rubbing himself down after a somewhat cold bath in Nickii's tepid water, John felt better than he had done for days. He was looking forward to their lunch with the Lewises, who had been friends of theirs right back from the old advertising agency days. A few years ago their friendship had been in danger of lapsing since, due to pressures and strains on both sides they did not meet up for over two years. After that they had made a pact that if nothing else they would definitely meet at least once year. They had agreed to have lunch together at some mutually convenient hostelry or restaurant somewhere between their two homes. This time they had chosen The George and Dragon at Houghton. When he pulled the bathroom curtains, before going through to the bedroom to get dressed, he noticed that the fierce wind that night had blown down not one, but two trees in the churchyard. Then they had an ample breakfast of toast and marmalade and coffee, giggling over Nickii's contraptions on the fire; and they wondered why the newspaper was late, which was a nuisance because without electricity there wasn't a lot either of them could do. But it wasn't until they got in the car and set out that either of them began to realise the full force of the storm that had ravaged the countryside during the night.

Then it hadn't taken them long to discover that this had been a gale with a difference. The lane was littered with branches, twigs and green leaves that weren't yet ready to drop from the trees; sirens were sounding in the distance as they drove, and they had only gone about a mile down the road, when they were amazed by the sight of a huge tree lying right alongside one of the most beautiful houses in the neighbourhood. The tree had only missed the house by what looked like inches; but it was the size of the hole it had left in the ground and the root ball still attached to its base that was the most incredible. A huge ball of earth, nearly as tall as the house itself, it seemed, was stuck up on its side as though some angry monster had plucked it out with one stroke of its giant hand and then tossed it down like some unwanted toy.

Now, having reached Slindon, they pulled up behind a line of half a dozen or so stationary cars. Obviously the road was completely blocked by a very large fallen tree. There were a couple of police vans slewed across the road at the front of the queue and a gaggle of activity surrounding them. A grey haired woman was craning her neck out of the passenger window of the car in front, but the driver's seat was empty. Turning on his hazard lights to warn the next intrepid traveller, John switched off the engine and opened his door.

"I'll go and see what's happening," he said to Nickii.

Nickii immediately opened the passenger door.

"I'm coming too!" she said. "I'm not sitting here like a tuppenny lemon!"

As they walked past the other cars they could see that the night had had a cataclysmic effect on the view for as far as they could see. What was once a wood had been flattened. There was hardly a tree left standing. When they reached the scene of activity, they discovered that already there was a large pile of bits of broken tree and debris neatly stacked on the verge. They found themselves in an atmosphere of camaraderie and team work in defiance of the elements. Three young policeman, with one chain saw and a couple of hand saws between them, were stripped to their shirt sleeves and covered in grime; they had obviously been sweating away for some considerable time, aided and abetted by an assorted band of drivers. Gripped by the spirit, John was quite ready to take off his coat and pitch in with some lifting and carrying, but within minutes it was apparent that the team had virtually achieved their goal. Just a couple more branches and there would be ample room for the cars to pass around the head of the tree. The gleam of satisfaction was already appearing on several of the sweated brows. They stood for a few moments laughing and chatting with the small cluster of onlookers and then, when it was clear that the signal for the off had been given, they walked back up to the car. John took hold of Nickii's hand as they walked. He was still feeling surprisingly cheerful and elated. There was something about this little excursion that was making him feel young again; taking him back to the times when they were barely into their twenties and enjoying one of their precious leave days together.

The small posse of cars moved slowly forward as each edged up on to the verge and around the fallen tree. Then they gathered speed and spaced out. Meandering around more fallen branches and wind swept detritus; they drove off into the distance and their separate lives. This small incident would be a series of the same story, each told in their different ways, about the great gale. Buckling her seatbelt as they drove off, Nickii said how refreshing it had been to see those young policemen laughing and joking and working so hard, shoulder-to-shoulder with the general public. Reaching the roundabout at the entrance to Arundel Park, John turned off towards Houghton and, rounding a bend after only about half a mile, they were confronted by another storm-built roadblock. This time there were no policemen or band of workers; just their car and a mound of dejected beech tree right across its path. Nickii's infectious giggle beside him made John turn to look at her.

"Looks like we're stumped now!" she said.

"Ho. Ho. Very funny! But I'm not beaten yet," he responded, determined not give up after getting this far.

"I'm going to have a closer look."

But a closer look only proved what was already obvious. They were not going to get the car any further along this road. Nickii was still laughing and shaking her head at him behind the windscreen.

Walking back to the car and opening his door, he bent down to talk to her.

"OK, clever clogs, I give in on the car; but we could walk from here! I think we could just about get through on foot and it can't be much further."

Nickii leaned across the steering wheel to look up at him. Her smile waned a little.

"What's got into you today!" she said, and looked from him to the tree and back again, "well I suppose I'm game for a try; but we'll get filthy clambering over all that lot and how do we know the Lewises will be there anyway? They're probably having the same trouble as us!"

✦✦✦

But the Lewises were there, and sitting by the telephone table in the candlelit dining room of the cottage that evening, Nickii was telling Claire about their day.

"You should have seen us clambering over all those branches. Daddy was absolutely determined to get there. It was good fun, actually, we both really enjoyed it."

"So, what happened when you did get there? Did the Lewises turn up?"

Nickii could tell from her voice that Claire was smiling but still thought they were both quite crazy.

"Yes, they were there; but they were a bit late. They had walked all the way from home because they couldn't even get their car down their lane!"

"Well I'm glad you enjoyed yourselves! Michael's been having fun too; sawing up the lilac tree with Charles from next door half the morning. It fell right across their front garden! And we lost a few roof tiles; the runner beans and the tomatoes have totally disappeared, just spirited away and it's really eerie to see all the trees in the garden completely bare of leaves overnight, just as though the fairies came and picked them all off! But have you seen the news? Did you see that beautiful Mercedes completely flattened by that enormous tree?"

Nickii looked round at the shadows flickering on the walls of the kitchen, and through the door of the sitting room, from the dozens of candles they had put around to make the cottage more cosy.

"No. What news? We're sitting in the dark!" she said into the mouthpiece with a tinge of sarcasm.

"Actually, yes, we did hear a bit of news on the car radio on the way home; something about the trees in Kew Gardens. But we haven't got any electricity so we haven't seen the news all day!"

Claire was suitably sympathetic, especially since they had got their power back sometime during the morning. Aware now of John's chair creaking and then the clang of the coal scuttle as he dropped more coal on the fire, Nickii answered Claire's questions about how they were coping with cooking and without hot water. And then Claire asked.

"And how's Jackie? Did she stay at home while you were clambering over trees?"

"Well, no" Nickii replied, wishing she knew how Jackie was, "we took her back to the house yesterday. On Tuesday night, when we were having supper, she suddenly said she thought she would like to go back. I've tried to ring her today but I haven't been able to talk to her; still I expect she'll come back for the weekend as usual."

Then just as Claire was telling her that she was hoping that Pippa and David were coming for the weekend, John appeared in the sitting room door. As he passed her on his way to the kitchen, he smiled and raised his eyebrows. Holding up his hand he clacked his thumb and four fingers together in the sign of a chattering mouth and disappeared. She could hear him filling the kettle at the sink. When his shadow appeared on the wall, she was waiting for him and poked out the tip of her tongue at him as he appeared. But then turning back to the mouthpiece, she said to Claire.

"Daddy's making signs; I suppose we have been on here rather a long time; I guess we'd better go!"

And so, after another couple of minutes, she replaced the receiver and stood in the sitting room doorway. John was standing by the drinks cupboard in the corner of the room.

"You're like a couple of old hens clacking!" he teased.

She pulled a face at him as she retorted, "there was a lot to talk about! And anyway what else is there to do?"

"Well I was thinking that we should get set up with some coffee and a drink and play a game. What do you fancy; backgammon, scrabble, Othello...?"

Nickii looked round and saw that he had balanced the kettle on her masterful cooking contraption and thought that that seemed like a reasonable plan.

"Oh, I don't know, you choose, probably all three I should think. I'll go and get the cups and the coffee; and, would you believe, I'm just going to try Jackie again first!"

CHAPTER ELEVEN

Over the next few days, John remembered the day of the storm with nostalgia. He wished he could conjure up the lighthearted cheerfulness he had felt then. The weekend was dismal. For some unknown reason they seemed to be the last corner of the country to get their electricity back; so he could not even shut himself up in his study with the computer and get on with his book. Jackie was withdrawn and illusive, padding softly around during the night and disappearing, and reappearing silently by day. The imagined and unuttered conversations between them when they did meet built up into a tension like leaking gas seeping up from the floor, until finally he had exploded, snapped and shouted at her, banging his fist on the kitchen table at the same time. She had looked at him with absolutely no change of expression, and then slowly walked away. Immediately he felt a huge wave of remorse, then a sharp pain that flashed through his head like lightening. It wasn't her fault. Time and again he had to tell himself that it was not her fault; but he seemed to be dogged by a rising impatience and peevishness over which he had no control. No matter how hard he tried, he could not stop the irrational irritability that seemed to make his very body tingle. It crossed his mind that perhaps this was some small indication of how Jackie felt. And he was not making it any easier for Nickii either. She struggled through the weekend, trying to keep the peace and juggling with saucepans of hot water on the fire.

On Monday morning they went to Waitrose and took Jackie back to the house. He sat in the car while Nickii went in with Jackie to sort out some of the shopping for her. Suddenly he longed for Jackie to turn round and wave to him before she disappeared into the house; but she didn't look back and the door closed. That afternoon the phone rang and he answered. Claire wanted to know how they were and before he knew it, he had snapped at her too. Why keep worrying and ringing when there's nothing you can do, he told her sharply.

On Tuesday morning when they woke up, miraculously the bedside clock was flashing and the power was back on. He spent most of the day struggling with the tumbling green words on his computer screen. It was the night for his writing class with Tim; usually a treat in store but that night he could hardly raise the energy to get in the car. The room seemed stuffy and hot; Tim's voice droned on in the distance. John could not keep awake and his notebook sat blank before him on the desk. He was aware of Tim announcing the assignment for the week. He tried to write it down and the letters jumbled under his eyes. The road appeared to rise up to meet him through the windscreen on the way home, and he was tired, so very, very tired. He woke up, the headlights blaring through a hedge and into the gloom of an empty field. Luckily, there was no other traffic. The road was completely still and quiet. He had to pull himself together. The car had stalled. He put his foot on the clutch and took it out of gear, then, as he turned the key in the ignition, it spluttered back into life. He pulled carefully off the grassy verge and drove very slowly home. Nickii was waiting there with a concerned look and a hot meal. They ate in their chairs beside the fire; then he dosed fitfully in front of the television, while Nickii too nodded on and off over her embroidery. When eventually they went up to bed, Nickii beat him to it and was lying on her side reading her book when he came out of the bathroom. On an impulse he walked around the bed and planted a gentle kiss on her forehead before he got into bed.

***

Claire was standing at the kitchen window in a patch of early morning sunlight. It was one of those calm mornings when everything appeared to be in slightly slow motion. She was about to take the second bite of a piece of golden buttered toast when the phone rang. As she walked towards it, it flashed through her mind that it was a bit early in the morning...

"Is that Claire? Claire Parsons?"

"Yes. Speaking."

"I am very sorry to have to tell you that your father has had a stroke."

The thoughts and questions came tumbling all at once. Her mind was screaming 'oh no, please, please no!' Rationality sent question after unanswered question; and intuition told her that, after this moment, her life was never going to be the same again.

And then Michael was beside her with his hand on her shoulder, and the gentle voice on the other end of the phone was saying.

"Are you alright dear, is there somebody with you?"

"Is.... is he conscious?" she stuttered into the mouthpiece.

"Yes, he's awake and he's quite comfortable and your mother's sitting with him."

"Can he speak?"

"No. I'm afraid he can't, but..."

A gulp of despair welled up in Claire's throat; she was handling this really badly. She couldn't think. Michael was holding both her shoulders now. The phone was shaking in her hand.

"I'll come down..." her voice was hardly more than a whisper.

"What I suggest...." the ward Sister said softly but firmly in her ear, "... is that you go and make yourself a cup of tea and sit down for a few moments; then I'll ring you back in ten minutes and give you some more details. You did say there was someone with you?"

Claire put down the receiver. She stumbled back into the kitchen and looked around. Their unfinished breakfast things still covered the table. She hadn't had her shower or got dressed. She needed to pull herself together, tidy up, pack a bag and get in the car; but her body was rooted to the spot, her mind numb. Michael was still holding her firmly by the shoulders, staring into her eyes.

"What is it, tell me, tell me what's happened," he was saying.

"It's Daddy!" she said, looking back into his eyes. "He's had a stroke!"

She started to shake herself free.

"I must go, I must go down there."

"No," Michael said, he refused to let go. "No not yet! Of course you must go, we'll both go; I'll come with you. But first you sit down for a moment; you look like a ghost!"

He propelled Claire towards the table and gently pushed her down onto a chair.

"I'll make some more tea!" he said, picking up their mugs, "while you tell me exactly what they said. Who was that anyway?"

Sitting on the chair now, her body felt like jelly, but her brain more calm.

"It was a Sister from the hospital. She did say her name, but I can't remember it. I can't even remember which hospital. But she's phoning back in ten minutes. She said that he's conscious but he can't speak. Look, I can't just sit here; I must get on."

Claire stood up again and stacking up their plates, took them to the sink.

"Do you think I should pack a bag? Do you think Mummy will want me to stay? She might not? Well I could take a bag anyway in case!"

"I should think there'd be no question. Of course your Mum will want you to stay. Now, will you please sit back down, at least until the Sister rings back! I can do that, and it won't take us long to get ready!"

***

By the time they set off there was a fine drizzle in the air. The roads were wet but it was not actually raining properly. The cars in front chucked muck all over the windscreen. They couldn't see, and the windscreen washer bottle was empty. They stopped in a garage to fill it and Michael couldn't get the top off. The journey seemed to be taking forever, and all Claire wanted was to be there. But she knew that they could not rush it. She knew now that she must stay cool and calm. The unimaginable had arrived. Something had happened to one of her parents and now, after forty one years and all that had happened in them, it was truly her turn to react like an adult. There was silence in the car as they drove; there didn't seem much they could say. Claire's mind passed the miles by remembering snippets of things about her father; in and out of her brain like birds flitting from tree to tree. And for some reason, she kept thinking about the car they were driving; he gave us this car, she kept telling herself; and she could have sworn she could still smell the trace of his pipe tobacco even though she knew that was ridiculous. He had given up his pipes probably even before he bought the car. Then she remembered when he had first bought it; long before she ever met Michael, and when David was still at boarding school. Her father and mother had taken herself and Pippa there to visit one Sunday. The Celica was brand new and her father was so pleased and proud of it. Suddenly he had stopped on a country lane and asked Claire if she would like to have a go. She remembered how surprised she was at his generosity; this was his new toy, and he was offering it to her to play with. It felt like a bucking stallion, she remembered, and he didn't even groan when she kept crunching it into the wrong gear. Then they had taken David to that strange hotel for tea and played Canasta at the table to pass the time before they had to take him back to school.

Driving past the turning they normally took at Singleton, which went up over the Downs, the road going straight on into Chichester seemed unfamiliar. Claire again felt the tension welling up inside her and tried to concentrate on remembering the directions that the Sister had given her to find the hospital. She thought, for the second time that morning, how stupid it was that she had been visiting Chichester for four years now and still did not know where the hospital was. However, they found it easily enough and were soon driving around the car park searching for a space.

"If you want, I'll find somewhere to park it and you can go on up!" Michael said. But Claire felt her legs trembling in her seat again and knew that she wanted Michael beside her when she went to find her father. Luckily, just then, they saw the taillights of a car backing out of a space ahead of them.

They crossed the car park and trotted up a few steps to a faded and unprepossessing door. Michael's shoes squeaked on the flooring of the corridor. They dashed in, immediately looking above them at the maze of white on grey notices, with arrows pointing every which way. Hurrying past a shop selling cards, flowers, chocolates, etc., it flashed through Claire's mind that they had got nothing for him; no flowers, no nothing. Oh never mind, she thought, later, time for that later. I just want to get there.

"The sister said it was up in the lift or take the stairs to the second floor." she said, searching for a notice that said Lift or Stairs. Michael took her arm.

"Look here we are. Let's go in the lift."

Out of the lift and turn left; through the double doors. Claire fought the lump in her throat. There were a hundred muted noises against a background of silence and that, forgotten but unmistakable, general smell of hospital. They passed several single rooms on their left, what was obviously the kitchen on their right, and then they came to a row of glass fronted offices with wards to their left and right. Floundering, they turned right and caught a quick glimpse of the beds lined along each wall. The curtains were drawn into the middle of the room around two or three of them. A nurse came hurrying in their direction. Her shoes squeaked on the lino too.

"Can I help you?" she said without breaking her stride.

"We've come to see Mr Tolley...."

"Oh, this is the ladies ward, the men's is behind you!" she said, pointing and smiling briefly as she disappeared through a door. They turned and walked back past the offices. A sister in her dark blue uniform, busy on the telephone, looked at them quizzically through the glass as they passed.

In here there was a mirror image of the ladies' ward; the same rows of beds, but with a different pattern on the curtains, a sea of pillows, flowers and strange faces. Claire scanned them, her eyes searching and flitting from bed to bed. Then she heard her mother's voice, right there beside her.

"Oh look here's Claire!"

And there they were; just there, right beside them, the first bed on the left. Her mother was struggling with the things on her lap to get up out of her chair. She was smiling, there was relief on her face at seeing them, but Claire was surprised by her composure.

"Don't get up!" she said.

And she walked forward to give her mother a kiss. As she put her arm around her, she took a second, longer, look at her father in the bed. The first was just a glimpse, a split second glance as she had taken in the scene. He looked alright. He looked just like her dad, propped up incongruously against a pile of hospital pillows. She put the other arm out and took his hand lying down on the sheet. The hand gripped hers. He blinked and smiled at her. His smile was crooked. He looked round at Michael, dropped Claire's hand from his and raised it in a wave. Michael greeted John from the end of the bed. Then looking vaguely around the ward, he said.

"I'll see if I can get some more chairs!"

The chairs were quite large armchairs, which took an embarrassing amount of space around the bed. Claire shuffled hers down as close to the locker as she could. Her father's locker was bleak looking and empty; the sign of a new arrival. Just the customary water jug, topped with a glass, and the Daily Telegraph with his glasses case on top. Michael squeezed a chair down beside her, hemming her in. They sat uneasily, questions racing but not quite knowing what to say.

"Did you have a good drive?" Nickii asked, as though they have just driven down for the weekend. Michael answered, talked about the traffic, and the fun and games with the windscreen washer.

Claire now on the other side of the bed, again put her hand over John's. He was watching Michael – listening. The hand did not move or flinch. It felt cold.

"What time did you get here?"

Claire directed the question at both her parents.

"Oh, about eight o'clock, I think, I don't know really. But we haven't been here in the ward very long;" Nickii said, "apparently we shouldn't really be here, because this is a surgical ward, but they haven't got any spare beds upstairs yet."

A very large physiotherapist, in size enormous navy blue trousers and a white tunic, shuffled into the ward, creating a diversion for them to look at. She looked as though she could benefit from her own exercises. She shuffled out again, and they heard her telling a nurse that she needed some assistance with lifting one of her patients. They smiled at each other. John caught the joke from his pillows. His smile was still crooked. Michael leant forward and touched Claire's arm.

"I think I might as well be off," he whispered, "there's not a lot I can say or do, and there's too many of us in here really. What do you want to do about your bag?"

Claire's insides panicked again. Why do you have to go so soon, she thought. But she could see that he was distinctly uncomfortable. And he was right, there was nothing he could do.

"I've brought some things to stay if you would like me to?" She said across the bed to Nickii.

"Oh, yes please, I hoped you would!" Nickii said.

Back down in the fresh air of the car park, Michael lifted Claire's bag out of the back of the Celica. They walked along the rows of cars looking for Nickii's. Claire struggled with the unfamiliar lock on the boot of her mother's Fiesta, and then they slowly retraced their steps back to their own car. Standing beside it, Michael put his arms around Claire; said he would call her tonight. Claire had the impression that a huge black cloud covered the sky. She clung on to him thinking, please; please don't go; let me come home with you as though everything was alright. She lifted up her face to give him a kiss; stood leaden as he got into the car and closed the door. Then she whispered.

"Drive carefully!" And watched until the car had disappeared out of sight.

CHAPTER TWELVE

Marjorie Minster parked her dusty white Mini in the last space before the white bus stop lines; just as she had on three days of every week for the last eighteen months. Looking across at a row of dismal, pebble-dashed, houses across the green, she grabbed her handbag from the passenger seat and struggled out of her car. She told herself, not for the first time, that she really must do something about her weight. Walking across the grass and aiming for the front door with the yellow paint, she looked at her watch. Ten-thirty. She was here a whole hour earlier than she usually came. With her bulging bunch of keys in her hand, she rang the doorbell and waited, listening for any sounds behind the door. This is their home, she always thought, well for the time being anyway, and it is common courtesy not to go barging in willy-nilly. But, as so often happened, no-one came to the door, and there was not a sound behind it, so she used her key and stepped into the hall.

"It's only me, Marjorie!" she called out, as usual.

The door to the front room was open and there was nobody in there. Marjorie walked along the short corridor to the back room, and that was empty too. The, somewhat dingy, beige curtains were still drawn blocking out the daylight. She marched across to them and pulled them back in two brisk motions allowing a weak gleam of sunlight into the room. The piano, probably donated by somebody before her time, was littered on both of its flat surfaces by piles of old newspapers, magazines and post, some opened, some not. The night store heater was draped with greying white underpants. Marjorie was glad she didn't have to live with that. An old manual typewriter sat in the middle of the table, surrounded by more paper, and, perched on the edge, a bowl with the dried remains of somebody's breakfast cereal. She was used to all this, but this morning Marjorie gave just the smallest sigh, and then quickly bustled through the door into the kitchen.

Standing over a sink full of unwashed washing-up, she looked out into the tiny garden, and the fence-to-fence scruffy grass, adorned in the middle by a rotary clothesline. There was a white blouse and a patterned sweater forlornly pegged on one plastic rod. Probably

Jackie's, Marjorie thought, and hoped that she really was upstairs as she suspected. Getting down to business again, Marjorie decided a nice pot of tea brewing before she went upstairs would be a good idea. The kettle was thick with finger marks, and she had a hard job to get it under the tap above a plate sticking up out of the tangle of dirty dishes. This was one of those mornings when she briefly asked herself why she was doing this job at all. But the doubt was always brief. She was doing it because she believed in it, because she had had a son once who was just like... Well, never mind that, most of the time it gave her some sense of satisfaction and it kept her busy in between visits to her own family. She poured a little water into the teapot to warm it, swilling it around over the draining board. There is nothing like a proper pot of tea over the dusty old dregs they put in those tea bags. Reaching up to the shelf she took down a packet of tea, which she knew was there because she had bought it herself on one of her stock-up days. But then, closing the lid on top of the steaming brew, she was dreading the approaching moment when she would have to haul herself up those stairs. Even she, the ever bubbly and efficient Marjorie, with all her old nursing experience, was not at all confident of how to approach Jackie with this news.

Up on the landing she found that two of the doors to the three bedrooms were open and their occupants out. But the door to Jackie's room was closed. Pulling back her shoulders and thus thrusting out her ample bosom a little further. Marjorie knocked on the door; just a couple of soft little taps.

"Jackie, are you there dear? It's me, Marjorie, I need to talk to you for a moment," she said.

After a few seconds of silence, Jackie called out.

"Yes. I'm here!"

Opening the door just enough to pop her head around it, Marjorie asked Jackie if she may come in. There was always such a striking difference in Jackie's room from the rest of the house. The colourful pattern on her duvet cover matched the curtains Jackie's mother had helped her to put up. They had made a point of telling Marjorie that the old manky ones were neatly stored in a polythene bag in the bottom of the cupboard. Not that Marjorie cared; she had just been jolly pleased to see some brightness about the place. And when Jackie's parents had helped her to move in, they brought an extra little bedside table and a small deep-buttoned bucket chair. Jackie was sitting in it now, still in her dressing gown, with her feet neatly placed together and her hands in her lap. When she looked up at Marjorie, there were dark circles around her eyes again, and her face was very drawn.

"Have you come to talk about the rent money?" she asked. "It's downstairs on the mantelpiece; I haven't touched it!"

The poor child thinks I've come with an inquisition, Marjorie thought, remembering the little spot of bother they had before.

'No, dear, it's nothing to do with rent money;" she said, her hand on the back of the small upright chair by the chest of drawers, "do you mind if I sit down?"

I do wish she wouldn't call me "Dear", Jackie thought, I'm not a child! But she didn't change her expression, just shook her head to indicate that Marjorie should sit down if she wanted to.

Marjorie moved the chair a little closer to Jackie's and sat down. She felt her bottom spilling over the edge of the seat.

"No dear," she started, "I've come because I have to tell you that your father is not well."

Jackie looked at her with a puzzled frown.

"I am afraid he was taken into hospital this morning because he has had a stroke. But they say he is quite comfortable and your mother is with him!"

Jackie's hands were clenched together in her lap; her knuckles turning whiter and whiter as they stretched. Her eyes opened wide and her mouth gave a little gasp as it dropped open. Then quickly she shrugged and shook her head.

"No, that's not possible," she said. "He was perfectly all right at the weekend!"

She paused for a moment, as though thinking how he was when she last saw him; trying to take in this strange information. It was not logical. It didn't fit. It could not be so.

"If it's true, why are you telling me? How do you know? Why didn't my mother ring me?"

"I'm very sorry, dear, but it is definitely true. Your mother couldn't ring you because she's had a nasty shock too, and she's been with your father all the time. But she asked the hospital to ring me, so that I could come and tell you myself. I've made some.." Marjorie said.

But Jackie interrupted.

"I see," she said, standing up from her chair, "well thank you for taking the trouble to come to tell me. Now I'll get dressed and go to see him."

This was Jackie's cue for Marjorie to leave the room, but Marjorie knew that it had brought her to the part of her task that she had dreaded the most.

"I'm afraid you can't see him, dear;" she said firmly, "not for a few days anyway. Why don't you sit back down for a while? I've made a nice pot of tea downstairs. I'll go and get us both a cup."

"I don't want tea."

Jackie's hands trembled now as they scrabbled at the buttons on her dressing gown.

"I want to see my father! Why shouldn't I see him if my mother is with him?"

Marjorie puffed up off her chair and tried to put her arm around Jackie's shoulders, but Jackie shook her off, taking a step towards the chest of drawers.

"They won't let you in Jackie, if you go there!" Marjorie said to Jackie's back.

"He is much too ill to have visitors."

***

In the hospital, John was drifting in and out of sleep. In between, the nurses interrupted his dozing to check his blood pressure, move him or fluff up his pillows. They certainly seemed to have a knack for that, as he looked quite relaxed and peaceful propped up there with a cotton hospital blanket around his shoulders. While he slept, Claire and Nickii talked across the bed in hushed whispers; both of them thinking to themselves, for the first of so many times, how disconcerting it was to be talking about him and across him in the bed, as though he wasn't there.

Claire watched his closed eyes and the rise and fall of his chest as he breathed; to be sure he really was asleep. She was becoming impatient with talking about the news and the weather now, and was desperate to answer some of the questions racing around in her brain. For some time she had been trying to pluck up the courage to go and ask the Sister, but somehow felt that that would be going behind her mother's back. Carefully she leant forward so that Nickii could hear her whisper.

"What have the doctors said?"

Nickii turned to watch him for a few seconds, before she too leaned closer to Claire.

"They seemed to give him quite a few tests when we arrived; and then the doctor told me that he has had quite a deep stroke. I don't really know what that means. But they said they wouldn't be able to tell how well he will recover until after a fortnight. They said he must just have complete rest for the first two weeks."

As her mother sat back in her chair, her tummy gave an embarrassingly loud rumble. Claire suppressed a giggle, asked herself how she could be so superficial. Nickii was giggling too.

"Have you eaten anything all day?" Claire asked her.

It was 3.30 in the afternoon and she could bet her mother hadn't even had breakfast. Come to that, though, neither had she, well hardly; and she was not in the slightest bit hungry.

"Well no I haven't actually. The nurses did offer to get me something but I didn't want to trouble them. It's all right though, I don't feel hungry."

"No, I don't expect you do; but it's not good for you! Why don't I go and find us a sandwich or something?"

"OK if you feel like a little walk, there is a sort of coffee bar place in the main reception, but I don't know what times it's open and then there's the shop near the other entrance. Perhaps you could get Daddy some orange juice or something at the same time; he's only got that plain water!"

Just as Claire was trying to move her chair silently, so that she could get up without making a noise, the sister appeared at the end of the bed.

"There's a telephone call for you from somebody called Marjorie!" she said.

Claire was puzzled by who Marjorie might be and watched for Nickii's reaction.

"She says she's speaking on behalf of Jackie Hildegaard."

John opened his eyes and looked around him, as though wondering where on earth he was. Nickii started to get up from her chair.

"I'll go, if you like!" Claire said.

She had completely forgotten about Jackie; she hadn't even asked if Jackie knew. Nickii joined Claire at the end of the bed, with their backs to John.

"Would you?" she said, looking relieved.

"Yes, of course, but what does she know?"

"Well, I'm afraid I asked the night sister this morning to ring Marjorie Minster. She's the lady that sort of looks after them in the house. I asked them to ask her to tell Jackie; and..." she hesitated for a moment, "...and, I asked them to ask her to look after Jackie but keep her away from here. You see I...."

Now the distress of the whole day was written in the lines on her mother's face.

"It's alright!" Claire whispered, "I'll deal with it."

She followed the Sister out of the ward and into her office. Indicating the phone lying on her desk the sister went out, shutting the door behind her. Picking up the receiver and putting it to her ear, Claire looked out through the glass at the ward. It was as though she were in a soundproof box.

"Hello?" she said quietly into the mouthpiece.

"I am trying to speak to Mrs Tolley!"

The voice was brisk and business like.

"Yes," Claire said, "I know. My name is Claire. I'm Jackie's sister. Can I help you?"

"Oh, hello dear!"

The voice was friendlier now, motherly even.

"Well, you won't know me; my name's Marjorie and I've got Jackie here with me. She's very upset and I would like to be able to give her some news about your father. She wants to know how he is! Actually we came up this morning; I wouldn't let her come in, but she saw him through the door and that made her feel a little better. But perhaps *you* could talk to her, dear?"

"Yes, of course..." Claire stammered, already struggling around for what she would say. It was years since she had had a proper conversation with Jackie, let alone in circumstances like this.

"Hello, is that Claire?" Jackie's voice sounded bright. "How's daddy? I saw him this morning, through the door. He looked quite well!"

In seconds, irritation mounted to anger within Claire; her hasty rehearsals instantly forgotten, she snapped.

"Of course he's not well, he can't speak!"

A loud wail sounded in her ear. The papers on the sister's desk were blurring under her eyes. Claire wished that she could rip out her tongue. She heard a scuffling, then Marjorie saying, "We'll try to call you tomorrow!", with a cool efficiency.

Closing the door of the sister's office slowly behind her, Claire then peeped around the corner into the ward. Nickii was leaning close to John's bed, holding his hand and talking to him quietly. His eyes were wide open and frightened; his head was turned towards Nickii as he listened. Claire decided not to go in. She tiptoed a few steps backwards, then turned and walked down the corridor, past the kitchen and the private wards and down the stairs beside the lift. With Jackie's wail still ringing in her ears, she vaguely remembered that she was going in search of sandwiches and orange juice. Immediately after her own emotionally exasperated outburst at Jackie she was consumed with guilt at her insensitivity and short temper. But now as she plodded heavily down the stairs, her steps echoing off the walls, her heart was hardening. A cold determination was forming within her. Jackie had been the focus of attention, trouble and worry for quite long enough. She would just have to look after herself, at least for the time being. It was her father's turn. Absolutely the most important thing now was that he recovered. During the next two weeks, he must have completely stress free, tender loving care and her mother would need all the support she could get. By the time she found the deserted reception area and the closed grille of the coffee bar, Claire had quite glibly decided that Marjorie Minster, 'they', somebody or just anybody, as long as it was not them, would have to take care of Jackie.

She walked back down the long corridor the way she had come. The odd figure in a white coat appeared, and then disappeared, going slickly about their business. The Hospital Friends shop was closed too. She looked at a row of Robinsons Orange Barley Waters in the dimmed light behind the locked glass door, then, thinking that it might be as well to leave Nickii alone with John for a while longer, she pushed open the door and stood on the steps that she had come up with Michael what seemed like days and days ago, but was only that morning. Standing there for a few moments, she watched two or three young men with assorted children going into the maternity unit opposite. So much joy, and so much heartache, under the auspices of one roof, she thought. Finally the chill gnawed through her sweater and she began to shiver. She started to walk slowly back. On the landing at the top of the stairs, she noticed the Ladies and realized that she hadn't been in there all day either. On the walls of the cubicle there were scrapings and scratchings of graffiti; *Paula loves John,* and *Sharon woz here.* Claire stared at it, as she readjusted her jeans, and felt that she needed to pinch herself to show that she was not just having a ghastly nightmare. But back in the ward the truth was quite stark. Her father had dozed off again, and her mother was just sitting there looking very pale and tired. Claire sat down; whispered that both the shops were closed. They stayed there until the evening visitors started to drift in. The ward noises changed to a hum of hushed chatter. Her father slept and woke; slept then nodded off again. The visitors began to drift out. They didn't want to leave him; but as the last few friends and relatives walked waving through the doors and the nurses came in with their trolleys, Nickii stood up and kissed him softly on the cheek. He opened his eyes.

"We'll be here first thing in the morning!" she said.

He turned his head and watched them as they walked backwards until they couldn't see him anymore.

CHAPTER THIRTEEN

They hardly said a word on the way home. The car was misted up on the inside, and Nickii couldn't find the switch for the fan. She had not driven her car very regularly at all, and hardly ever in the dark. The stream of headlights coming in the opposite direction dazzled her eyes. It was a huge relief when she could at last turn into their own quiet lane. She pulled up onto the drive; the headlamps shone on the white garage doors. Nickii put the handbrake on with an exhausted sigh.

"I can't be bothered to put it away," she said, "we'll be out in it again first thing in the morning anyway."

As she got out of the car and stood waiting for Claire to take her bag out of the boot so that she could lock it, she remembered all the struggles she had had out here when she left. They walked outside the hedge along to the front gate. John's car was sitting there in the dark in the church car park, the windows and roof all misted over with dew. Claire stopped and looked at it.

"I had to back it out of the drive this morning to get mine out."

Nickii said, standing beside her.

"It was ghastly. The ambulance just drove off up the lane and left me in the dark and I wanted to be with him so I was in a terrible hurry. Then I dropped his car keys and couldn't see where they were; then I had to shut the garage doors behind me. Still never mind I got there in the end. But look, his car is covered in mud all along this side!"

Bending down she rubbed at the bottom of the passenger door with her hand.

"I think it's mud; I don't think it's scratched but it's difficult to see in the dark."

Suddenly Claire moved towards the gate.

"Listen!" she said, "I think the phone is ringing!"

Nickii fumbled in her coat pocket with a muddy hand for the door key, and hurried up the path still wondering what could have happened to John's car. It's funny he didn't say anything, she thought.

The phone call was from Ellie, who lived opposite and had seen the ambulance in the morning. She wanted to know if everything was alright. After that the phone didn't stop for nearly three hours. Nickii rang her sister, thinking the family would wonder why she hadn't if she didn't. Claire rang Michael and then, as the news travelled, neighbours, friends, relatives and Pippa and David too, all rang, sending their love and wanting the address at the hospital to send cards. While one of them was on the phone, the other tried to make teas or coffees that never got drunk. Half way through the evening, they realised that they still hadn't eaten anything. They looked for something quick, and ended up with kippers. God knows why! Neither of them ever ate kippers. But there they were in the freezer; quick and easy to grill, and eat with a bit of bread and butter. They took them out and put them back under the grill so many times between phone calls, that when they came to eat them they fell about with hysterical laughter. Shoe leather would definitely have been tastier. Then, after the laughter came a reflective silence while the trays and remains of dried up and half eaten fish sat at their feet on the sitting room floor. Neither of them would ever forget the smell of those kippers.

"Shall I make some more coffee?" Claire said, bending forward to collect the trays together. While Claire went out to the kitchen, Nickii sat there, recalling all the consoling words from her telephone conversations.

"Patricia Neale made a full recovery!"

Someone had said, and several others had all had friends or acquaintances who had had strokes and made it back to normal lives. It was funny that. It was the same when he had had his heart by-pass. Suddenly, everybody you met knew somebody who had had one too. That was when Nickii remembered that she hadn't asked Claire what had happened about Jackie when she rang the hospital that afternoon. She remembered because she had realised that it wasn't like that with Jackie. Nobody talks about all their friends and relatives who are *mentally* ill; probably not because they don't exist, she thought, but because people simply don't want to admit it.

Sitting up in bed now beside the empty space, she remembered that she still never did ask. They had talked about something else when Claire came back in with the coffee. She knew Claire was not asleep; she could call out and ask about Jackie, but she decided she could not face any more talking tonight. She would remember to ask tomorrow. She picked up her book; a biography of Gwen John. She read a page, turned over, and then realising that she had absolutely no knowledge of what she had just read, she laid the book on her lap. The clothes he took off last night were still lying over the chaise longue at the foot of the bed. How many times would she go over and over the way he looked this morning when she came back upstairs with their tea! It was no good; she would have to keep busy. She got out of bed and went through to the dressing room to get a hanger to hang up his trousers. After that she could pack his sponge bag, and then decide what else she would need to take in tomorrow.

***

Before she had even opened her eyes, Claire was aware that she was not where she should have been, and all too quickly she remembered why. The room was pitch dark, but a glimmer of light was seeping around the edges of the door. She fumbled for the light switch and looked at her watch, 5.40 am. Shivering on the landing in her nightie, she found Nickii's door pushed to, the light glowing around it. Impossible to open quietly, the door creaked as she pushed it. Nickii was sitting up in bed, her book on her lap and her dressing gown around her shoulders.

"Hello. Would you like some tea?" Her mother said, lifting the lid of the pot on the tray beside her, "on second thoughts I think this is too cold. Shall we go downstairs?"

Nickii must have been awake for some time; she seemed pleased to have some company.

They sat on either side of the kitchen table, in front of the electric fire. They tried to decide when was the earliest they could go back to the hospital. The nurses had said that they could come whenever they liked, but they didn't want to be in the way. Nickii said that she would go and have a bath and wash her hair, but there was masses and masses of time and they seemed to be stuck to their chairs. They drank more tea, and then more tea. Nickii told Claire about how it had all been yesterday morning. And then how everything seemed to fall into place now it was too late; and how she wished she had done something about all the symptoms that she had not recognised. How John seemed to be searching sometimes for the right words for things. How he had shouted at Jackie and then put his hand up to his head as though something was wrong. How he had confessed that he had been to the doctor's because his eyes seemed funny, and the doctor had said that he just needed an eye test; but that he would get him an appointment for a blood test too, just in case. And then Nickii remembered to ask Claire about her conversation with Jackie yesterday.

"Don't worry," Claire said, "she sounded alright. Marjorie said she would ring again today. Perhaps I'll walk over there sometime and see her."

And so they talked their way to 7.15 and at last they were able to get ready to leave.

Just over two hours later, Claire was briskly scuffling leaves on her way along the Chichester ring road towards North Street. It was a crisp, clear, blue-sky morning, and the sun glinted on the roofs of the cars as they glided along the dual carriageway. Claire's emotions were gripped by a vice and yet she was still getting pleasure from the swish of the leaves beneath her feet, the freshness of the air, and the feel of the sun on her skin. There were two worlds; normality and nightmare, and somehow or another they locked fingers with each other. When they were hurrying up those, now so familiar, steps this morning, she had had a vision of her father rested and refreshed, greeting them with that old grin and a 'Hello', followed by news of his night, and what time they had woken him up for breakfast. A picture born out of previous visits; like the time when he had the angiogram, and ripped all the leads to the heart monitor off his chest because he wanted to go to the loo; and then got into trouble with the nurses because he didn't know how to stick them back. Then, before that, years and years ago, when he was in hospital with the hepatitis he had mysteriously contracted after a blood doning session. That time, Claire and her mother had got back to the car after visiting, only to find that he had beaten them to it in his pyjamas and dressing gown, and was determined to escape. And even after the heart by-pass, he was always self-possessed and as jovial as he could be, however weak. But this morning when they had turned the corner into the ward his twisted lower lip trembled with relief. He had looked lost, vulnerable and frightened; like a child who has been left by its mother for too long, and thinks she is never coming back.

Turning into North Street, Claire walked briskly past all the shops without giving a thought to her shopping list. She had been stupid, and selfish again, she was telling herself, to expect any different. It was, after all, only just over twenty-four hours; and twenty-four hours of not being able to even tell anyone that you want to go to the loo. How must that feel? She had reached the Cross at the centre of Chichester and she stood there, not knowing which way to turn. The strains of a familiar tune were playing in her ears, as she tried to remember what she had come to buy. A bearded young man, in jeans and a worn leather jacket, was playing his clarinet on the corner outside the shoe shop; the odd coin chinked into the open case at his feet. She watched him and listened. She could not concentrate on her shopping until she had remembered the name of that tune. People jostled past her, a baby started crying behind her. And then she got it. *Sailing. I am sailing ... stormy waters... cross the sea....*

Right; – fruit juice, some flowers or a plant, shaving cream, something for their supper that would be quick and easy and would *not* smell of fish; and then the difficult bit, a personal stereo, so that her father could be cheered up by some of his own music tapes. She and Nickii had had that idea last night, but Claire hadn't really got a clue of how to choose a good one. But, never mind, first she had got to find the shops that fitted the list. On cue her brain clicked into gear. OK, she thought, Superdrug for the shaving cream, and M & S for the fruit juice and food. Turning round, she walked off with a sense of purpose. She was back on track.

It was nearly eleven o'clock when she got back to the hospital. Walking across the car park, arms just a bit stretched by the weight of the potted azalea and two different bottles of fruit juice, Claire had a satisfied sense of mission accomplished; although she was not one hundred percent confident of her choice on the stereo. Just as she reached the steps, she suddenly remembered that she had said she would go and see Jackie. How stupid. She had walked all the way to the town and back without thinking of it. It would have been sensible to go that bit further while she was there. Putting two carrier bags into one hand to push open the swing doors, she told herself that perhaps she had better walk back again, sometime this afternoon.

Up in the ward, there were two surprises. Her father was sitting out in an armchair with her mother beside him. He had his glasses back on, and the newspaper was on his lap. As Claire walked in, he raised his eyebrows in an expression of greeting. And there was another visitor. Jumping up out of a chair on the other side of the bed was her son.

"Hello mumsy!" David said, giving Claire a big bear hug before she could even put down her bags.

Claire, always amused by David's use of the 'you're smaller than me now little mumsy,' expression, smiled and struggled to return some of his affection, while locked in his grip and loaded down with shopping.

"Oiy!" she laughed, "You're squashing Granddad's azalea! How long have you been here? How did you get here; you crazy boy?"

David released her, took the carrier bags and plonked them down unceremoniously beside John's locker.

"I've been here about half an hour; and I came on a train; you know, chuff, chuff? And I'm not a crazy boy! I'll have you know I got out of bed early to... well actually that is crazy, yes. But it was worth it! And here I am...."

Her father was raising his eyebrows again, and making a brave attempt at a smile. David stood behind the chair he had been sitting in and indicated that Claire should sit down. He looked well. It could not be possible that he had grown in a few weeks. Ever since he had reached his teens, Claire had been incredulous that the cheeky little schoolboy with dirty knees, and his cap on all crooked, were one and the same person as this giant. But his thick blonde hair was still flopping in his eyes, to be tossed back occasionally with a shake of the head. Some things didn't change!

"Sit down, Mother, you're making the place look untidy!"

She did as she was told and he leant over the back of the chair and pretended to massage her shoulders; another trick of his. It actually felt quite good. She asked him how he was. "Had he spoken to Pippa? How was he getting on?" he said.

"Fine, fine and fine. No seriously, I've already told Grandma and Granddad all my news. You can get it from them. I think I ought to be going in a minute; there's a lecture this afternoon I ought to go to and I don't know how long it will take to get back."

Claire stretched her neck back to look up at him.

"But you can't go yet, I've hardly said hello!" she moaned.

"Oh, keep your wig on mother!" he taunted, "I'll come again. Now, I had a jacket somewhere, where have I chucked it? "

After fooling around looking for it under the bed, and behind the curtains, he picked the jacket up from beside the wall where he had laid it and added.

"You could walk downstairs with me, if you're that bothered!"

David's comic humour evaporated like smoke in the wind as they passed through the door.

"Will he be alright?" he said quietly as they reached the stairs.

They traipsed down slowly; the echo of their footsteps in that stairwell was becoming as familiar to Claire as the steps outside. But then, walking across the car park, David perked up again.

"How do I get back to the bloody station, anyway?" he said, with a smile, "I got just the teensiest, weensiest bit lost on the way here!"

They ambled across to the road and stood on the pavement. Claire pointed and gesticulated, telling David the quickest way to the station. He kissed her on the cheek, took a few paces, then turned and came back.

"I forgot..." he said, "...how's Auntie Jackie? I didn't like to ask Grandma!"

"She's OK. I talked to her yesterday."

Claire felt pangs of guilt. She was lying.

"Does she know?" David asked.

He had always been fond of his Auntie Jackie, and she of him. She used to babysit, throw him in the air and make him laugh when he was tiny.

"Yes. She knows."

Claire said simply. She kissed him again, remembering the stage when he used to refuse to be kissed, and he swaggered off along the pavement. Watching him go, she thought, yes, he is a crazy impetuous boy, but it was a lovely, lovely surprise. Then, striding back across the car park, her brain was humming *Sailing.... I am sailing...*

She could not get that wretched tune out of her mind now.

***

Two perfectly formed tears rolled down his face and dropped onto his pyjama top, spreading into a small dark stain. Nickii was looking the other way and did not notice them. Claire watched them on every microsecond of their journey, and then she scrambled to her feet.

"Excuse me, I've just got to go out for a second."

She gulped, and fled out of the ward. There was an open door, a room with a television and a lot of empty chairs, a large window, and bright light. She dashed in there, pushing the door behind her, reeled through the chairs to lean on the windowsill. Through the mist of her own tears she saw the tops of trees, the cathedral tower in the distance. Why? Why did this have to happen to *him*? Why hadn't she done more? Why didn't she help them more with Jackie? Her shoulders began to shake; her arms trembled on the windowsill. There was a noise, a strange voice behind her.

"Are you alright, love?"

Quickly she straightened her back; wiped her bare hand across her cheeks, and under her nose.

"Yes, I'm alright." Her voice was strangled.

She did not look round. She heard the door close softly and then she turned. The room was empty. Sitting down on a chair, she stared at the blank grey of the television screen. You are doing it again, she told herself, sharply. He is perfectly entitled to cry. He has every reason to cry. What you should be doing instead of moping around in here is growing up and giving a bit of support. She got up, opened the door and walked along to the lift lobby, and then into the loo with the graffiti walls to fix her face.

CHAPTER FOURTEEN

The rumble of wheels, the clank of metal on metal, and an imperceptible mixed aroma of food, heralded the arrival of lunch; there was a buzz of anticipation in the ward. Two young nurses danced in with the trolley.

"Here we go, here we go, here we go...."

Chirped the short, pertly attractive one with the dark hair.

They stopped by John and Nickii as their first port of call. The same nurse, her white hat clipped in amongst her dark curls, consulted a clipboard on the bottom shelf, and then the charts hanging at the end of John's bed.

"Ah, Mr Tolley," she said brightly, "you didn't get to filling in your form yesterday , so I'm afraid we've chosen for you today."

Bending down she took a plate from the second shelf; its contents hidden by a dull metal cover.

"Cod in parsley sauce, with mixed vegetables! Should be nice and easy for you to swallow anyway!"

She put the plate on the table beside John's chair.

"I think they might be moving you upstairs this afternoon. We'll miss you..." she turned to Nickii. "What about you Mrs Tolley, can we get you anything? I'm sure we could find something in the kitchen."

"That's very kind of you, but no thank you," Nickii said. "My daughter's here somewhere and I think she bought us some sandwiches this morning; but thank you anyway!"

They clattered on with the trolley to the next bed. John looked with indifference at the covered plate on the table. The pillows had slipped behind him in the chair, he looked stiff and uncomfortable sitting there, as though most of his concentration was needed to keep himself upright. Nickii stood up, tried to pull the pillows up behind his back, make him more comfortable so that he could eat his lunch. She wished they would put him back into bed, he had been out for a long time; he must be tired. Suddenly one of his legs jerked forward. His head lolled back awkwardly over the top of the chair. His eyes rolled back in their sockets, the pupils out of sight.

"Darling, what is it? Oh my poor darling, what's the matter?"

Nickii looked up. Both the nurses had their backs to her. She wanted to shout; but she could not. He started to slump down. She struggled to stop him falling. His body was leaden.

"NURSE!" Claire shouted behind her.

Both the nurses turned. And then they were there, holding him up.

"Mr Tolley! Mr Tolley!" They patted his cheeks.

Claire and Nickii were scooped out of the ward. There was a bell ringing in Nickii's ears; people were running. They stood in the open door of the television room. Two female patients sat watching, one with her leg in plaster.

"I'll be back in a moment!" The nurse muttered and disappeared.

Claire's hand was holding hers. She was holding so tight she was hurting Nickii's fingers. Nickii tried to work them free. The pert, dark-haired nurse came back.

"You'll be more comfortable behind here." she said, ushering them to some chairs behind a screen.

"How is he? What...?" Nickii was afraid to ask.

"We've got him back in bed and the Doctor's with him now. I'll try to bring you some tea in a moment!" she said and rushed off.

They sat behind the privacy of the screen. The chairs were grey, plastic and hard; the screen covered in dull brown baize. The television was turned off, and Nickii heard a shuffling, as the two women left the room. Claire's hand was resting on her lap now, but Nickii could hardly feel the weight of it. She watched Claire's shoulders trembling, and wondered why. A whole part of her had shut down, and a strange, cold and fatalistic calm had taken hold.

"I suppose there'll be a funeral and people, all those people!" she said, quietly.

"No. No there won't;" Claire said, "he's going to be alright!"

And then they sat in silence; close together on the hard chairs, just waiting.

Until, suddenly, Nickii heard footsteps. She expected the nurse with the promised cup of tea. Her face appeared around the screen. Her hat was a bit askew. She was smiling, a little half smile.

"You can come back in now!" she said.

Nickii stood up; the floor seemed to sway under her feet. She followed the blue dress, black stockings, and flat shoes. She could sense Claire behind her. He lifted his head from the pillow, raised his eyebrows.

"Sorry about that!" his eyes seemed to say.

***

Claire watched clear gin glisten as it slid into a glass over two large ice cubes; the cubes cracked and made her jump. Mesmerised by her thoughts, she had poured too much. She contemplated sloshing some back into the bottle, but then she decided she needed it. It had been a day from hell. She had already taken a large glass of Bristol Cream to Nickii who was slumped in the chair in the dining room. She was back on phone duty. Again it had already been ringing when they got to the door, like an echo of the night before. Though tonight the mat was also littered with envelopes. Those were lying in a neat pile, next to the bottles on the kitchen table, waiting for Nickii to open them. Claire refilled the ice tray and went out to the walk-through to put it back in the freezer. How many times, she thought had she watched him do this, as she slid the tray back on top of its snowy brother. He always did the drinks. And scenes from the day kept appearing in her mind like patterns at the end of a child's kaleidoscope.

When she and Nickii had returned to the ward from behind the screen in that television room, the cheerful little curly-haired nurse stood beside them at the end of the bed.

"Just keeping us all on our toes weren't you Mr Tolley!" she said jovially. Then she turned to Nickii and added, "He was probably sitting out for a bit too long. He just fainted, that's all. But he's much better now; aren't you Mr Tolley!"

Her father had raised his eyebrows again and given a little nod. A faint hissing sound came from his lips. Her mother walked around the bed and gave him a kiss on the cheek; then she grabbed her handbag from the floor and bolted out of the ward. Claire and John, faces turned, had watched her go. She was as white as the sheets on the bed, and Claire realised then that Nickii hadn't left his side since they had arrived that morning. Claire had retrieved one of the chairs that had been cast aside in the scuffle, and sat down on the side that moved. It had taken her until today, she thought now, as she took a big gulp of the gin, to realise that the other side didn't, move that is. The whole of his right side from top to toe was as though it didn't belong to him anymore; he wasn't even aware it was there it seemed. She took another big slug. The liquid moved down the glass. Through the kitchen door, she could hear her mother still talking quietly on the telephone. Supper; she should think about their supper! They didn't want to have shades of the kippers episode from the night before! She turned to look for the carrier bags; so much travelled since they were filled, and remembered how the good hand had gripped hers when she offered it. How the newly arrived heart monitor had demanded her attention, with its mesmeric bleep, and flashing green signals. And how he had tried to speak, and the frustration on his face as his head flopped back on the pillow when he couldn't get the words to come. Then her mother had come back. She had a completely new brave face, and a bit more colour in her cheeks. Claire had swopped chairs so that she could have the good hand, and then they had sat there, talking about the world, the weather and David coming all that way on the train just for an hour's visit, until the last of the evening visitors had filtered their way out of the ward and they had to leave him again.

There was a soft ping as Nickii put down the phone. Coming into the kitchen, she walked straight to the window, pulling the curtains over the inky black squares of night. The shopping still littered the kitchen table where Claire had unloaded it. Two M&S individual Linguini with Prawns, a mini bread stick with a French flag on the label...

"Oh look, we brought the shaving cream home, how silly!" Nickii said.

And just as she was picking the top envelope from the pile on the table, the phone gave its piercing ring yet again making them both jump.

"Do you want me to go?"

Claire made a move towards the door. But Nickii had already dropped the unopened envelope and retreated to the dining room. Claire picked up the triangle packs of their uneaten sandwiches. She was wondering whether to throw them away or put them in the fridge, when Nickii called out that it was Michael on the telephone.

It was good to hear his voice; although her mind has been too full to realise it, she had obviously been missing him.

"So how's John?" he asked, after they had said their initial hellos.

Claire told him about David's visit and her father's fainting fit; and then, once the flow of words had begun, she carried on with every little detail, as though pouring it all out to him might exorcise the day's events.

"After that, one of the nurses came and said they were ready for him to go up to the other ward. You should have seen us all; talk about palaver! They moved the whole bed with him in it, lock, stock and barrel. We had all his things, and our shopping, piled on top of his legs as though he were some sort of removal carriage; then we all squashed into the lift; porters, bed and Mummy and I. If Daddy hadn't looked so weak, it would have been funny; well, I suppose it still was in a way!"

"So what's it like up on the new ward?" Michael asked.

"It's amazing how different it is, actually. It's on the opposite side, where the women's ward was downstairs. It's bigger, about fourteen or fifteen beds I should think, and it's noisier. There seems to be more going on. I suppose it's because on a surgical ward people are either waiting for their operations or recovering, so it's more subdued. But most of the patients up there have been there for a while; they've had time to bring out their characters, get to know each other, and the staff. There was quite a lot of chatter across the beds!"

"Well, I wouldn't have thought John would like that much!" Michael said. "He likes his peace and quiet doesn't he?"

"Yes I know, but it does mean there's more to watch, and us being with him all the time will be easier. They didn't say anything, but we did get the feeling that we shouldn't really be there downstairs, whereas the nurse this evening said Mummy could get there as early as she likes in the morning. They seem to encourage the relatives to be there. They even showed us everything in the kitchen and said we could use the fridge for anything we wanted. Anyway you'll see at the weekend. Are you coming down tomorrow?"

Yes, Michael told Claire, he was planning to leave work early and drive straight to the hospital in time for evening visiting. Then he said the washing was about to flow over the top of the basket, and he was running out of clean shirts. By the time Claire had explained the intricacies of the washing machine and tried to impress on Michael that he should separate the white clothes from the coloureds, Nickii had tidied the kitchen table, laid two trays for their supper and sorted all the post.

"There's a nice lot of cards for us to take in tomorrow," she said, as she slid a baking tray containing the two linguini into the oven, "and there's a note there too, which says his glasses will be ready to collect on Monday."

CHAPTER FIFTEEN

Jackie was staring at a dirty mark on the pale grey carpet of her room. Her forehead was burning, her body shivering. She hunched her knees up closer to her chest, curling up into a tighter ball; as she did so her head moved further towards the edge of the bed; but still she kept her eyes focused on the mark. She had been watching it for a long time; an amoebic stain spoiling the continuity of the clean carpet. It was like her, she thought, Jackie Hildegaard, an ugly nuisance of a blob in a world of normal people. A shaft of bright light from the middle of the undrawn curtains fell across the dark patch. It sliced her blob in two, two halves, before and after, normal and ill? It was only a small mark; small mark, small life. Yards of clean carpet, one small blotch; hundreds and hundreds of ordinary, well people and her. She had seen them all yesterday; had watched them, swarming about their normal lives all day, while she walked.

She had walked and walked; around and around and up and down for hours and hours. She had woken early. Lay in bed, eyes open, for a long time, just as she was doing now. But as she had lain there, she pictured them all up there in the ward; her father in the bed, Claire and her mother sitting by his side. And she had become angry, very, very angry. He was her father too! She had got up and dressed and out of the house in a flash. She had walked, fast and purposefully, through the town and out to the hospital. Then she stopped. She stood in the car park and looked across at the building; and she could hear Marjorie's voice ringing louder and louder in her ears.

"They won't let you in Jackie, if you go there!"

"They won't let you in Jackie, if you go there!"

"THEY WON'T LET YOU IN JACKIE, IF YOU GO THERE!"

And suddenly it had hit her. They wouldn't let her in, not because he was too ill, but because they didn't want her! She had seen his fist, as it thumped down with a crash on the kitchen table, and the agony written on his face when he had shouted.

"I can't stand it. I just can't stand it any more!"

And so she had turned and walked away. She just walked, slowly and doggedly all day long. Back up into town, then up South Street towards the house and then out on the ring road past the Leisure

Centre; round to the theatre, along near the hospital then again back into town. And she had watched the ordinary people; couples laughing and holding hands; families, mothers with babies, fathers with children; she hated them. How she hated their laughter, hated their love; hated their luck. She sat in the Cathedral. Watched clusters of them coming in and going out, talking in hushed voices. None of them noticed her.

Finally, when it was getting dark, she had come back. Bob had been in the front room when she stood in the hall. He said Jackie should be sure to ring Marjorie because she had been looking for her. But Jackie didn't ring. Whatever for? She did try to ring Lytton; but his new woman answered; MJ or whatever she was called; she said that Lytton wasn't there he was in London. Then she had spoken to Flavvy. She asked her how she was, and Flavvy said she had just had a bath and she was going to watch *Eastenders*. Then she said.

"You're my real Mummy, aren't you?"

Jackie just said, "Yes". Then she hadn't known what else to say. Flavvy put down the phone and Jackie just heard the harsh buzz of the dialling tone. She had put the phone down too and walked straight upstairs and got into bed.

Now she was still shivering. The bed had that crumpled, uncomfortable feeling of one that had been occupied for too long. But Jackie was barely aware of either. When a light warning tap sounded on the door, she still had her gaze firmly locked on the blotch on the carpet. Then the door burst open with a confident flourish.

"Right, up sit dear, you're going to eat some brunch."

Jackie looked up as Marjorie marched towards the bed carrying a tray. She sat down heavily on to the bed, dangerously close to Jackie's curled up legs, and rested the tray on her lap.

"Come along, you can't possibly refuse after I've gone to all this trouble to get it ready for you!"

Actually, I could, Jackie thought, but I haven't got the energy; and there is something very appealing about the smell of that toast. She struggled to sit up, her legs being somewhat trapped by the bulk of Marjorie. There were two boiled eggs on the tray, each neatly wrapped in clean hankies as makeshift egg cosies, and a toast rack. Jackie had never seen that in the cupboard. It was full of toast and flanked by two mugs of steaming coffee. Marjorie took one of the coffees off the tray and slid it across the bed on to Jackie's lap.

"You look dreadful dear; if I might say so. You really must look after yourself or you can't hope to carry on up your ladder, can you?"

Jackie just looked at her blankly, her hands still under the duvet by her sides, and the tray balanced precariously on her outstretched legs.

"Oh, I know you've got a lot to put up with at the moment; that's why I'm here dear! But you must just try and take it day-by-day, hour-by-hour, and this is the hour for eating. Come along, look sharp, or I might eat the toast myself if you don't hurry up. I've already put lashings of butter on it!"

Jackie took one hand from under the duvet and reached for a piece of toast. Nibbling slowly at the corner of it, she looked at Marjorie and began to wonder why she was doing this for her. A little smile of satisfaction crossed Marjorie's face as Jackie took a larger bite and then another, actually enjoying the slice of toast.

"So what were you doing yesterday? I came to see if you were alright, but you were out all day. Did you go to the hospital?"

It's none of your business, Jackie thought, instinctively. But then she reminded herself that Marjorie was making a huge effort to be kind.

"No. Well.... no, I was just walking," she said.

"Hum, I see!"

The smile had gone from Marjorie's face now and her brow was puckered in thought.

"Would you like me to go downstairs now and ring the hospital to find out how things are?"

There was a pregnant silence in the room as Jackie asked herself the same question over again. Then she decided; yes, she very much would like to know what was going on. She looked at Marjorie and nodded, murmuring a quiet "Thank you."

Left on her own in her room again, Jackie felt a sense of irrelevance heaped on the confusion that was already her life. What was she doing here in this strange bed, in this strange house, with this strange woman running up and down the stairs for her? Particularly when Marjorie had said to them all more than once, "I'm here to keep an eye, not to play nursemaid to you folk, you know!"

With indifference she lifted the hat from one of the eggs. The top was sliced off and replaced, like an, extremely neatly repaired, Humpty Dumpty. Jackie remembered how her father used to carefully scoop the piece out of the top, and eat that before he started on the egg itself. She picked up a spoon and did the same. By the time Marjore came back, she had completely emptied the shell, and then automatically turned it upside down in the egg-cup; like they used to do when they were children, pretending that the eggs were brand new.

"Well, I've had quite a little chat with the Sister!" Marjorie said, landing back in the same spot on the bed with a thump. "They've moved your father up to the medical ward now, and she says he's settling in nicely. They can't tell us much about his condition, because they like to wait a few days and let him rest and recover from the shock before they investigate too much, but they'll be able to say more next week."

Next week! So he won't be home for the weekend, Jackie thought. "How long do you think he'll be in there?" she asked Marjorie.

"It will be several weeks at least, dear, I'm afraid. It could even be a few months. But don't worry, just give it a few more days for him to have a complete rest, and then I'm sure you'll be able to go there regularly to see him; that will make you feel better about it all. In the meantime, tomorrow I'm coming in the morning to fetch you, and you're going to come and have lunch with me. No ifs and buts; I know you would have been spending the weekend with your parents. But you can't do that, so you'll have to put up with fat old Marjorie; and it will be nice for me to have some company. Now are you going to eat that egg?"

Jackie picked up the spoon again and gave the egg a tap on the top, disintegrating the shell into the egg-cup. Marjorie smiled at her warmly as she stood up.

"There you are you see, you've even found the edge of your sense of humour! Now see if you can eat the other one, then pamper yourself somehow for the rest of the day and I'll see you tomorrow!"

Jackie couldn't imagine what going to lunch with Marjorie would be like. She didn't really think she wanted to go; but then what else would she do for the whole weekend, and then the week after that, and then....

"Thank you!" she said, as Marjorie opened the door.

"You're welcome dear. See you tomorrow!" Marjorie replied.

And then Jackie heard her walking slowly and heavily down the stairs.

***

A man of late middle age, with greying black hair and a round florid face came gliding into the ward in a wheelchair. He was going at quite a lick.

"Hello Jack," somebody called from one of the other beds.

Jack let fly a string of loud and cheerful, but unintelligible words. Half-running to keep up with him was a short, dumpy woman with the sides of her anorak flying behind her in her haste; inches of white flesh showed between the top of her boots and the hem of her skirt. She seemed to have understood his noisy greeting.

"Shush, Jack," she chided, as they approached his bed further down the ward. "They don't all want to know where you've been!"

Michael looked over the top of his newspaper at John and said quietly.

"Jack's one of the live wires then!"

John raised his eyebrows, looked towards the end of the ward, where Jack was now whizzing around visiting other beds, then looked back at Michael and nodded twice.

"Does it get on your nerves?" Michael asked.

John gave a slight shrug of his shoulders with a little half smile and shook his head. Then they both went back to their reading. They had quickly developed a friendly, mutual acceptance of the situation. A decent two-way conversation was impossible. So the only sensible course of action seemed for them both to enjoy each other's company while reading the newspapers. Although Michael had, in the last few minutes, been asking himself whether John could actually *read* the paper? Just before Jack had come bowling into the ward, John had been struggling to turn the pages and fold his paper with the one hand; then he had laid it on the bed, and firmly pointed at the uppermost financial page. Michael had leant forward, looked at the article where John's finger landed. Then he had commented that he wasn't really much into stocks, shares and investments, since they hadn't got any money. Now it had just crossed his mind that John may have been asking him to read or paraphrase it for him. On the other hand, if he couldn't read, he couldn't find the page, could he? Michael could have just simply asked him, but somehow it didn't seem right to say to a distinguished and intelligent chap like John. *"Oh, by the way, old chap, can you actually read that?"*

That was the thing that had struck Michael the most when he came into the ward last night – that John didn't really look ill. On Wednesday he had done; his face was flushed and he looked frightened, shocked and vulnerable. But after two days, he seemed to have regained his composure. His complexion was back to its normal healthy olive, and apart from the paralysis in his arm and a slight droop to his lip, he could have been just sitting up in his own bed. He glanced at him again now. He did appear to be reading the paper.

Looking round at the door, Michael hoped that Claire and Nickii would be back soon. They had gone out, over an hour ago, for some fresh air, and a walk around the shops. Before that Michael had enjoyed a good walk around on his own. It was the first time he had explored Chichester alone on foot, and he had discovered some interesting buildings. He had wished that he had taken his camera with him, to take a few shots of some of them. Turning back to glance at John, before returning, disinterestedly now, to the newspaper, he thought that although he had chided Claire this morning for worrying too much in advance, there was some truth in what she said. She had allowed the details of the situation to crowd in and flood her brain with panic after a chat with the sister yesterday. And that morning, after Nickii had left for the hospital, and they were alone in the cottage, she had told him all about it, building up into a crescendo of staccato questions.

"He's going to be in there for at least eight weeks. The more support and care he gets from his relatives the better his recovery will be, but we have to face the fact that he will probably never walk and may not speak again. He will have to have speech therapy to be taught how to speak. How will Mummy cope? How will they both cope when he comes home? What about the cottage? It's not suitable for a wheelchair? How will we cope? How will I cope? How can I be in two places at the same time?"

"How we cope and how you cope is not really the issue is it! We'll manage," he had said firmly. "It's the quality and speed of your dad's recovery that's important, and that you give your Mum as much support as you can."

That had done the trick; like a quick tap on the face of a hysteric. However, she was partly right, working out the visiting patterns was not going to be easy. Lost in the possibility of working out some pre-ordained timetable, which probably wouldn't work anyway, Michael was aware of John looking at him. He was nodding in the direction of the door, with that slightly twisted little smile that was becoming familiar. Before he could turn round, Claire and Nickii were standing at the end of the bed. They both looked better, refreshed and smiling, and were carrying some ominous looking bags that meant money spent! He stood up, so that one of them could have his chair.

"It looks to me as though they've had a good time, John!" he said, with a wink in John's direction. And then to Claire and Nickii he said.

"I thought I would go back now, and leave you two to show off your purchases. Perhaps I'll get some dinner ready for when you come back!"

"Well, that'll be an experience!" Claire teased. "Anyway, I'll walk out to the lift with you."

As they approached the lift well, Michael asked her about the cheerful chappie in the wheelchair.

"What's with Jack; the chap in the wheelchair, what's wrong with him?"

"Let's go down the stairs;" Claire said, as though she hadn't heard him. "I'll come down to the door."

They started to walk down the stairs, although Michael couldn't see the point in not using the lift.

"Have you got a key to get in?" she asked him, and then, before he had time to reply, added,

"He had a stroke, similar to Daddy's I think, about nine or ten weeks ago."

Walking across the car park to the car, Michael began to recognise the panic that was in Claire that morning. He could not somehow picture John careering about in a wheelchair like Jack. But opening the boot, and dropping in the carrier of food that Claire had given him, he dismissed the thought and concentrated on his determination to prove that their dinner certainly would be an experience!

CHAPTER SIXTEEN

Claire had to admit that Michael was right about the dinner. She and Nickii had arrived home to the smell of roast potatoes. There was a bubbling cauliflower cheese with a crispy brown topping in the oven, and expertly sliced runner beans in a colander on the worktop.

"You will have to hurry up and cook your own steaks," he had said, "because I'm not getting my fingers all bloody. Just getting them out of the freezer was bad enough. But I also have to confess I don't know what to do with them!"

They had forgiven him that, and for the fact that he hadn't opened the wine, since, not only had he done all this in a completely alien kitchen, but he had cleared and washed up what must have been a considerable mess as well. The only thing to spoil an extremely tasty meal, for which neither Claire nor her mother had had to lift a finger, was the fact that there were only three of them to enjoy it. After that she had even managed to get partially engrossed in a film on television. She and Nickii hadn't switched the box on once since Wednesday, but Michael jollied them along and insisted, partly because of his own addiction but also, she suspected, because he was trying to encourage them to switch off their problems, in the same way that he had learnt to deal with his own.

However, one can't learn the lessons of a lifetime overnight, and the next evening, after Michael had left for home and she and Nickii were alone again, the television was forgotten. Left to their own devices, they had developed an evening routine like working women catching up on all the mundane chores. They had both been pleased to get a few things done so they could be ready to get to the hospital by eight o'clock on Monday morning. By now they had come to an unspoken arrangement with the staff that Nickii would arrive in time to help John with his early morning ablutions. This pleased the nurses, who were grateful for any help they could get. And it pleased John too. However kind and attentive the nurses were they were still strangers. If he had to be washed and shaved by anyone, he far preferred it to be his own wife.

Claire surveyed the line of red plastic chairs opposite the lift as her mother walked on into the ward. There was no-one here waiting at this time of the morning, so she could take her pick. She chose one of the middle ones next to a red Formica topped table, which was still stained with the dark coffee rings that were there when she had first sat there the previous week. Since then these had been added to and smudged by newer marks. An overflowing, luminous red, foil ashtray spilled screwed-up sweet-papers and dustings of ash around its edges. She dropped her handbag on the floor and crossed her legs, leaning one arm on the filthy table. This area was becoming as familiar to her now as her own sitting room. How many hours had she sat here? There was a spare bed, regulation hospital type with metal frame and plastic-covered mattress. It stood along the wall on the left, empty and expectant. People sometimes sat on it when this space became crowded, or kids clambered all over it, bored by visiting time. Behind her, on the high windowsill, lurked a nearly dead chrysanthemum, covered by the tiny whitefly sucking the life from the leaves. It had obviously been banished from the ward and forgotten in this no-man's-land.

I will never forget that chrysanthemum, Claire thought. So many times she had sat there thinking the same things. She should read her book, write her diary, file her nails, and make some use of the time. But she could never summon the enthusiasm. Instead she sat, enveloped in a numb inertia, listening to the drum of the lift machinery and other people's footsteps on the stairs. As she was doing again now, waiting until it was time for the shops to open. Then, with something constructive to focus on at last, she went off to buy lunch for herself and Nickii.

Sometime later, she was bending down in front of the fridge in the empty ward kitchen, hesitant about where to put the ice cream and yoghurts she had bought for her father. A voice from behind startled her.

"Feel free to make tea and coffee for yourself or your mother whenever you want! Has anyone showed you where everything is?"

It was the bubbly staff nurse that they had chatted to over the weekend. Claire and Nickii had already picked her out as one of their favourites. Claire admired the skilfull things she did each day with her ash blonde hair and the way she made the uniform look subtly more stylish than some of the others. But most of all they appreciated her friendly manner and the fact that she was so much more caring, hard working and efficient than any other nurse they had come across so far.

Claire looked round from the fridge.

"Yes, we have been given a quick tour, thank you. Does it matter where I put these?"

"No, not really." The nurse said, looking over her shoulder as she filled a kettle at the sink on the opposite side of the kitchen. "Strictly speaking you should put his name on them so we know what's whose, but don't worry for now!"

Then, leaving the kettle switched on, she was gone at the speed of light. Claire wondered how she had had the cheek to consider herself good at doing several things at once. Closing the door of the fridge she decided that compared with these nurses she was a complete novice.

When at last Claire walked back into the ward there was a bit of a kerfuffle going on. A skinny, wizened little man with pointed features, who resembled a little old elf and had spent a large proportion of the weekend screaming abuse at the nurses, was in the process of vacating his bed again; much to the dismay and consternation of several other patients who were each yelling in their turn for a nurse. The fact that they had fitted cot sides to his bed to try to prevent his wanderings was obviously not going to deter him, since he was nimbly clambering over the end, clattering his charts to the floor in the process. To add further spice to this scene, and causing Claire great difficulty in restraining an outburst of giggles, he tottered across the ward, dressed only in his pyjama top, and tried to join the opposite patient in his bed. Realizing that she was guilty of gawping, Claire walked quickly along to the left side of her father's bed and sat down with her back to the situation. Her mother was smiling too.

"But it's not funny really!" she said. "He must be a perfect pest; I think Daddy is saying he tried to get in with him last night!"

"Really?" Claire looked at her father, still trying to suppress her laughter "What did you do?"

John raised his eyebrows, shrugged his shoulders, and then his bedclothes gave a sudden jump as he demonstrated a kick with his left leg. At that, Claire could contain herself no longer and let out an, embarrassingly loud, cackle of laughter. At the same time the glamorous staff nurse walked briskly into the ward, also laughing, fortunately for Claire.

"Come along Fred!" she said sharply, as she approached the bed of the poor patient who was still grappling with the interloper. "You really are a very naughty boy! We will have to handcuff you to your bed if you don't look out!"

For which she was called a 'silly bitch'.

Eventually, everything returned to normal and Claire turned round to see if there were any additions to the cards on her father's locker that she could look at. He already had so many, that there was only room for the newer ones to remain standing. Then as they were replaced, they joined the growing pile in the shelf below. Out of the corner of her eye, she caught sight of his heart monitor on its shelf above the locker, and then wished she hadn't. Once she had noticed it, she could never keep her eyes off the beastly thing. It was as though it was only by watching it that she could will it to keep to the right patterns; not that she knew what the right patterns were.

"We've done a lot of communicating this morning!" Nickii said, providing a welcome distraction. "Daddy wants me to put his car in the garage, and keep mine out on the drive-in, which is easy enough. Then I think he wants me to ask Ellie to get him a wheelchair."

First Claire thought that they had indeed done a lot of communicating, and she wondered how they had managed it. But she was puzzled about the wheelchair. Her parents' neighbour, Ellie, did voluntary work for the Red Cross and sometimes stored some of equipment in her garage. But why would he think that she would get him a wheelchair.

"Surely they'll give him one from here, won't they?" she said.

"I think he's just impatient to get on with it;" Nickii said, looking at him, "he doesn't like being upstaged by Jack down there, and he thinks he'll get it quicker if we get one from Ellie I suppose!"

John gave a couple of determined little nods. Claire was beginning to loath this business of talking over him while he sat there looking from one to the other of them. Then he held up his left hand and clutched his little finger by his thumb, leaving three fingers in the air. Nickii carried on.

"He was so eager to get moving that he tried to get out of bed when we'd finished the washing routine this morning. He very nearly fell over, taking me with him! He's feeling a bit better and getting obstreperous already!"

Her father totally ignored Nickii's teasing, apart from a quick twisted grin which might have said 'oh phooey on you', and repeated his three finger gesture moving his arm three times to emphasise the point.

"Yes, I know!" Nickii carried on, "three things, I know; but I've deliberately left the other one till last. I think you ought to ask her yourself!"

There was a brief silence and whatever it was, Claire thought, since they had obviously developed their own workable method of talking, which must have taken some time, her mother might just as well spit it out and relay the message. Her father was looking at her with his eyebrows raised, probably wondering how to repeat the process with her, when Nickii took pity on him.

"He wants you to carry on with his book, but I don't know exactly what that means!"

Claire's very first reaction was to feel flattered that he would trust her with something as important as his novel.

"Well of course I will, if that's what you want! What do you want me to do; carry on with the editing?"

He rested his head back on the pillows with an air of satisfaction, gave another nod, another lopsided grin, and another one of those faint hissing noises that they were coming to understand as 'Yes'.

As she began to take in his request more deeply, Claire quickly understood that he must have come to terms with the fact that his recovery was going to be slow, and he didn't want his novel to just sit there waiting until he could get to it; too much time would be wasted. But then she started to think about it in practical terms of what she would actually have to do. It was some months since she had read his very first draft, and she knew he had chopped it about quite a bit since. Then he had been feverishly re-editing it after the writer's day. She wondered how far he had got, how much he intended to change, whether he wanted any additions or subtractions. And the more of these questions that drifted into her mind, the more frustrated she felt, because, of course, she couldn't ask him! She could only ask him questions that demand a 'yes' or 'no'. The whole exercise would have to be accomplished like a game of Animal, Vegetable or Mineral. She had better start with the basics. He was still looking at her, as though he had been following her every train of thought.

"So, all the copies and what you've done so far, are in your study?" she said.

"Sssss." he tried to say with a determined nod.

"And you've been re-doing it on the computer?"

"Sssss."

"Is it user-friendly? Have you got manuals for it?"

As she spoke she realized that two questions at once were not fair. She would have to learn. A shrug, a little nod and the raised eyebrows is what she got. Which seemed to say.

'I've got every faith in you, you'll work it out!'

Soon it was time for the diversion of lunch. Mealtimes in the hospital were like mealtimes on long haul air flights. They provided some relief from the long spells of self-entertainment. Except, of course, that plane trips come to an end much sooner than most spells in hospital. Nickii started to clear a space on his table ready for the ritual. Claire was trying to remember what he ordered, with some vague recollection that it was something peculiar that she wouldn't have chosen herself in a million years. Then when the magic metal cover was wafted away from the plate, she remembered. It was something, something and something with dumplings. The somethings were mashed potato, dull green peas, definitely not petit pois, and, what they used to call at school, 'flat meat'. Resplendently positioned amongst them were the grey dumplings. Claire looked at them with consummate horror, and at the same time thought that perhaps it was not such a surprising choice, since her father had often said that in his advertising days of expense account lunches, he used to long for some plain ordinary food; and he had discovered that they did the best toad-in-the-hole at The Ritz, and the best bubble and squeak at The Cumberland. She watched Nickii cutting the flat meat and vegetables up into fork-size pieces; a process John visibly hated. But not so much as he hated being fed like a child. Before her mother had finished the job to her satisfaction, her father reached forward and took the fork out of her hand. She hadn't started on the dumplings, but she surrendered compliantly and wheeled the table further up the bed so that he could reach. He was beginning to be very skilfull with his left hand, and, with a determined concentration, began to separate the contents of the plate into neat piles, as though in order of preference. When he had arranged it all satisfactorily, he began to eat, slowly and deliberately, forkful by forkful, selecting carefully from each section. It must be ghastly, Claire was thinking, to be eating under the scrutiny of an audience; on top of which they thought his throat must be sore, because he seemed to find it difficult to swallow. That was why they had started buying him the ice creams and yoghurts. Rather than watch him too closely, she concentrated her eyes on the dull glutinosity of the two little dumplings. Was he savouring them as a final treat? Surely, really, surely not! Finally a good proportion of the ready cut piles were gone. He put the fork down on the plate and leant back, resting from the effort. Nickii leant forward, picked up the fork and knife. Then standing up, she said.

"Shall I cut you up a bit more?"

As the knife hovered over the, supposedly savoured, morsels of delicious dumpling, John leant forward from the pillows in a flash and snatched the fork from Nickii's hand. She looked up in surprise; a worried frown flickering on her brow asked whether he was angry. He carefully laid the fork down on the table, but only to pick it up again as a drummer might his stick. Then with a completely straight face he landed a series of sharp taps to each dumpling, and with each tap the fork bounced a little higher in the air. His straight face crumpled and he was laughing. They were all laughing. Claire laughed until her lungs were piercing her ribs and she had to bend double to stop the pain. When at last she could catch her breath, she sat up and looked at her father, and quite involuntarily, the words just fell out.

"Oh, I do love you!" she said.

And then she was covered in confusion, as she realised that she had never said that to him before.

CHAPTER SEVENTEEN

Gazing out of the window, over the top of her typewriter, Jackie studied the garden fence. She looked to the upstairs windows of the house opposite; their curtains were bright orange. She seemed to spend so much of her time just gazing at things and thinking; or even gazing at things and not thinking at all, her mind vacuous. However, this time she was giving herself a lecture about persevering with all the plans that she had made on Sunday afternoon. But the days were passing so slowly; and as the time dripped relentlessly by, the plans had a way of losing their purpose. Today was Wednesday; one whole week since Marjorie had first told her that her father was ill, and they had both gone up there to the hospital; and five more days to go before she had told herself that she would go there again. It was quite simple; all she had to do was stay with the positive mood she had been in when she made out her plan of action. Those two little words, 'stay with', that were always coming up at the group sessions in the hospital. *Stay with* that thought; *stay with* that feeling; *stay with* that time in your life! It was all very well, but what happens when other stuff gets in the way? But, this time, she instructed herself, I will try harder. And she reminded herself again of the small high she had experienced on Sunday, after drawing some kind of a map for herself. It was the first time she had done that in a long, long time.

It was the day with Marjorie that did it. When she had got back on Saturday night, Jackie realised that she had enjoyed it. She had had a nice day. Before Marjorie picked her up she had been dreading the whole thing. She had even thought of going out for a walk so that she wouldn't be there when Marjorie arrived. But she couldn't quite bring herself to do it because Marjorie had been so kind to her the day before. Although she still could not bear the prospect of Marjorie's chattering, talking at her all day long and calling her 'Dear'.

As it was, the only thing Marjorie said in the car was.

"Don't forget your seat belt, dear!"

And then she had just driven along, leaving Jackie alone in her own space. The sun was shining and she had almost enjoyed watching the scenery and the colours of the autumn leaves. Marjorie lived in a flint cottage near Fishbourne and, although Jackie had never given a thought to where she might live, when they arrived outside it seemed that the house and Marjorie went together like some dogs do with their owners.

Marjorie led her straight into the sitting room, which had French windows leading on to a small walled garden. Two white plastic chairs and a table were still standing outside on the patio, left there from the summer; but now they were covered in brown leaves and splattered with mud. Again Marjorie had left her alone, with time to acclimatise herself to the strange surroundings.

"Make yourself at home, dear, pick whichever seat you fancy; read the paper if you want! I'll go and put some coffee on for us," she said.

And she had gone briskly out of the room, closing the door behind her. Jackie didn't sit for a while, although the two chintzy covered deep armchairs and the sofa had all looked most tempting with their cushions well squashed down where many people had sat before. She walked to the window and looked out at the garden, and then she walked slowly up and down the room. It was a long time since she had been a guest in the home of somebody that she didn't know well; it felt almost like being abroad. The fireplace bore the cold ashes and charred remnants of a previous fire, and the rug in front of it was stained with the scorch marks of years' of spitting logs. There were photographs everywhere; the front windowsill, the mantelpiece, the top of the television and the mahogany side table, all had photographs standing in a medley of different frames. One of the largest ones, standing on the table next to the lamp, was a posed studio picture of four children, with their hair brushed shiny and obviously wearing their Sunday best; three girls and a boy, two older girls behind and a younger sister and even younger brother arranged carefully in front of them. All the other pictures told the story of their growing up; various stages of school photographs; three weddings and then more babies.

When Marjorie came back, bashing the door open with a tray of coffee and biscuits, Jackie had been standing with her back to the unlit fire.

"I like your house," she said, as Marjorie balanced the tray across the dips in the sofa seats.

"Thank you, dear!" Marjorie said, looking round. "It's small, but it does very nicely for me, and I'm happy here."

Jackie's face must have been expressing the slight puzzle that was crossing her mind, because Marjorie added, "What's the matter, dear? You look perplexed! And aren't you going to sit down?"

"Yes, thank you," Jackie sat in one of the nearest armchairs beside the fire, "no I'm not perplexed, but I suppose I thought..."

"You thought I'd have a husband lurking around somewhere, and you wonder where he is? No, dear. I'm here all on my own and that's the way I like it. Booted the husband out years ago; best thing I ever did. You don't need a man to live, dear, you know! And you don't need a man to be happy either."

Then Jackie had asked her about her children and the photographs. She didn't have to say much for a long time after that. Marjorie told her the life story of all three of her daughters; one living in Canada that she didn't see very often, but talked to on the phone once a week; one in Suffolk, and one in Kent. And then she heard about all the successes, illnesses and quirks of the nine grandchildren that her daughters had given her between them. What had been strange though, was that she didn't mention the boy in the picture on the table at all, not once. Jackie didn't like to ask, but she did wonder whether he had fallen out of favour, or what may have happened for him to be obliterated from Marjorie's memoirs.

They had had an extremely pleasant lunch, sitting at the dining table with Jackie positioned so that she could still see Marjorie when she was talking back at her from the kitchen; still about the grandchildren. But Jackie hadn't minded that after all. She enjoyed hearing about children and it stopped her having to think what she should say. Marjorie had made three courses and even put a little posy of white chrysanthemums in the centre of the table. It was only when they went back to the sitting room with their coffee that Marjorie had started to talk about Jackie's life and her problems.

At first Jackie had begun to squirm and go into instant recoil. She had been sitting in the same armchair by the fire, and Marjorie was perched on the sofa pouring the coffee, her skirt hitched up over her knees, and leaning down between her legs to the tray in front of her on the floor.

"Have you spoken to your mother, or your sister? Silly, but I can't remember your sister's name?"

Jackie didn't answer. A few seconds before that she had felt almost peaceful, but suddenly a tense pounding pressure began to build up from the top of her neck and behind her ears, a flash of temper lurched into her mind, and she wanted to shout.

'NO, I haven't.'

Marjorie had looked up at her as she slurped coffee into the second cup.

"No, I didn't think you had;" she said, then looking back down and picking up the milk jug, she carried on, "and I can tell by your silence, that you've clammed up and you don't want me to talk about it! But there is just something I want to say to you, dear, and you can listen or not listen, just as you please, but I'm going to say it anyway!"

She shuffled and struggled and stood up then and handed Jackie her coffee. Jackie remembered how her hand shook when she took it. Then she balanced the saucer on her knees and held it with both hands not knowing what to do with it. Marjorie sat back down on the corner of the sofa nearer to Jackie. She could feel her looking at her. And then she had started.

"Now Jackie, dear, I know that on top of all your other problems, which were already quite enough for any human mortal, you are now feeling very hurt and left out while your sister, what *is* her name?........"

"Oh well, never mind, while your sister and your mother are up there in the hospital with your father, leaving you with not so much as a phone call. But what I want to tell you is that it's your illness that they're leaving out, not you! They love you, Jackie! I know it. I've seen it. Well, actually, I can't speak for your sister, I haven't met her. But I have met your parents. I have seen how much they love you. And it's because they love you so much that you're being left out. Now I want to try to explain to you why I believe that is. You see, you and your family have known each other ever since the day you were born, which is what, thirty something, nearly forty years? But you've only been ill for a part of that time; how long is that? Anyway, about seven years let's say. So for nearly thirty years you lived together as a family; mother and daughter, father and daughter, and sisters. You laughed with each other, cried with each other, had holidays, Christmases, birthdays, talked, got on each other's nerves and generally lived the way all families do, one way or another. And then your illness came along. And an illness is what it is, Jackie dear, just in the same way as you might have had a very long attack of the measles; but the illness changed you into a different person. Slowly you stopped laughing, you stopped crying, started saying things, and behaving in a way that was totally alien to the old you. And because they were so close to you, and because at first they didn't know that it was the illness that was doing this, your family began to think that they must have upset you in some way, that you didn't love them anymore; that you really believed some of the things you said to them, that some of the strange things you did, you did to punish them. And the more they thought that, the more they struggled to get you back the way you were, to make you snap out of it. They probably smothered you with affection one minute, and bombarded you with questions you couldn't answer, the next. And all the time you were thinking that they, of all people, should be the ones that really understood. But they didn't. And that made you angry, because they were the people closest to you, and they should have understood. So you see, it's the illness that pushes its way into the family and messes it all up."

Marjorie cleared her throat. She had been going on so much that she was making herself hoarse. Jackie was rigid in the chair, the cup and saucer still clutched on her knees. But still Marjorie hadn't finished.

"Now take you and me for instance! You've given me one or two rough moments; quite a few of your steely glares and long silences, but I can cope with it; partly because I had some nurse's training, but more because you're not a part of me. I happen to like you a lot, dear, though, God knows, sometimes I've wondered why; but you're not my family, and I don't love you. Do you remember that time when I came to fetch you from the police station? Well, if you were my daughter, that would have been one of the worst days of my life; as it is, we coped and I actually think it was all quite funny."

She wriggled her way to the edge of the sofa and stood up again.

"Well, anyway, that probably all sounded very garbled, and I don't know how much of it has gone in; but I'll just say again what I said at the beginning. It's your illness that they're leaving out, not you. And I think that you can safely say that the more a parent loves a child the more they are upset by the illness; so it's because they love you so much that you can't be there until your father is a little more rested. If he saw you right now, it would just remind him of how upset he is because you are ill, and that wouldn't help him get better would it! And you're not really in a fit state to be supporting other people, which is what your mum needs. The reason they don't phone you is probably because they simply can't think what they can say without upsetting you, and therefore making you feel worse. So it's a bit of a stalemate situation, but it won't last long. And what you've got to do is to concentrate on looking after yourself and keeping as cheerful as you possibly can, so that when you do see him you will be able to help him by looking more like your old self!"

Then Marjorie had stood in front of Jackie and gently reached forward for her cup.

"End of sermon! Come on, dear, you can come back to me now! Here let me take that cup and I'll go and make some fresh coffee!" she said.

Then she disappeared out of the room again with the tray.

For a while Jackie didn't move a muscle. She had hated every moment of Marjorie's speech. It sounded like a load of sentimental claptrap; all that talk about love. What did Marjorie know whether they loved her or not? But after a while the silence in the room had soothed her, and she leant back in the chair. She found herself looking at the photograph of Marjorie's children and then, in retrospect, she realised that Marjorie's voice had been very emotional while she was talking, and when she took her cup she had looked really upset. What *had* happened to that little boy? Jackie had thought. Could it be that Marjorie really *did* understand?

After a while she had bustled back in with the coffee as though nothing had happened. She got out more photographs in albums to show to Jackie, and talked incessantly as she turned the pages. Then she made tea and brought out a plate of homemade currant buns, and more biscuits. And, finally, she drove Jackie back to the house in the dark and dropped her off at the door.

"You won't mind if I don't come in will you, dear;" she said as Jackie got out of the car, "I'll see you on Monday!"

Jackie had gone more or less straight to bed when she got in. But not for the same reasons that she normally went to bed so early. She had been genuinely exhausted, and as she lay there she found she was thinking about the day, and not dreading the next one as usual. As she was falling asleep she had suddenly had the notion that she might go to church in the morning; it would be somewhere to go and something to do.

She hadn't enjoyed the service very much at all. She hadn't been to church for a very long time, and she could hardly remember The Lord's Prayer, let alone the various responses. She sat alone, next to a stone pillar, at the end of an empty pew and, several times, had asked herself what she was doing there. But when she got back, the very fact of having made a decision and passed some time was inspiring. She had gone up to her room and sat down in the chair and had then started to think about what Marjorie said the day before. She remembered how her father held her hand when they went to see Dr Bulstrode. Perhaps there was some logic to Marjorie's monologue after all. And it was then that she had made the plans. She had decided that she would wait one more week until she went to see him. She would go on the next Sunday. And in the meantime she would make a huge effort to do what Marjorie said so that she would be ready. First of all she supposed she should eat something. There had been a few bits and pieces left in her cupboard that her mother had put there; she couldn't remember what. And she knew there was nothing on her shelf in the fridge. She never bothered with shopping. She had looked in her purse and there wasn't much in there either. It was a whole week since she had seen her parents, and she never bothered to go to draw her money. She had had to pay the rent, and, anyway, everything always got in such a dreadful muddle with her finances. But she did go back out to the corner shop; bought some bread and cheese and a few tins, and forced herself to eat some lunch. Then, in the afternoon she had gone into the back room, and struggled to lift the typewriter from the floor by the piano on to the table. Her father had given it to her when he'd been pushing for her to get a job. She thought it would keep her busy if she tried some practice, and then perhaps she really would get a job some day. She had searched around and found some paper, and then she needed something to type. It seemed like a good idea at the time to use pieces out of the Bible. There was a list of the parables in the back of the old Bible she used at school. Laboriously she had typed out all of the parable of The Sower; then the Prodigal Son. But the small print hurt her eyes, she was horribly, horribly slow and when she looked at the results there were masses and masses of mistakes. After three whole days, the determination and renewed energy she felt were fast slipping away. Nothing had really changed. She was still here, alone. And all of the people in her life that meant anything to her at all, were out there – somewhere. And it was still a very long time till Sunday.

CHAPTER EIGHTEEN

As Jackie sat at her typewriter, wondering if she could ever really come to grips with her life, Claire was sitting on a train, that rattled and chugged through strange Sussex stations, and asking herself what all these sudden changes were going to do to hers.

In two separate places, she had seen the roofs of clubhouses that had been ripped off and deposited hundreds of yards away in their playing fields by the hurricane. She stood on Platform 11 at Clapham Junction Station waiting for a train to take her to Twickenham. It was the coldest, most bleak and windy station in the world. Since the changing of the clocks at the weekend, the light had faded as she waited and it was now almost completely dark. The platform began to fill with weary commuters as the time edged into rush hour. A masculine, recorded voice had announced the arrival of the Twickenham train three times, but still it was nowhere in view.

"Clapham Junction; this is Clapham Junction; the train now standing at Platform 11 is for Strawberry Hill..."

When, finally, it arrived, she edged into a vacant window seat and looked out, past her own reflection in the glass, barely seeing the steep banks of the cutting, and then the white tombstones in an enormous cemetery. She asked herself why she was doing this. Suddenly all her reasons for coming home seemed paltry, compared to what she had left behind.

That morning they were a bit later arriving at the hospital, and the nurses had already given her father his wash. Claire waited while Nickii finished off with the shaving and etceteras, and for them to have some prime time together, before she went in. Then later Nickii had gone out to get some shopping and fresh air. Claire told her father that she had been looking at his novel. The truth was that she had had no success at all with his computer. Try as she might, she couldn't even get into the file that he had been working on; and her mother had no idea at all how to work it. But she had found the print outs of what he had already done, and compared them with the original. She had told him that she was going home this afternoon, just to catch up on some chores and typing, and she would come back early on Friday morning. Then she had said that perhaps next week, if he felt up to it, she could bring in the drafts and they could try going through some of it together. He raised his eyebrows and nodded, but he hadn't seemed overly enthusiastic, and all the time she had been talking, he had looked agitated and uncomfortable. She asked him if he wanted a bottle; she had got quite used to finding clean ones in the sluice at the entrance to the ward. But he shook his head indicating, that that was not the problem. At the same time he was plucking angrily at the blankets with his left hand, wriggling around in the bed and frowning heavily with frustration. Claire looked around the ward for a nurse, but the only one around at the time was busy with another patient; she had decided she had better find out for herself what was wrong. Standing up she pulled the curtains around his bed, with difficulty since they refused to slide properly on their runners. When she had finally got them cocooned in their own little space she pulled back his blankets. It didn't take much investigation to discover that both of his legs were stuffed into one leg of his pyjama trousers. No wonder he was fidgety. The act of pulling down your own father's trousers and rearranging them like you would one of your children's, was at once weird, sad and very funny. She had got the giggles again, and so did he, which had helped to cover any embarrassment he was feeling. The train pulled out of Earlsfield Station, and Claire was thinking about how brown and healthy her father's legs had looked, and how unbelievable it seemed that they should be lying there, immobile, in a hospital bed. She had tried to avert her eyes from the private parts of his anatomy that were responsible for her very existence. But, in retrospect, from the small glimpses that she simply could not help, she realised that that was the only part of his physique that reflected his illness. Perhaps it's one of the first monitors, she thought. And then quickly she told herself that her mind was really wandering now, and she turned her head from the window and looked around the compartment. Life goes on; sullen faces looked at her, people read their Evening Standards, schoolchildren giggled and tittered behind their hands, and she was thinking about how this morning, she struggled to heave her father's pyjama trousers under his partially paralysed bottom.

    Walking up the street in the dark, she reached her front door. The familiarity of her own doorstep, the tired geranium in its pot, the leaves blown up in the corner beside it, the knowledge of the ordinary everyday chores that awaited her when she got inside, all brought the stark fact that was floating around in her mind on the train, rushing into her brain now, like a clap of thunder. This was her old life; the way it had been before she left. But things now were not the same at all. However fit his body may look, she had left her father down there, unable to speak and with half of that body totally unresponsive to the messages from his brain. She wiped the corner of her coat sleeve quickly across one cheek, and fumbled clumsily in her handbag in the dark, looking for her keys.

In the gloom of the unlit hall, she all but fell over one of the cats, the arrogant one, who was loudly protesting the fact that he had had to wait until later than this for his evening meal for days now. Trying not to be affected by his piercing whingeing, she switched on the light and went through to the kitchen. A pile of newspapers on the table indicated that she had not been around to weed them out to the garage, and thence to the dump for recycling. Putting her handbag on the table beside them, she gathered up all but today's and walked towards the utility room, bending on the way to pick up the encrusted cat bowls with her other hand and plonk them in the sink. Dropping the papers by the back door, she noticed that the tumble dryer was full of dry clothes, and the washing machine full of wet ones. Pulling the tangled multi-coloured dry ones into her wicker carrier, she told herself she should think herself lucky they were not still in the laundry basket upstairs and made a mental note to thank Michael. Then she thought. But why, why should I thank him for doing the washing? And immediately after, well, because he doesn't normally do it, I suppose that's why! The hum of the dryer made it feel more like home. Within fifteen minutes she had fed the cats, taken pizzas from the freezer, laid the table, sighed at the list of messages by the answerphone from her customers, including Dr Boffin; started a salad and a long mental list of all the things she would fit in tonight and tomorrow so that she could get back to Chichester first thing on Friday morning.

***

That night Nickii simply could not go to sleep. In the end she sat up in bed, with her dressing gown around her shoulders, and tried to draw some plans of how they could rearrange the cottage to cope with a wheelchair. They could change his study into their bedroom, but what would they do about the bathroom? She had visions of them laughing as they tried to get him up the stairs on his bottom. Then she told herself that with his strong will, he would probably walk again, eventually. But it would take time.

Still, with all of those visions of their future, she could not clear another, more immediate, problem from the back of her mind. Several times during the evening she had gone to the phone, hovered by it, or even picked it up, but then finally walked away without dialling. But she just could not stop thinking about Jackie, and whether she should ring in the morning before she went to the hospital. She hadn't spoken to her for over a week; didn't know how she was, or even for sure where she was. Two weeks ago it would have been unthinkable that she would just abandon her like that. But what could she say? How could she bring herself to say, 'I just phoned to see how you are, but I haven't got time to see you and I don't want you to come to the hospital'?

Finally she dozed off still sitting up and with the light on. When she woke, with a terrible crick in her neck, it was still dark but the red figures on the radio alarm told her it was 6.20 am. Thankful that the night was over, she got up and had a bath; still thinking about Jackie. But by then she knew that she wouldn't phone. She did not want Jackie to come to the hospital, not yet, maybe in a few days, but not yet. Yesterday afternoon, after Claire had left, John had seemed tired and rather depressed. In fact the whole ward was subdued. Even Fred was just lying still and quietly in his bed. She had tried to cheer John up by seeing if they could talk to each other by writing notes. But when he took the pen he didn't seem to be able to convey what was in his mind on to the paper. The fact that he had to use his left hand made it difficult enough, but they didn't seem to be on the same wavelength somehow. The letters didn't seem to have any meaning to him. He just looked blankly at her messages. She began to get depressed and asked herself how they had managed to communicate so well a couple of days ago. But, trying to keep positive, she had written all the letters of the alphabet down one side of a page and at the top she wrote, SPELL WITH TICKS. He took the notebook from her and laboriously tried to copy the letters horizontally across the page. She thought he was being obtuse and took the notebook away from him again, wondering how two people who had been so close for forty-two years could occasionally get their wires so crossed. Like all those occasions when they had agreed to meet somewhere and both waited in completely different places. In sheer frustration she had written 'SAY SOMETHING' on top of the next page and held it up in front of him. He just looked at her then, his head rested back against the pillows, and the sadness in his eyes was almost more than she could bear. Leaning forward she laid the notebook on his legs, and with her left hand, in very wiggly writing, she wrote, 'I LUV YOU'. He grasped her hand and squeezed it tight. That was better. But then, just as she was thinking that she really would have to go home, he had another one of those fainting fits. She sat alone and still in that television room again, waiting for them to call her. When they did, she sat with him for another half an hour. She tried to cheer him up; to tell him that they could still do all those things they hadn't done, and it wouldn't take as long as it seemed.

Now it was still only 7.55 am as she drove into the car park. There were plenty of spaces. She half-walked, half-ran up the stairs, thinking that the exercise would do her good; she was in a hurry to get there and she would be sitting all day. The glamorous staff nurse was in the corridor, still in her coat. She had obviously just arrived on duty.

"Morning Mrs Tolley!" she said cheerfully.

John's head was turned towards the door; he was waiting for her. As he spotted her, his eyebrows raised. She took his hand and bent across the bed to give him a kiss. The sister's voice behind her made her jump.

"We're going to move him this morning, Mrs Tolley, but if you want to give him his wash first, we can sort him out afterwards!"

"Move him?" Nickii turned round, "where to?"

"Well there's an empty bed up at the end in the corner now. We thought he would have more space down there, and a nicer view!"

There *was* more space. Nickii stood all his cards along the window ledge, together with the photographs she had brought this morning, and a couple of the soppy teddy bears that they had bought each other in the past; these together with his plants and flowers made it his own personalised little corner. It was a shame that, with his bed backed onto the window, he couldn't see the view behind him. But, on the other hand, probably just as well, Nickii thought, as she stood beside the bed. The paint had long since disappeared from the metal window frames, and where they met the glass there was a thick line of grime. Condensation was partially obscuring the view anyway. But in the distance, across the rooftops, Nickii could just see the spire of the cathedral. She had grown fond of the cathedral as a symbol of home and safety. When they had been off somewhere on a long trip, she could always spot it several miles away along the A27, and then she knew that they were nearly home. Though somehow on this day, from this window, it didn't look nearly so comforting. Turning her back on it, she sat down in the chair beside the bed. The floor was still sopping wet and suctioning at her shoes, where a disinterested and laconic cleaner had just sloshed the dirt and dust into the edges with his over wet mop. The glamorous staff nurse was walking down the ward towards them holding John's special socks to her cheek.

"I think his sexy leggings are dry now, Mrs Tolley, do you want to put them back on or would you like me to do it?"

These were the special elasticated stockings that they had produced yesterday, saying he should wear them for his circulation. Nickii had been quite staggered this morning when the nurse said she would rinse them out and put them on the radiator. Surely they had more than one pair! But considering the reason that Fred ran around flashing all the time was because the men had to share pyjamas, she shouldn't have been that surprised. Of course, she had been bringing John's in for him, so he had the luxury of a complete set.

"No, that's alright, I'll manage. Thanks very much," she said, standing up and reaching over the bed to take them.

The nurse smiled and told her to let them know if she needed anything and then, drawing the curtain across, she walked away. It certainly was a nicer space. Just the one curtain to pull across and they were enclosed in their own small alcove with windows on two sides. There was a disconcerting door on the wall facing the bed, through which, one felt, someone could burst at any moment. But nobody ever did, and Nickii presumed it must be a fire escape, or a disused cupboard or something. She pulled down the blankets on the bed and started to roll up the pyjama trousers on his right leg. His feet were cold; it was drafty by these windows. He needed some thicker pyjamas. Then, suddenly she realised that she had just taken something monumental for granted. She looked up at him with a surge of delight.

"You moved it!" she said, "You moved that leg!"

He looked at the leg, and then at her, then gave her the raised eyebrows signal of excitement.

"Do it again!" she said, holding her breath.

Her eyes flickered from his face to the leg. With an expression of fierce concentration, he too was gazing at his own right leg. And then it moved. Quite unmistakably, it moved a good two inches off the bed before flopping down again.

Nickii was so excited. She felt like shouting it to the whole ward; the whole world.

'He moved his leg. He moved his leg!'

But she tried to keep a sense of decorum as she rolled the creamy elastic of the special sock up the performing leg.

"There you are, you see!" she said, looking up at his face with a big smile, "I told you it wouldn't take as long as you thought!"

He looked back at her with a wan and wobbly smile as though he was still not very convinced. With the bedclothes neatly drawn back up to his waist, she made to pull back the curtain. But he raised his left arm sharply to stop her. Standing at the end of the bed in the corner of their new alcove, with her hand still on the curtain, she waited to see what was the matter. He raised his eyebrows again, opened his mouth, and with another burst of concentration, let out a protracted burble of incomprehensible speech.

"Ahhh, wahhh, yahh, yaaaaah, yaaaah....." he said.

Nickii spirits sank almost as far as they had risen. It sounded like the outcry of a deaf person in agony.

"That was very good!" she lied, "so you want to talk and wobble your legs about all at once! Do you want to practise some more, or shall I pull the curtain?"

He shook his head, and Nickii didn't know whether that meant he didn't want to practise anymore, or don't pull the curtain. But then he beckoned to her with his fingers, and she let go the curtain and went over to the bed. He stretched out his left arm and grabbed her sweater by the shoulder giving a little tug. It was a cuddle he wanted. With only the one curtain, there were less chinks for the world to gawp through and Nickii walked around and sat on the bed next to his left side, so that he could use his good arm for a proper hug. She remembered their 'Moaning Clubs' of old, and thought perhaps his little vocal outburst had reminded him of them too. When the girls were young, if anyone in the family had had a problem, such as that they couldn't do their homework, or the dinner had burned, or the car wouldn't start, they used to say, 'Oh never mind, let's have a Moaning Club!' Then they would all stand, arms around each other resembling a mini upright rugby scrum, and moan in unison. This was supposed to make the afflicted one feel better – and invariably did.

"Let's have a Moaning Club!" she said to him now, nestling into his neck, "but a quiet one though, eh!"

CHAPTER NINETEEN

Yesterday was bad, interminable. She had tried to dig the garden with a rusty trowel. That was pretty pointless. She had decided to write to the children instead. What had she to write about? Dear Flavvy, How are you? Love Mummy. She had considered telephoning Dr Bulstrode for help. What a notion! Was she mad? No, in the end she did nothing. She sat in her chair, forever, and waited for the time to pass. This morning, spontaneously, she had decided to neaten up her hair. She sliced decisively; a dark feathery shower floated down to the bathroom floor. She had already picked out what to wear on Sunday. The clothes were neatly folded over the back of the chair in her room. The hair cutting would take a while; then she would clear up the mess; perhaps go for a walk; buy a card for him; the time would pass, only one more day to go.

***

Claire was studying her father's eyebrows. She was studying them as quite separate entities on his face, as though she had never really looked at them before. Apart from his hands, the nod or shake of his head, and the occasional peculiar utterance, they had been his only form of expression during the past eleven days. Quite still now, over his closed eyes, they were slightly bunched up by the frown on his sleeping face. They arched into quarter moons pointing up to his temples, and the odd white, wiry hair escaped the rest with a curl in the wrong direction.

She could remember when they were black, and the objects of his fierce and angry look. And then she also remembered when she was seventeen, and she had first plucked her own.

"You've plucked your eyebrows!" he said to her, his own rising in dismay. They had met in the hall of the house where she and Jackie grew up in Surrey. Claire had come down from her bedroom, and her father had just come home from work. They were standing by the telephone table with the mirror on the wall above it.

"Yes," she said, preening in the mirror and then looking back at him, "don't you think they look better?"

"No," he said, "I liked them the way they were!"

He wasn't cross, just sad. And she was surprised; surprised that he cared that much about her eyebrows.

The frown eased and his brow smoothed. He was half-sitting, half-lying against the pillows. The old, red velvet, 'smoking jacket' that her mother made him years ago was wrapped around his shoulders. Her mother had struggled with the decision to bring it in here because it had got so scruffy, but he loved his old things best, and he got so cold by those windows. The light from the one behind him was growing dim and beads of condensation were working their way down from the top. Her mother had gone to find some thicker pyjamas to try to keep him warm. Claire looked down at the newspaper on her lap. She didn't want to rustle the pages for fear of waking him. He had had a dreadful morning.

Fred was letting out the odd expletive from his bed, but apart from that the ward was quiet. Jack was out somewhere with his relatives and afternoon visiting was over. There was just the wife of the man who was opposite her father's old bed, sitting there with her knitting. Claire looked back at her father. His head was still resting on the pillows but his eyes were open. He was beckoning with his hand for her to come closer. She pulled her chair nearer to the bed and leant towards him. He grabbed her hand quite fiercely and pointed it towards a small box fixed high on the wall at the end of his bed. He was making noises that meant nothing more than 'ahh....ahh... ahhh..'

"What is it?" she asked, "Do you want to know what it is?"

He let their hands fall onto the sheet and looked at her with an expression of relief.

The box had a glass cover. Inside was an oversized till roll of graph paper, on which a levered marker had traced signals, resembling the patterns of his heart monitor which, she suddenly noticed, hadn't been there since she got back yesterday. Quickly wondering herself what the box might be, she said.

"Well it looks like a barometer of some sort, perhaps it's measuring the air pressure in the ward?"

She was about to ask him if it was worrying him. Perhaps she could find out for him definitely what it was. But now the box seemed to have lost its significance. He lifted his head from the pillow and stretched towards her, squeezed her hand again, and, as though with his whole soul, said.

"Aahhhh...."

She looked at him blankly. What did he want? His head fell back again. He waited a second. He lifted it again, stared into her eyes, and said.

"Aahhh...."

"The book!" she said, "Do you want to talk about the book?"

He gave an imperceptible shake of the head; a tighter squeeze on her hand and an even more concentrated.

"Aaaahhhhh...."

Claire was floundering around in her brain. Why, oh why couldn't her mind be more in tune with his. This was her father, he wanted to tell her something that was of huge importance to him and she couldn't understand. Jackie. Could it be Jackie? Dare she mention Jackie?

"Is it Jackie?" she said, in barely a whisper, "do you want to see Jackie?"

The eyebrows raised a little. He looked surprised. He rested his head back as though pondering whether he did want to see Jackie or not.

A "Ssssss.." came slowly out of his mouth. But then his head was up again, and again he tried.

"Aaaaaaahhhhhh...."

She looked at him. She concentrated as she had never concentrated before. Oh, please, please let me know what it is, she thought. She failed. She spoke for the sake of something to say.

"I wish, oh, how I wish I knew what you are trying to say! Mummy will be back soon. She's gone to get you some thick warm pyjamas. She's alright, you know! She's coping very, very well. And I'm trying to help her. When we get home in the evenings I usually get her a drink; that's your job, I know, but I can do it for a while. And then we have supper and in the mornings, before we come, I always make her have her toast. But what else, what else can it be that you want to tell me?"

His head rested back against the pillow; his tight grip on her hand relaxed and his face softened into a tired acceptance. He lay there quietly looking at her. She looked away from him; still racking her brains for any other subject that might be worrying him then saw her mother and Michael walking down the ward.

"Look!" she turned back to him, "here she comes; and Michael's with her. They must've met up downstairs somewhere."

Her mother took two pairs of brushed cotton pyjamas out of a familiar green M&S bag to show him. Claire moved out of the good side seat, and went round to sit with Michael. He asked if they wanted to go out shopping again, now that he had arrived, but since her mother had only just been, and Claire was not bothered, the three of them stayed for a couple of hours, whiling away the time with games and chatter. All the time, Claire was still asking herself what it could possibly have been that he wanted so desperately to tell her. Whatever it was, he did not make any more efforts. It must have been something that he wanted to convey to her while they were on their own. When they had exhausted all the games, and the silences were getting longer, Michael put one hand on her arm.

"I think I'll go now. Would you like me to do the supper again, or do you want to come with me?"

She thought for a moment. If her mother was quite happy at the prospect of driving home in the dark alone again, it was probably good for her parents, and themselves come to that, to spend some time alone together.

"Will you be alright driving home if I go back with Michael?" she asked Nickii across the bed.

"Of course I will," Nickii said, with a hint of a tone of 'don't fuss'.

Claire stood up and took her coat from the back of the chair.

"OK, well we'll get some supper ready; say for.....what....about half past eight?"

She bent down to give her father a kiss.

"I hope you have a good night," she said, hovering over him, "and we'll see you in the morning!"

Suddenly, but slowly, his good hand stretched across and picked up Claire's hand, which had been resting on his tummy. With one gentle, graceful movement he lifted it to his lips and softly kissed the back of her hand. She, in turn, kissed his cheek, then turned and began to walk down the ward with Michael. There were tears in her eyes. She could still feel the touch of his fingers on hers, and his lips as they caressed her skin. She looked back. He was watching as they walked. She looked back twice during the length of the ward. He was still watching. At the door, she turned fully. He was still watching. She lifted her arm high in the air and waved to him. He waved back. They turned the corner in silence and walked towards the lift. It was not until they were in the car that Claire could trust her voice. Then she asked Michael.

"Will you come with me to see Jackie sometime tomorrow?"

CHAPTER TWENTY

The next morning, standing at the ironing board in her mother's studio, Claire looked at her watch. It was twenty to eight. She picked up another blouse. She could still do another couple of things before it was time to go.

Suddenly, she heard a thump as something fell in the kitchen, and then her mother's voice as she came hurrying through the walk-through.

"Claire, Claire, come quickly. We must go. We must go now. That was the hospital. They said they thought I should get there as soon as possible!"

Her mother's eyes were wide with fear. Claire stood the iron down on the board. She started to rip the rollers out of her hair, shedding them on tables and shelves as she passed, running for her coat and handbag. She hadn't even heard the 'phone. Standing at the bottom of the stairs she shouted up at Michael.

"The hospital rang. We've got to go. I don't think I turned the iron off...."

Back in the hall, Nickii was waiting with the front door open. The windows of the Renault were covered with condensation. Claire rubbed round them all with her coat sleeve. It started first time and she thanked it mentally. The gravel crunched as she backed the car round; the tyres slid a little as she pulled away. Quickly, she looked both ways at the end of the lane; there was nothing coming. She pulled out, raced the cold car through its gears, and guided it as fast as she possibly could around the bends. They travelled through Hunston village at more than twice the speed limit, but Claire knew she was driving well. Ninety per cent of her brain was concentrating on her driving. Ten per cent was praying silently, over and over again, 'Please God, please let us get there in time.' Beside her in the passenger seat Nickii muttered.

"Oh, please, let us get there in time!"

They flew around the roundabout at the A27, and straight on into the road into Chichester. Then just as they approached the level crossing, the gates swung down in their path. Never, in all the journeys they had made, had that happened before. They sat there, holding their breath. Claire had the car in gear ready to go. Her leg trembled as she held it down on the clutch. She took her hand from the gear lever and rested it over her mother's for a moment. They said nothing.

She slewed the car into a space in the car park. They scrambled out and pushed the doors shut behind them. Then they ran; up the steps, through the familiar doors into the familiar smell, along the corridor and up the two flights of stairs, along past the private wards and the kitchens and into the ward. The Sister blocked their path. Claire was craning her neck, trying to see his bed. The Sister asked them to come into her office for a moment. She asked them to sit down if they wanted to. They didn't; they wanted to see him. And then she said it.

"I'm really very, very sorry; but I have to tell you that Mr Tolley passed away about twenty minutes ago!"

Neither of them moved. Neither of them spoke.

"I promise you we did everything we possibly could, but in the end the struggle was just too much for his heart!"

"Can I see him?" Nickii asked with quiet control.

"Of course you can."

The sister turned and put her hand on the handle of her door.

Claire looked down the ward. The teddies and photographs were clustered round his empty bed. They were shown behind the curtains, right next to the sister's office. An inert shape lay on the bed covered with a white sheet. They stood, as inert, formally at the head of the bed. The Sister stood behind them. Hardly breathing, Claire reached forward and took the top of the sheet between her finger and thumb. She pulled it back.

Immediately Nickii moved forward in front of her. She bent down close to his face. She didn't cry. She talked to him quietly.

"Oh, my poor, poor Darling!" she said, "You look so beautiful!"

Claire stood, as leaden as a rock. She heard a rustle behind her, turned and saw the sister disappear through the curtains, leaving the three of them alone. She turned again. Her mother was kissing him now, stroking his hair, and still talking to him gently. He didn't look beautiful to Claire, not now. His hair had a sort of yellowish stain. Perhaps her mother put something funny on it last night, she thought. And people were meant to look serene and peaceful when they die, weren't they? Her father didn't look serene and peaceful, he looked cheated.

Another rustle, and the Sister was standing by her side. Her mother was hugging her father now, their cheeks together. Claire looked beseechingly at the Sister. She really did not know what to do for the best. Should her mother stay with him for a while or should they take her away. The Sister leant forward towards the bed.

"Mrs Tolley..."

Claire put her hands on her mother's shoulders.

"Come along, Mummy..." she said quietly.

"Just a moment..." her mother said, "I want to look at his neck. He had such a beautiful neck!"

And then there was another small room; one they hadn't even noticed existed. There were a couple of armchairs, and several more hard upright ones, a low table with magazines, and a tray with teapot, cups, milk and sugar. They both picked hard chairs; sat bolt upright, and ignored the tea. Each of them had in their hand a hard ball of tissue. Why? And where did they come from? Neither of them had cried. The door opened, and Michael appeared.

"I'm so sorry!" he said, taking another hard chair. But then immediately he stood again. "Shouldn't you have some of this tea?"

He poured it for them, handed them each a cup. Claire and her mother looked at each other bleakly. He sat down again.

"I know that anything I say is going to sound like a cliché...." he spoke softly, but his voice seems to jangle in the quiet room, "...but somebody once told me that grief is a selfish thing. When you grieve, you grieve for yourself and not for the person who's gone. Of course, with someone like John...; but you both know that the last thing he would have wanted....."

"Did you turn the iron off?" Claire asked him.

The Sister popped her head around the door. She looked directly at Claire.

"Do you think I could have a word with you before you leave?" she said, "When you feel up to it. I'll be in my office!"

"I'll come now," Claire said, standing up. Her cup shook a little as she handed it to Michael.

This time she accepted the offer of a seat.

"What time did you say it was?" she asked, before the Sister started to speak.

"Just after eight o'clock," she replied.

While they were waiting at that level crossing, Claire thought, he probably died while they were waiting at that level crossing. Could he see them sitting there? Did he know they were coming? Surely he must have....

"... and so it won't be ready until..." The Sister had been talking. Claire hadn't heard a word. She would have to confess.

"I'm sorry. I wasn't listening. Please could you tell me again?"

"That's alright. I understand and I know how hard it must be, but there are just a couple of formalities that we have to arrange. Now, unfortunately, because it's Sunday we can't have the certificate ready for you until tomorrow. So if you could come back after ten in the morning we should have it ready, and you can collect your father's things at the same time."

His things; his photographs, his teddies and his new thick pyjamas, Claire tried to swallow; there was no saliva.

"Is there anyone else you would like us to inform on your behalf?"

Oh my God, Claire thought immediately, they would have to tell Jackie. How were they going to tell Jackie?

"No I don't think so. Thank you for offering, but I suppose we'll have a lot of people to tell...."

"Alright then, we will see you in the morning, but stay there as long as you like. Don't leave until you feel ready, and until you think your mum's ready."

Claire stood up, said 'Thank you', and moved towards the door.

"I really am very sorry," the Sister added, as she opened it, "you're father was a lovely man. We are going to miss him ourselves."

Standing in the corridor, Claire tried to think. They would have to go and see Jackie. Supposing, just supposing, she should come up to the hospital? Looking round for the time, she couldn't believe it was still only five past nine. But she was also very relieved; that should at least mean that there was still time to think.

Down in the car park, the sun was shining out of a clear blue sky. Other cars had parked all around the crooked Renault.

"Are you sure you're alright to drive?" Michael asked her, his arm around her shoulder.

"Yes, I'm sure. I'm fine!" Claire said.

What would her father think if she smashed her mother up on the way home! She would get there.

"Where's the Celica?" she asked him, looking around vaguely.

"It's over by the gate;" he took a few steps away. "I'll see you back at the cottage then. Take it slowly!"

He's not normally a one to fuss, Claire thought.

But she did take it slowly. There was nothing to hurry for. The level crossing gates were up. They didn't say a word. Just after the roundabout, Nickii spoke.

"He was afraid of dying! That was the one thing, all the way along, I've always told myself I would not let him die without my being there, and I wasn't...."

She looked away, out of the window of the moving car. Claire couldn't see her face.

"You couldn't help it, Mummy. We did our very best. You know he would have known you were trying.... "

"I know but.... Well, I just wish I could have been there. I wanted to be there!"

With the car safely back outside the cottage, they both sat there. There was not a lot to get out for.

"It's All Saints Day!" Nickii said, "That's nice!"

Claire wouldn't have known that. She supposed it was the village life, and the sight of the church, that had reminded her mother. But she was not wrong, if people must die, then All Saints Day is a nice day for it to happen. Michael pulled up beside them, giving them a reason to move. As they got out of the car, Claire noticed that Ellie was standing by her front gate.

"Ellie's over there!" she said to her mother over the top of the car.

"Oh, yes!" Nickii looked over; gave a small wave. "Please would *you* go and tell her?" she asked Claire, and turned towards the cottage gate.

CHAPTER TWENTY-ONE

He would simply *have* to get out in a moment, Michael thought. Jackie might look out of the window; see the car, and wonder why the hell he was sitting outside her house. At least he recognised the house now that he had got there. He had actually taken a wrong turning, despite Claire's specific instructions, but finding the house was the least of his problems. Of course Claire couldn't leave her mother alone right now, and of course Jackie needed to be told as soon as possible, but knowing that his being here alone was the only sensible solution, did not make it any easier. He hardly knew Jackie. He simply did not know what he was going to say. How would she react? Would he be capable of giving her the support she needed? The clock on the dashboard gave a mechanical tick; nearly quarter to eleven. He got out and locked the door; then walked slowly across the wet grass towards the flat, characterless, pebble-dashed terrace of houses, and that ghastly yellow front door where he remembered dropping Jackie off one day.

After a considerable wait, he heard the sound of slippered feet behind the door. It opened slowly and a pasty-faced chap with drooping bags under his eyes looked out as though the light was blinding him. Michael's spirits sank even further.

"Hello," he said. Then just the very fact that he had used his own voice spurred him on, "I'm sorry, I don't know your name...."

"Bob, my name's Bob," the chap said, looking somewhere over Michael's right shoulder.

"Hello Bob, I'm Michael, and I'm Jackie's brother-in-law. I wonder if I could come in for a moment and talk to her?"

Bob opened the door wide, turned towards the stairs, and shouted.

"JACKIE, VISITOR!"

Michael stepped through the open door into the hall. He watched Bob's back as he slouched into the sitting room on the left. A door opened and then closed again upstairs. Michael looked up just as Jackie appeared at the top. She was looking far better than he expected. She was dressed in jeans and a brightly patterned sweater; she was thinner, much thinner than when he last saw her, but her face was alert and her hair looked good, newly trimmed and shining.

"Hello!" she said, as she came down the stairs, "what a surprise, it's nice to see you. I'm just getting ready to go and see Daddy. They said he would be well enough after two weeks and I promised myself I could go today. Perhaps you could give me a lift?"

"Is there somewhere we could sit down first, just for a bit?" Michael asked her.

"Well in here I suppose!" she said, taking a few steps into the sitting room, rather with the air of someone who is not really bothered about sitting down, but would rather be getting on with things. Bob was sitting in the chair by the empty grate, hunched over a dog-eared Private Eye. He did not look up as they walked in. I can't do this in front of him, Michael thought.

"I'm sorry, Bob, I don't mean to appear rude and ask you to move in your own home, but do you think I could just talk to Jackie alone for a moment!"

"Oh yes, sure!" He stood up abruptly and shuffled out and along the corridor.

Jackie stood in the middle of the room, waiting for whatever it was Michael had to say. And he knew he must say it; now, this minute. There was no easy way.

"Jackie, I'm afraid I have some very bad news, do you mind if we sit down?"

She looked at him with no change of expression, but sat down on the edge of the small sofa. He sat beside her.

"I'm so very sorry to have to tell you this, but your father died this morning at about eight o'clock."

Michael felt a surge of relief that the words were out. Jackie sat very still. She looked at him and said nothing. He carried on to fill the silence.

"The hospital rang very early this morning. Your Mum and Claire left immediately but he had gone before they got there. The ward sister said it was very peaceful and he didn't suffer any more pain but the strain was just too much for his heart."

He paused. Jackie didn't flinch. She was still watching him.

"I'm sorry too that I'm the one to be telling you this, and not one of your real family. But we all thought that you should know as soon as possible. We couldn't possibly tell you on the 'phone; your mum didn't feel strong enough, just yet, to tell you herself, and Claire didn't feel she should leave her on her own this morning. So I'm afraid it's just me. But they send their love and if there's anything at all I can do to help, you only have to say."

Still she didn't move, or speak.

"Would you like me to make you a cup of tea or something?" he asked her quietly.

She shook her head a little, and then she said.

"But would you like one?" Her voice was quite normal.

"Yes please," Michael said, though he didn't really want one at all. They had tea at the hospital, and then coffee back at the cottage, while they were trying to decide who was to come here. But he didn't know what to say next. They couldn't just sit here. Jackie stood up and walked towards the door. He followed her. Bob was hunched over his magazine at the table in the back room now, but Jackie took no notice of him at all and went straight into the small kitchen. Michael stood leaning against the worktop, as Jackie slowly went through the motions of making tea. A part of him sensed that he should be doing it for her; while the other decided that it was probably better for her to be occupied. She made no reference to the terrible news he had just thrown at her, asked no questions, made no comments; in fact she did not speak at all. But she showed no visible signs of feeling any different now, than when she had first come down the stairs, looking so bright and cheerful. He wondered whether he should carry on talking about John, and the person he was, or whether he should just find something mundane and ordinary to talk about.

"This is quite a nice little kitchen, isn't it? I've heard stories about how you used to make your own bread every day; do you manage to do any cooking here?"

"No. Not really. There doesn't seem much point. And it's not really my kitchen!"

He was pleased to see her take two mugs down from the cupboard. She had obviously decided to have some tea after all.

"No. Well I can understand how you feel. But it must be nice to start to get your independence back. This must feel like the first step on the road to a home of your own, and a new life?"

She looked down at the mugs, waiting for the kettle to boil.

"Well, I don't know how much longer I will be allowed to stay here, and I don't know where I can go next."

Michael could have kicked himself for blundering on. He remembered the way it was with Anne. It didn't matter how hard you tried, whatever you said, you always touched one or other raw nerve. So now he muttered some, hopefully comforting, words about things only being able to get better. And then as they stood there drinking the tea, he resorted to the usual conversational gambits of the weather, reading material and films. Jackie gave him monosyllabic replies. She was beginning to withdraw into herself again, and that initial gleam of hope that only he had witnessed, had gone.

"Would you do me a favour?" he asked her after a while, when he could think of absolutely nothing else to say. She moved her head and gave him a quizzical look, but her eyes had gone quite dull.

"I could really do with some fresh air. Would you come for a walk with me? Not a long one, just around the block for a bit!"

***

"I can't stop thinking about the sherbet lemons!" Nickii said, "We used to say that life was like a bag of sherbet lemons; as the time passes, so we slowly eat the sherbet lemons from our bag until there are fewer and fewer left. Now his sherbet lemons are all gone!"

Claire hadn't heard about the sherbet lemons before, but she did remember some of their mortality conversations. They used to tease each other about who was going first.

"If I die before you, you're going to be a really scruffy old man!"

"Oh no I won't, because IF that happened, which it won't, I would sell the cottage and travel round the world, so there! But it's not very likely now is it!"

He would grin, as if to say I'll win this one, because the odds are heavily stacked in my favour. They were joking of course, but Claire used to cringe inside and wish they wouldn't.

But now this was the reality and Claire and Nickii had been going over it all; not moving from the kitchen table since Michael left. Sitting opposite each other, fiddling absent-mindedly with any object they could reach on the pine surface, and half drinking yet more, and then even more, cups of coffee, they replayed every little detail of the morning.

"I knew before the sister told us," Nickii said at one point, "when we ran down the corridor that gentle little nurse with the dark hair gave me such a sad look and she mouthed 'I'm sorry' at me; she was nearly in tears."

Claire hadn't noticed the nurse at all.

"I suppose I'll have to write letters to everyone to tell them!" Nickii said dully.

"I suppose so; but you can't really start until we know when the..." Claire could not say the word. Somehow the thought of that was even more final than the word death, as though until then there was always the possibility that it may all be some ghastly mistake.

"...Perhaps we should make a list, and I suppose there must be some people that we should be phoning right away; like David and Pippa, I ought to phone them. Good heavens, look, it's nearly half past one! Michael's been gone a long time."

Nickii looked round sharply at the clock on the oven.

"I suppose we ought to get some lunch. Oh dear, I hope Jackie's alright. I should have gone with Michael. I know I should have gone with him, but I really couldn't face it. I want to see her, and I don't want to see her. Her problems all upset Daddy so much. All through his life, if there was a problem he would work away at it until he could find a solution, or until it went away. But this one would not go away, and however hard he tried, he couldn't solve it. All his efforts were in vain. He just couldn't see that it was beyond his control. Now he's gone, and Jackie will still be ill just the same. It's not her fault, and I should have gone to see her. But I just wish she could get better. How am I ever going to cope with it all on my own!"

Claire could not imagine how her mother was going to cope. First of all she was going to have to come to terms with the loss of the man who had been by her side for virtually all her adult life. Then she must start learning to live alone. And on top of all that, she must accept the fact that her younger daughter's life was in tatters and she seemed to have no capability of rebuilding it for herself. Not to mention Jackie's moods, her disappearances and ghastly unpredictability. How could her mother possibly cope?

She was about to say that they would do whatever they could to help, when there was a small tap on the front door. She had hardly got to her feet, before her mother was through the dining room to open the door.

"How was she? How did she take it? I'm really sorry I made you go on your own."

"She was much better than any of us expected I think; and she took the news very well considering, so don't worry!"

Joining them as they stood in the hallway, Claire could see the strain on Michael's normally relaxed face. She said nothing.

"We went for a walk, that's why I've been rather a long time. But she's fine, really! I said you'd see her sometime this week."

It was only after her mother had dashed off to the loo, that Michael told Claire that perhaps one of them should go back and see

Jackie again later. That she hadn't really seemed to accept the news at all, and he was worried about what might happen when she did!

But Marjorie had done that for them. And Claire was never more grateful than she had been for Marjorie's kindness and understanding that afternoon. She had felt very nervous of ringing her; not least because it was a terrible cheek to disturb her on a Sunday, but also because at the end of their last conversation in the hospital, Marjorie, quite understandably, had not sounded best pleased. But finally, sitting at the desk in her father's study and fiddling with the corners of his manuscript, she had plucked up the courage to dial the number she'd found in her mother's address book. She was really ringing for Marjorie's advice, but after Claire had explained everything to her, Marjorie just took over with a brisk and sympathetic efficiency. She completely pooh-poohed the fact that it was Sunday, and said she would drive straight over and make sure that Jackie was alright. Then she said she would keep a special eye on her over the next few days, and not to hesitate to ring her again if they were worried. And all after Claire had expected a massive lecture about shirking their responsibilities and Jackie needing them too.

Now she grabbed one of the pillows from Michael's side of the bed and, leaning forward, pushed it behind her back, so that she could sit up more comfortably. She gave the duvet a tug too for more warmth, and the bright orange folder lying on her outstretched legs slid closer towards her. She could hear muffled music from the late night movie that Michael was watching down in the sitting room, but not a single sound from her mother's bedroom next door. Claire hoped, stupidly, that Nickii was alright. But then realised that of course that was a ridiculous notion; how could she possibly be alright! The music was irritating Claire. It meant that she couldn't concentrate on any sounds that her mother might make. But that was Michael's way of shutting out the world, and she was grateful too for his support; and the fact that he had stayed on to help them out tomorrow.

Tomorrow. Mentally she started to make lists again for tomorrow. Go to the hospital first, then to the undertaker's. Giving a shiver, she pulled the duvet even closer and looked around the small bedroom. She could see her father standing there, remembered him coming in on that Sunday morning of the first weekend she had brought Michael here.

"Are you decent?" he had said, putting his head around the door, and then coming in when he could see that she was making the bed.

"I just wanted to tell you that I approve!"

She could still see the old familiar grin.

"He's a lovely chap, one of us; our sort of person, if you know what I mean! When's the wedding?"

She had teased him back. Told him to hold his horses, she hadn't known Michael all that long.

Undertaker, Under Taker, Taker Under. Burier. She hadn't thought of that before. She gave another shiver. Go to see Jackie. Fetch Pippa from the station at 11.20. That would be nice. Pippa absolutely insisted that she wanted to come and help, and Claire would be so pleased to see her. After that, they should try to be back at the house by a quarter past twelve, when the vicar was coming to see Nickii. She gave a small involuntary sigh, and reached forward for the folder. Stuffed full of paper, she needed two hands to bring it close enough to handle. Thirteen hole punched computer sheets of her father's second draft of his novel were tucked in on top of the wodge of typewritten sheets of the original. This is virtually all I've achieved so far, she thought, just to tidy the papers and fail to work his computer, but I will do it. I will definitely do it. After all I don't think he ever asked me for anything else! Tucked in the flap on the left were several scraps of paper with handwritten notes. She pulled out the top one and read:

Introduction – *As a work of fiction this leans on the truth. It is said that truth is stranger than fiction. It is also less kind. But in life who knows what is true and where the fiction starts.*

Suddenly there was silence downstairs, then the sitting room door opened and closed again. For some reason, Claire didn't think Michael would understand her reading all this right now. She scrabbled the folder together, and put it down on the floor beside the bed. But, long after they had turned out the light, she was still thinking about the difference between fact and fiction, and reality and fantasy, and wondering whether her mother was asleep.

CHAPTER TWENTY-TWO

For Jackie the line between fact and fiction was like a sheet of polythene. Nothing seemed factual to her at all, apart from the throbbing in her head and the cracks in the ceiling above her. They formed counties on a map, the outlines of two faces, or the sea between two islands. It just could not be true that her father had died; was no longer there at the cottage, sitting in his chair or working in his study; that he would no longer be around to care where she lived, or whether or not she got a job. And yet she knew that it must be true, otherwise why did Michael turn up here and why was she out walking with him alone? Then Marjorie had come too in the afternoon, on a Sunday; and the next day Michael again, with Claire and Pippa; Pippa looked well. It had been a very long time since Jackie had seen her; dressed in neatly belted smart trousers, and her hair in an efficient French pleat, she seemed so grown up and capable. She had calmly made coffee in the kitchen downstairs, while Michael and Claire sat with Jackie in the sitting room. But it was as though all of these things had happened on the outside of a huge bubble, inside which Jackie sat alone. Like one of those soap bubbles that her mother used to blow at bath time when they were small. But those bubbles had smears of pretty rainbow colours, and there were no colours to this bubble. It was only a plain, filmy, grey. She could see and hear through it; but it blurred her vision and toned down the sound, and it stopped her touching. She could not touch or feel anything, so how could it be real?

It had been quite strange to sit there and watch while Claire stammered and stuttered, and finally came out with a lecture about how they didn't want any histrionics at the funeral. Somewhere, way away, there was a small voice that told her that she should fight back at this bossy elder sister telling her how, or how not to behave, but it had been as though the words were bouncing off the walls of her bubble, and held no real meaning for Jackie at all.

She closed her eyes. Staring at the cracks was hurting them now; increasing the pain of the tight band that was being squeezed tighter and tighter around, from the back of her head to over her eyebrows. She needed to go to the loo, felt the pressure pushing downwards, but her body was like a huge rock; completely unwilling to get up off the bed. And then her mother had come with Claire. Which day was that? Not today, because today was the day the letter had come; so was it yesterday? Her mother had looked tired and distant, as though she was in a bubble too. She had wanted to know if Jackie had anything to wear, whether she had got her nice black suit here. Jackie didn't answer because she didn't know. And then her mother had come up here and started sorting through the cupboard. The suit was there. It was hanging on the outside of the cupboard door now. If she opened her eyes and turned her head she would see it.

As though somebody else's brain was giving her body instructions, she dragged herself off the bed and propelled herself to the bathroom. Mechanically, she locked the door behind her and undid her jeans. Barely noticing the relief as the long stream of warm pee released the pressure on her bladder, she sat there and thought about the letter that arrived this morning. It seemed that even that, she had read through the filmy grey, protective, polythene walls of her bubble. Neatly printed words, formally arranged on smartly headed solicitor's paper, told her that Lytton had applied for a divorce, and custody of all her children. He needed to be free to marry again the letter said; marry the woman who was looking after her children and now, apparently, expecting her husband's baby. And it didn't mean anything. After all this time and all that hurt; after reading the letter that brought the news that she had dreaded more than anything else, she felt nothing. Nothing more than a numb acceptance that that was all she deserved. She had felt nothing; she was nothing, nothing but an amoebic blob of worthlessness inside a polythene bubble.

Now shut in the silent bathroom her body was glued to the loo seat by the heaviness in her head. She had read the letter through just once and then carefully refolded it, replaced it in the envelope, and put it in the top drawer in her bedroom; the drawer where she kept her other bits and pieces of paper, and her photographs, photographs of the children, photographs of Lytton, and the photographs of their wedding day. The one of them swinging around the lamppost in the Kings Road that her father had taken; and the one of them standing together and holding the bread knife, about to cut the sponge cake that her mother had hurriedly made the night before. It was a lovely day. No white dress, no flowers, no church, no guests, but Jackie enjoyed every second. They didn't need guests or flowers, or presents or trimmings, Lytton said. It was their own private day and none of anybody else's bloody business. They didn't want their material presents and traditional values. All they needed was a couple of witnesses off the street, he said. But, at the last moment, Jackie really wanted her mum and dad to be there. Finally he had given in.

"But it's only because I love you, you crazy little bitch!" he said.

So she had phoned them the night before and told them she was getting married tomorrow and would they come. And they did. Her father in a smart suit, her mother all dressed up, and wearing one of her 'wedding' hats, and they brought the cake and a cheque for a wedding present.

The hard plastic of the loo seat was pressing into the flesh of her bottom, telling her to stand up. Her father didn't hate Lytton then, she thought, and like an automaton found herself sitting back down, fully clothed, on the closed seat of the loo. He would be pleased about the letter but she wouldn't show him. The letter was hidden now and she would not tell him until she was ready. But of course, she remembered, he wasn't there anymore. He would never know about the letter. She heard the stairs creaking. Someone was standing on the landing outside. In fact he would never know what she did anymore, whether she ever got better, or...

Someone tapped gently on the door of the bathroom, and Marjorie's voice sounded muffled in the distance.

"Jackie, are you in there dear? It's me, Marjorie! Are you alright?"

Silently, Jackie watched the closed door. She could picture Marjorie outside, her ear pressed against the paintwork listening for sounds. She probably wonders if I'm dying, or dead, she thought; blood seeping out, all over the bathroom floor, or streaming in a gory stain into the bathwater. Why isn't she? Why doesn't she? Quietly, she looked around the room for something sharp. There wasn't anything. Why was it that she never thought of that in her numbness? Perhaps it would be the very best thing that could ever happen to her. And probably they would all be pleased to be rid of her. There was another tap.

"Jackie!" Marjorie repeated outside.

Slowly Jackie stood up, and moved to unlock the door.

"Ah, there you are dear; and not looking too brilliant, if you don't mind my saying so. You look like a walking headache to me. Have you had anything to eat today? No, I don't suppose you have. Hunger can cause headaches you know, dear, I've told you that before, and if you don't look after your body, how can you expect to cope? Come along, down you come, we are going to find you something to eat!"

Following her obediently down the stairs, Jackie wondered how Marjorie could possibly know about the tight throbbing band around her head.

It had become a routine. She didn't know how many days it had been now that Marjorie had appeared in her room at some stage and taken her downstairs; chattering cheerfully away while she bustled in the kitchen, and then sat opposite her, there at the table, while Jackie struggled to eat what was on the plate.

"When's your next hospital appointment dear?" she had asked once.

"I don't know" Jackie said. What was the point anyway?

"How are you getting to the church tomorrow dear?" she asked now.

Tomorrow! Jackie thought. Is it tomorrow already?

"I think Michael's coming to fetch me," she whispered. Isn't that what they said? Michael would come to fetch her on his way?

***

He drove straight past the end of the lane. For a moment, Jackie wondered where he was going, then he turned into the pub entrance. Claire's Renault and her mother's car were sitting there, next to each other in the empty car park.

"There won't be much space up by the church, so Claire came up here and asked them if we could put some cars in their car park," Michael explained.

She got out; tottered a little, being totally unaccustomed to her high-heeled shoes. Michael looked a different man. Jackie had never seen him in a suit before. He locked the doors, testing all the handles, before they walked off. They said nothing in the short distance up to the cottage. The familiar lane seemed foreign, as though it were years since she had been there, not just the few weeks it could only be. How many weeks? She didn't know.

Standing inside the front door, she could hear Claire in the kitchen.

"You look nice!" her mother said, coming out and giving her a kiss on the cheek. "Would you like a cup of tea; I think we've still got time. Have you had any breakfast?"

"No thank you," Jackie said. She didn't want to be any trouble. She remembered Claire's lecture. In the sitting room, the furniture had been moved around, making space in the middle of the room. There were bowls of crisps, nuts and olives, cheesy straws and piles of paper napkins, strategically placed on the windowsills and tables. She went through the alien space and into the loo, relieved to be shut in the quiet by herself. The lining of her skirt rustled as she smoothed it down, felt silky against her legs. Back again, standing at the kitchen door, Claire was turned away from her, towards the sink. Every surface was covered with plates of different food.

"Are you sure you've had some breakfast?" her mother asked again.

"Yes thank you, I'm sure," she said. She felt sick.

They put on their coats. They stood around by the door, waiting and peeping out. Tyres crunched on the gravel outside. A man in a black tail suit appeared at the gate.

"They're here!" Somebody said.

Then she was walking slowly, very slowly, up the path to the church. She looked round and found that her mother was walking next to her. Her mother reached out and took her hand. Inside there was a blurred sea of shapes and faces. The church was bursting with people. There were not enough seats. People were standing at the back and along the sides. The coffin wobbled as they placed it on the stands. They all filed trembling into the front pew. They sang.

The Lord is my shepherd; I shall not want.....

She could hear her mother's quavering voice singing quietly beside her. Claire was not singing. She and Michael stood, rigid, on the other side of her.

Outside in the daylight, there was colour again; splashes of bright colours against the black of the people's clothes, the green of the grass, rainbows of umbrellas, and the soft reddy brown of the mud. There was mud everywhere. They stood on a mound of it; a dense circle of people blocking any escape. Jackie stood alone. The rain splattered on her cheeks and the shoulders of her jacket. Claire was standing over there; her arm around their mother. The vicar's words, although barely audible, still seemed to boom over the silence of the crowd. Jackie shivered. Suddenly there was a strong arm around her shoulders; it gave warmth, support and comfort. She looked round and found that it was David, grown tall, strong and adult, from the chubby little baby that was once her nephew. He gave her shoulders a squeeze. She thought she was going to cry. She never, ever cried. But not now, she could not cry now. She stared ahead and stiffened in his grasp.

The service ended. The vicar stood for a moment, then walked slowly away, his robes billowing behind his lone figure on its way back to the church door. It was over. There was complete silence. The crowd stood, stock still, not knowing whether to move or speak, until her mother and Claire moved slowly towards the cottage. Then, suddenly, the sitting room was bursting with people, uncles, aunts, cousins, friends; some that Jackie hadn't seen for years, others that she didn't know at all. The silence broke. The air reverberated with chatter as they greeted each other. Jackie was trapped amongst them. Her mother brushed by.

"Would you mind taking some coats, Kee?" she said.

Jackie took an armful. Their owners smiled, kissed her cheeks, asked her how she was. She fled with the coats, through the hall, and into her father's study. It was all hoovered and polished, quiet and empty; his desk all tidied and cleared of papers. She dropped the coats onto the sofa and then stood looking out into the garden where her father used to lean over the style to feed carrots to the horse in the field.

Now it was getting dark outside. The front door closed on the last person to leave. The sitting room was littered with empty glasses, and some half-filled plates with dried grains of rice and withered garnish. Crisps and crumbs ground into the carpet. Claire wandered amongst it all with a tray, vaguely picking things up. Michael was getting ready to leave. Jackie went to fetch her jacket, but her mother appeared from the door of her father's study. She looked pale and drained.

"You don't *have* to go with Michael," she said, "stay for a little while. You haven't eaten anything all day! We can take you back later."

As they went through to the kitchen, Claire was saying goodbye to Michael in the hall.

"We'll see you on Thursday!" Jackie heard her say.

"Claire is staying on for a bit," her mother explained, "and then she wants me to go and stay with her for a few days. I expect I'll go; it probably is a good idea."

Jackie sat down at the table.

She ate; enough to take the sickness away, and to ease the worried frown on her mother's face. While she was eating, her mother sat beside her, talking quietly. Jackie didn't remember what she said. It was quite late when they eventually left, windy and still raining. They forgot that the car was around the corner, and had to walk up the lane in the pitch dark. Jackie stumbled in a hole in the road. Claire grabbed her arm to steady her; but she hadn't spoken to Jackie once all day.

Back in the stark little house that was her home, Bob was hunched in his chair by the fire. Melanie was in too, sounds were coming from the television in her room upstairs. In the kitchen her mother piled Tupperware boxes into the fridge.

"You must have some of this food, Jackie!" she had said as she packed them up, "there is so much left over!"

Closing the fridge door, she turned to Jackie. Claire was waiting in the car. Her mother looked as though there was so much she wanted to say, but couldn't. Jackie's head raced with words, but she too could not find any to say. Her mother looked away and walked along the hall to the front door. Jackie stood behind her. She turned and put her arms around Jackie.

"I'll see you when I get back from Claire's! Please, please look after yourself!" she said.

And Jackie just stood there as the front closed behind her.

CHAPTER TWENTY-THREE

<u>Creole</u> – Creole stood on the steps of his front door a moment too long. He was on the way out. And for the first time he looked, really looked, at the street into which he had committed his life. Never before had he been committed....

<u>Creole – Chapter One</u> – It is said that the sins of the father will be laid at the door of the child. Creole was a very sorry lad. It was with such a spirit of adventure and confidence that he had stormed off from his home, his school, all the people that he knew and the surroundings that were familiar to him.

Claire read the first lines of these two, completely different, opening chapters for what seemed like, and could easily have been, the five hundredth time. Sitting in the middle of an old bedspread on the lawn, she was surrounded by piles of paper.

"Why don't you take it all out in the garden, get some sun, make some pleasure out of it!" Michael was always saying. Well its more trouble than it's worth, she thought irritably, replacing the garden trowel and her bottle of sun oil on two of the piles to stop them blowing in the wind. She had made her head throb with concentration; reading and re-reading, making notes, and trying to work out what order to put it all in and which part she should re-write next.

Allowing the noises of the children playing in the garden next door to bring her back to earth, she realised that she had become completely disassociated from the world around her, and all to no avail. She was still no closer to knowing what to do next. Picking at the moss in the grass at the edge of the bedspread, she dug in her fingers and pulled at a dandelion, then saw another and another, and yet more stretching across the grass to the shaggy edges of the lawn, which blended with the weeds in the flowerbed. She would achieve more by doing some gardening, she thought. And then she remembered how her father used to patiently dig the weeds out of the lawn with a knife, leaving a trail of dark, muddy, little holes behind him, as he travelled slowly across it on his knees. He probably did it for a bit of peace and quiet, to get away from the hubbub of domesticity indoors. She wondered what he used to think about while he was out there alone; work probably, business deals, problem solving, Jackie, Lytton, Lytton, Lytton, Creole, Creole....

With a huge sigh, she laid back full length on the bedspread, amongst the flapping piles of paper and her notebook, pencils, pencil sharpener, rubber. Is this what madness feels like? This complete inability to concentrate on any one thought for more than a split second; this brain overload to the point of bursting, and this complete despair of ever being able to sort it all into anything worthwhile. Closing her eyes, she gave herself a mental slap on the wrist. No, of course, it isn't. How dare she compare a few moments discomfort and lack of concentration in a sunny garden, with all the pain and sorrow that Jackie had been through. And in any case 'mad' is a word that she had thought many times should be banned from the dictionary. Illnesses of the mind should be known by their proper names just like illnesses of the body; in exactly the same way as golliwogs are considered unacceptable and nicely brought up children no longer sing *'Eenie meanie, miny mo, catch a nigger by his toe......'* Those vaguely derogatory words like luny, crackpot, bats in the belfry; they all help to increase the stigma that helps to increase the pain, for everyone. But thoughts like these, Claire knew, were partly borne out of her own guilt, guilt that she had been less than sympathetic herself in dealing with Jackie's problem. The sun moved out from behind a cloud and beat down on her face. The warmth of it was as relaxing as a healing massage. Perhaps Michael was right after all.

But the pleasure was being scarred by a memory of how she had shouted at Jackie.

"Go; just GO, you have got to go, I can't cope...." she had screamed.

It was not long after her father had died. Claire was tired. She had been working hard to catch up on her typing for Dr Boffin. And she had been worrying about money too; they were broke. Michael's firm were running out of work, and she had lost some of her clients during the weeks she was away in Chichester. She needed to earn more and she had been scouring the local papers for part-time work. She worried all the time about how her mother was coping; though, of course, she was coping perfectly well; and at the same time, she had been spending the evenings working on the novel. One day, in the middle of all that, there was a quiet tap on the front door; a tap that she wouldn't even have heard, if she hadn't been standing right by the kitchen door at the time. It was Jackie. Completely unexpectedly, on a weekday afternoon, Jackie was just standing on Claire's doorstep.

Claire had tried to hide her surprise; no it wasn't surprise, it was shock. Shock and fear, she was still ashamed to admit, even to herself. What she had wanted to say was, "What are you doing here?" What she should have said was, "Jackie, how nice to see you. How are you; is everything all right?"

What she did say rather blankly was.

"Oh, Jackie! Err... you'd better come in!"

She had trembled; she actually trembled with fear, she remembered as they went into the kitchen. But then she had told herself to get a grip, make an effort, talk to Jackie and see if she could help. She had taken Jackie's coat. Jackie just stood in the middle of the room until Claire suggested that she sit down. She made some coffee, tried to make small talk while she did it, but Jackie didn't say a word. She sat down with her at the kitchen table. She asked her how she was feeling. What her new room was like. Did she have any special reason for coming up? Did she want to stay? How long did she want to stay? Jackie only said yes and no. Some of the time, it was as though she hadn't heard Claire speak at all. Claire thought she should give her more time. Perhaps she was tired and cold after the journey; she might open up a little after she had rested. So Claire had got up, opened the fridge, surveyed the contents, and tried to decide what they might eat for dinner that night. She might as well be using the time, as sitting there wasting her breath.

But Jackie didn't open up. No matter how hard Claire tried during that afternoon, Jackie uttered hardly more than half a dozen words. The strain of wondering what to do, what to say next, what lay behind it all, and where it was all going, had built up in Claire until she didn't know what she was doing herself. She remembered pouring water into the sugar bowl instead of onto the tea bags in the mugs. Clearing up the sticky mess had made her even more irritable and tense. But in the hours of thought that Claire had given to the incident since, she had realised that she hadn't tried hard enough; not anywhere near hard enough. Her questions were trite and clipped, asked through the tight lips of fear and animosity. Why hadn't she reached out to touch Jackie? Given her a cuddle, asked what it really felt like, given her some hope, shown even an ounce of genuine sympathy?

Once again the recollection of her inadequacy suddenly hurt enough to make Claire sit bolt upright. She started fiddling with the moss again, picking the little green fronds from between the blades of grass. She hadn't done those things because there had been a wall between them, built by Jackie's illness on her side, and Claire's total lack of understanding of that illness on hers. The wall might just as well have been built of bulletproof glass. They hold first aid classes to save bodies, she thought now. Why can't they hold first aid classes to save minds? Surely there must be some simple skills that one could learn; some artificial respiration to stop that wall of blind panic. Michael had relieved the tension a bit when he came home. He seemed to be better at making small talk and getting reactions from Jackie than Claire was herself. But the evening was strained nonetheless. Jackie had gone off to bed early, leaving them to talk in hushed whispers downstairs.

"I've got an interview tomorrow at twelve, what am I going to do?" Claire had moaned selfishly.

"Offer to drive her to the station on the way!" Michael replied practically.

When finally they had gone to bed themselves, Claire got very little sleep. The landing light was on for a lot of the night and she could hear Jackie creeping around the house. Jackie was obviously unable to sleep, but Claire just lay there wondering what she was doing. It never occurred to her to get up and offer to chat, make tea, and be sisterly. In the morning she had given Jackie hours of warning that she could give her a lift to the station on the way to her interview. But at ten to twelve Jackie was still upstairs, moving around in the spare bedroom. Claire called up the stairs to see if she was ready.

"No I'm not!" Jackie shouted down, "I'll make my own way to the station when I am!"

Claire didn't get the job, and Jackie was still upstairs in the spare bedroom when she got back. That afternoon had been worse than the one before. By half past four Claire's head was pounding, she felt near to breaking point herself. She went up to their bedroom and rang Michael asking him to come home early. She told him about the day; said she couldn't cope any longer. He had arrived just after five, and firmly told Jackie that Claire hadn't been feeling too well lately either. He was worried about her and he was afraid that Jackie would have to go home. He would give her a lift to the station, now. Jackie said she didn't want to go. And that was when Claire had shouted at her.

"Go, just GO, you have got to go. I can't cope; I feel as though I'm breaking up myself and I'm not going to let you drag me down. Just GO AWAY AND GET BETTER. Daddy's dead and all he wanted was for you to get better...."

Little piles of drying fluffy moss now surrounded her. She realised that she had shifted her position several times to get at more picky patches of grass. Still she could not believe that she could have been so cruel. Struggling to stand up with her legs stiffened from kneeling, she wandered up the garden asking herself if she would ever be able to talk to Jackie about it; apologise for her lack of sensitivity; probably not. Standing in the vegetable patch, she realised that the sun had moved off the tomatoes. She ought to water them.

Of course Michael had told her not to be so hard on herself over that day.

"Knowing that the person is sick doesn't make the frustration of their behaviour any easier to bear," he had said once. "You are entitled to respect your own intuitive feelings; especially when you have just lost your father."

Feeling better with a task to focus on, she walked briskly back down the garden to fetch the watering cans and fill them. But soon her mind was off, flitting around like a butterfly again. She remembered how the storm had destroyed all last year's vegetables; then thought that this time last year, her father was still alive. How everything had changed since then.

Not long after that fiasco with Jackie, she had been offered a place as a doctors' receptionist. It was hard work, and most days she came home with a headache from the noise of the children, the telephones and the tension, but she still enjoyed the job. Busy though it was, they were a friendly bunch; they laughed a lot, and she developed a rapport with the patients; well, most of the patients. There were some that were never going to have a rapport with anyone. On the whole, Claire was confident that she did the job well, but even there she shied away from the mental patients; hid away behind the shelves of notes, and hoped that one of the other women would go to the reception window. It was instinctive in spite of her self-reproach, and she wished she could shape up and conquer her fear. She sloshed water around the roots of the tomato plants, and wondered whether she should get the sprinkler out and give the bed a proper soaking. Looking across the dry earth, she saw the robin sitting there looking at her out of one eye. She talked to it; asked it how it was feeling today and said she was sorry but she wouldn't be digging so there weren't going to be any worms right now. Often the robin had sat on the fence, or a branch above her head, warbling and twittering away as she gardened, as though it were trying to tell her something. Half knowing it was ridiculous; she still could not quite discount the concept that he might be her father's spirit in disguise. She could talk to her mother about such things, but not Michael. He didn't like it. He believed that death is final, finish, end of story; and he got quite niggly if she tried to discuss the robin or other ethereal phenomena.

She upended the second watering can, draining the very last drop of water onto the last tomato; then decided to fill them again, just to wet the runner beans. She would have to get the sprinkler out tomorrow evening, if it didn't rain. Then she remembered that they did not want it to rain tomorrow because Jackie's children were arriving at the cottage to stay with Nickii for their summer holiday. And she would not be phoning her mother at six o'clock tonight as usual, because Nickii would be driving into Chichester to pick up Jackie.

Dumping the two watering cans under the garden tap outside the conservatory, she went back to her writing base on the lawn. Kneeling down, she gathered all the fluffy piles of moss into one heap; looked at the folders and separately stacked sheets of paper, and then at her watch. It was ten to five, time to feed the cats, think about dinner and wash her hair ready for work tomorrow. This was her one completely free day this week and she had achieved nothing. Tomorrow she was working at the surgery, and then Pippa was coming home for the weekend with her boyfriend. The next weekend they were going to Chichester to stay with Nickii. And so the time passed. It was over nine months now, and in spite of all the writing and re-writing, re-typing and racking her brains, Claire still felt that the work was no further forward today, than it was on the day her father died. Even the encouragement she had received from Tim Stanley had begun to fade. She had telephoned her father's evening class teacher in the spring, reminded him that they had met at the Writers' Day, and asked him if he would mind giving her some advice. He had remembered her immediately and asked how Nickii was; then he had apologised for not coming to the funeral; said he had been away that weekend. Claire had really appreciated the fact that he would have liked to come. She sent him the whole of her father's original manuscript, and all the chapters that she had rewritten. He contacted her again a few weeks later with some helpful advice and encouragement on what she had achieved so far.

But the more editing and re-writing she did, the further away it moved from the book her father had written. And now Claire felt herself to be in a completely hopeless mess with it all. But she had promised him; she had promised him she would do it. How? How was she ever going to finish it, if she frittered away her days like this? With an overwhelming sense of disappointment and failure, yet again, she replaced the papers in their folders and carried them back down the garden towards the house, wondering as she went whether her innate urge to write was passed to her in a gene by her father and, if so, was it a blessing or a curse?

CHAPTER TWENTY-FOUR

"Another thing, Jackie, that has occurred to me after looking through your notes, is that although you have been ill for quite some time; let's see... nearly eight years? Anyway, from what I can see, there has been no record of any serious suicide attempts! Is that right?"

Jackie had just nodded, and said nothing.

"So, presumably, however desperate you have felt during that time, you have never actually decided that you no longer wish to live. Therefore you must, somewhere inside yourself, believe that you have a future."

She looked up at him then, full in the face. She was completely gob smacked.

"I believe in your future too, Jackie;" he continued, looking her straight in the eye, "and I believe it can be better than your past. I want you to do two things. I want you to come back and see me in one week. During that week, I want you to think about your future and what you want from it. If you find yourself thinking about your past, and it hurts, forget it. Don't look back, look forward!"

He had stood up then, actually risen from behind the desk, and walked around it. He took her arm.

"Come with me and we'll make an appointment for next Tuesday," he said.

That was the first time Jackie saw Dr Andrew Smith. She had walked out of the hospital in a complete daze. Having gone in expecting the usual, terse waste of time, she was confronted by this stranger. Nobody told her that Bulstrode was retiring, that there would be someone new. And there he was, sitting behind Bulstrode's desk, wearing no white coat, but a navy blue Guernsey sweater, with a crop of dark hair, a six o'clock shadow where he hadn't shaved that morning, and a charming, friendly and sincere smile. He had sat there for a few moments flicking through her notes. And she sat thinking how much younger he looked compared to Dr Bulstrode; probably in his early forties, not much older than her. Then he had looked up and said.

"You haven't been taking your tablets regularly, have you?"

She was still dazed from the shock of seeing him. She didn't have time to feel irritated but she didn't reply.

"How do I know that? Well, I can make a fairly safe guess by looking at the size of you. Your notes mention some weight gain and you're pretty skinny now!" he said. Jackie just glared at him.

"You probably think that's a very personal remark; but it's the truth, the one obvious hint that tells me that you can't be taking them properly. And if I'm open and honest with you, Jackie, then I hope you will be open and honest with me. That way I may be able to help you. Anyway don't fret about the tablets for the time being. I want to study these notes and then we'll see, perhaps we can find you something new."

Then he had sat there flicking over the pages and come out with the bit about her future.

That week passed quite quickly. She went to the cottage for the weekend. Claire and Michael were there. The four of them went for a walk by the sea. She could remember walking along next to her mother, with the cold wind hurting her ears, and thinking that Dr Smith was truly different from any of the other doctors she had seen. He had taken a risk going on about her future and suicide. Supposing she had taken it as a suggestion? How had he known that she wouldn't? How could he know that she had any future? A home of her own, a job, a normal life; they all seemed much more impossible than the prospect of walking into the sea until the waves closed over her head and swallowed her up.

But, when the Tuesday came, she found herself actually looking forward to the appointment, and wondering what he was going to say next.

"Jackie, has anyone ever explained to you what might be the causes of your illness?" he asked. Once again she was too dumbfounded to make any reply. She shook her head. Then he had started to tell her about nerve cells in the brain, synapses and transmitter chemicals, all of which seemed to make some sense at the time. He said it could either be a lack of the right chemicals, or that they were all being used up in the wrong way, that made her feel and act differently from a so called 'normal' person. He said it was always very difficult to know what caused the imbalance in these chemicals. It could be that it was an illness, just like having too much acid in your stomach and getting a gastric ulcer, or it could be that too much pressure and stress in her life had caused the chemicals to overreact, like too much heat under a saucepan of milk.

Jackie had sat there transfixed. She saw mental pictures of all the little cells in her brain with brightly-coloured liquids trying to jump between them, and rows of saucepans with milk frothing over the top and fizzling into a brown stain on the metal sides. What it all meant was that there was a cause for it all; an explanation with pictures, something to blame, a reason why it was not just she, Jackie, who was so hopeless.

"Have you thought about what I said about your future?" he asked her.

She muttered something about a home and a job.

"I see no reason why you shouldn't have both of those and even a bit of fun and laughter too!" he said.

But then he got more serious. He said he wasn't going to pretend that it was going to be easy. She would have to work at it, very hard indeed; sometimes she would feel that she was going backwards, but then she would have to carry on thinking forwards, and above all she was going to have to trust him. He wanted her to change her GP to one he recommended. He wanted her to go to the hospital and have some blood tests to test out her hormone balances. He said they were going to try some new drugs, but it might take a while to get them right and they might have some unpleasant side effects. He would explain to her what these might be as they went along, but she would have to take them regularly and properly; come and see him every week for four weeks, and then every two weeks for a while after that. She would have to tell him exactly how she felt and what she thought the drugs were doing to her.

"And..." he said, "...when, and as, you are ready, I will want you to tell me a bit about your past; what things make you happy, and what things make you sad, what makes you angry even. Not now, and not all in a rush, but when it feels right. That way I might be able to work out whether it's the gastric ulcer or the saucepan of milk, or a bit of both."

That was well over a year ago now; and he was right, it hadn't been easy. The drugs did have some nasty side effects. They made her tremble badly to start with, and they made her feel so painfully slow at everything. Some days she seemed to spend most of her time in the loo, and on others she felt dreadfully sick. And the looking forward business was all very well when Dr Smith talked about it so glibly in his office; but that turned out to be the worst of all. All those failed interviews for jobs, all those people who wouldn't take her on because she was honest about her past, all those long dreary evenings alone in that dismal room of the residential wing at the hospital, while she longed for a flat to become available; how could she look confidently forward through all that. All it did was remind her constantly of all the things she had lost. The children; she missed her children dreadfully, especially after that first summer holiday. For a whole week they were with her every day. They talked, laughed, swam, built sandcastles, played games in the evening, read stories at bedtime. It was the first time she had ever washed Flavvy's hair. And then it was over. Lytton's mother came and took them away; the pain was unbearable. The headaches began again; she started to slip.

"But they'll come again, Jackie," Dr Smith said, "and I wouldn't mind betting they know who their real mother is. Nobody can ever change that wherever they live!"

And Lytton; she had lost Lytton, and she loved him.

"Better to have loved and lost, than never to have loved at all!" Dr Smith said.

"A lost love can be as lacerating as a bereavement, but just as we tend to remember more of the best in those that we have loved and lost through death, so we do with those we have lost through break-up. But it wasn't easy, was it Jackie, loving and living with Lytton! It caused you a lot of pain as well at the time. But nobody can take the memory of the good bits away from you!"

Now she gave a quick last look around the flat to make sure that everything was ready and checked the table, yet again; she very much wanted this afternoon to be a success. She was lucky the cake and the scones turned out so well; just like the ones she used to make years ago. Think forward, think forward, she said to herself, and smiled. Think forward or not, there was no doubt that two or three years ago, the huge responsibility of making a simple cake would have been completely beyond her capability. The doorbell startled her, even though she was expecting it.

"Hello, Jackie dear, I hope I'm not too early!"

"No, no you're not! I'm all ready. Come in; let me take your coat."

Marjorie looked just the same. Breathing heavily, she struggled to get her arms free of the sleeves of her mac.

"Phew, thank you dear!" she said, as Jackie relieved her of the damp coat from behind, "I've been doing a few errands since lunch, and it's a bit blowy and drizzly out there!"

Jackie walked through the open door of her bedroom, and dropped Marjorie's coat on the bed, while Marjorie stood, nearly filling the doorway. Jackie thought she must have put on a bit of weight; surely she wasn't quite that big before.

"Oh, it's so nice to see you in your own place, dear!" Marjorie said, as though she really meant it, "And so kind of you to ask me to tea..."

Jackie smiled again. She found herself doing that more and more now, spontaneously; and after all that time when she thought she had forgotten how.

"Well it's only small, but I still get a little shiver of pleasure every time I put the key in the front door. Would you like to see the rest of it?"

She showed Marjorie the bathroom, and the cupboard in the hall, just to make the tour seem longer, and her tiny kitchen and then the sitting room with the French windows that she could open and sit by in the sun when the weather was good. She asked Marjorie to sit down and was amused to watch her choose an upright chair, rather than struggle down into her somewhat spongy settee.

"It's a lovely flat, dear. And you've made it very cosy and comfortable. How long have you been here now?"

Jackie mentally counted the months from the 10th December; she would never forget the date of moving day.

"It's a few days over nine months, now. I can't believe the time has gone so quickly. I've wanted you to come to tea with me for a long time.... after you were so kind to me; but there never seemed to be a suitable afternoon when I wasn't working. But today..."

"Oh yes dear, tell me...." Marjorie interrupted her before she had time to tell her that today was the first day of a whole two weeks of holiday.

"I knew you'd been working but I couldn't remember where?"

"In the office at the Leisure Centre..."

Marjorie interrupted her again, asking her how long she had been there and whether she enjoyed it.

"Well I started just before I got the flat; and actually it was very hard at first; particularly when they found out. I lied you see. Well I didn't lie exactly; I just didn't tell them I'd been in hospital; because every time I went for an interview, and was honest about having been ill, I never got the job. But then they found out at the leisure centre; and I had to go for more interviews and.... Anyway, in the end they very kindly kept me on; even sent me on a day release computer course ... and now the work is getting easier and I get on quite well with them all."

"Well, I take my hat off to you Jackie, dear!" Marjorie said, with a huge and motherly smile. "Just think, this time two years ago.... well I never would have thought it possible!"

Jackie said that perhaps she should make some tea now, and standing in the kitchen she remembered Dr Smith that morning when she left.

"Have a good holiday with the children, Jackie...." he said, "...and, although I must say that in some ways you are one of the lucky ones, you can still give yourself a little pat on the back for being the only patient I've got to have kept their job so long!"

Then he had said that, if she liked, they could leave it for eight weeks before her next appointment. Before she had met Dr Smith, Jackie would never, never have advised anyone to seek psychiatric help; but now? Dare she believe that she had turned the corner at last?

Back in the sitting room, Marjorie was standing by her sideboard, looking at her photographs.

"Are these your children, dear?" she asked, picking one up as Jackie reappeared.

"Yes;" Jackie said, joining her, and pointing the children out over Marjorie's shoulder, "That's Flavvy, she nearly seven now, and that's Jodie, she's ten, and Dane is going to be fourteen in September."

"They haven't taken your dark hair, have they dear? They're all quite blonde; but that little one looks just like you!"

"No, well my husband was... he's got fair hair. Anyway, I'll be seeing them all tomorrow. They're coming for a holiday."

The kettle switched itself off in the kitchen and Jackie left Marjorie holding the photograph.

"Well, that's nice, dear. I'm so pleased for you; are they coming to stay here?"

Carrying the old family teapot, that Nickii gave her when she moved into the flat, back into the sitting room, Jackie explained that they were all going to stay down at the cottage with her mother. She couldn't quite visualise herself coping with them all squashed into the flat. Well not yet anyway. Marjorie ate a healthy tea, but still managed to chatter merrily away, just as she always did. Jackie heard all about who had been in and out of the old house since she left, and how Marjorie was still trotting along there every morning with her bits of shopping, and keeping an eagle eye. Apparently there was quite a young girl in her old room at the moment.

"But it's such a shame, dear, because her time's nearly up. They're trying to move them on much more quickly now, you see; the

Society's got such a waiting list. But her feet have hardly touched the ground; came out of hospital much too soon anyway, if you ask me. She wasn't ready. It's a pity she's not with that new Dr Smith. He's a bit special it seems to me. Got a bit of a reputation for being a nuisance; but that's because he fights much harder for his patients. You see him, don't you Jackie, dear! "

Jackie nodded; was about to comment on the merits of Dr Smith, and offer Marjorie some cake. But before she could open her mouth, Marjorie was off again.

"I thought so; he took over all of old Dr Bulstrode's patients, but I suppose he can't see everybody, poor man. Anyway, our little Jenny's got nowhere to go. Parents are divorced; father's remarried and gone off to foreign parts; and mother lives up north somewhere, and doesn't want to know anyway; washed her hands of the whole thing, apparently..."

Then she asked Jackie how her mother was, barely waiting for her reply before enquiring about Claire, and then telling her, again, how well she had done herself.

Jackie need not have worried about what she was going to find to say; or indeed about her cooking. When Marjorie stood up and said that she really must be getting along now, there were only two scones left and, between them, they had made a sizeable hole in the cake.

Closing the door after all the goodbyes, and Marjorie saying for the umpteenth time how kind it was of Jackie to ask her and "do be sure to keep in touch, dear", Jackie felt a surge of relief and satisfaction together. She had done it. She had actually had someone to tea in her own flat. It was only when she was hastily clearing the table to be ready in time for when her mother came to pick her up, that she remembered that she meant to pluck up the courage to ask Marjorie about her son. The moment when Marjorie was looking at her photographs would have been a good time. But, never mind, Jackie thought, on reflection, perhaps it was just as well that she didn't; and then she dashed into the bedroom to put a few last things into her case.

CHAPTER TWENTY-FIVE

"Shall I choose your card for you?" Nickii said, without thinking.

Then she quickly looked around the shop to check that nobody was giving her funny looks for talking to herself. She often did it at home; said aloud things like, "Why don't you help me then?" when she was struggling to make the lawn mower start. Or, "Oh, alright then what am I doing wrong?" when she was wrestling with John's tools, trying to do repairs. She should stop it, then she wouldn't have to worry that she might do it in public. But of course there was no-one looking. The rest of W. H. Smith was carrying on in its own sweet way. Really she was there to find a birthday card for Claire, but it would have been their wedding anniversary tomorrow.

"Don't you think this is a bit silly?" he had half-whispered in her ear, having already made her jump by playfully poking her in the ribs.

"What's a bit silly?" she had hissed back, standing right here, by this very shelf unit.

"Well we both stand here in the same shop, at the same time, choosing cards which we then take home and give to each other. Why don't we just show each other here, it would be much cheaper!"

"Why you old skinflint!" she had said, with a return dig to his ribs, "Oh, alright then..."

"That one's yours!" she said now, with her lips firmly sealed, and then she moved along to the birthday cards.

She had picked out, looked at, and replaced three, before she realised that she simply was not concentrating. Forty-five years; forty-five years it would have been but they had only made forty-two; forty-two and a half, or three quarters to be precise. When people had told her that time would heal, she could remember thinking she didn't want it to. She could remember wishing that time would stand still, because when it moved, it was taking her further away from him. She even had an appalling dread that she might forget what he looked like, imagined, with horror, that there might come a day when she could no longer picture him in her mind. And later she read somewhere that it is not the people that die that leave, but the ones who are left living; as though the dead have just stepped off a train that goes racing on without them. That seemed to make sense with the way she felt, and she was right, the time had taken him further away. But at least she could still see him. She just did, as plain as a pikestaff, exactly as he was three or four years ago, standing there with the card in his hand and that familiar, and so badly missed, grin. But all those well wishers and sympathisers had been right too; because she could smile at the joke now, without the knife twisting around so hard in her heart. She finally chose a card for Claire. There wasn't a suitably funny one, they all seemed too corny, so she opted for a painting; an ethereal painting of a table and two deckchairs in the garden of a cottage. Having paid for the card and got out of Smiths, she was pleased to have finished all the niggly bits of shopping so that now she could go back to Waitrose and get the food for the weekend. She made a mental note, again, not to forget the baked beans and Daddies sauce for Michael.

As she walked briskly down South Street, dodging on and off the pavement around the lingerers, there was a man a few paces ahead of her in a beige coloured jacket; same height, same gait, same upright back, same silver grey hair, wrong neck. She looked away, concentrated her eyes on someone else. That still happened, all the time, everywhere she went. She supposed that it always would. But she was getting used to it; that fleeting gasp of hopeless excitement, followed by the obvious plunge back to the awful truth.

It took several trips from the garage to the front door to unload all the shopping from the car. Taking the last few bits out of the boot, she pushed down the lid and went to close the garage doors. Every time she did that now, she remembered the day when she had come home in the dark after being out all day. She was very tired, having fitted her shopping and a visit to the library in between her morning and afternoon art classes. As she had closed the garage doors there was a loud thump from inside the garage. She had opened the door again to see what it was, and immediately noticed that she hadn't turned the car lights off; then she had found that two library books, which she had put right in the middle of the car roof when she got out, had fallen to the floor. It had been amusing to wonder whether John had given the library books a quick shove off the roof, to save her from a flat battery. It did not do to share that kind of thought with everyone, but it was comforting nonetheless.

On her last trip today she noticed that there were enough winter iris in bloom against the cottage walls to fill two small vases. That's good, she thought, I could come out later and pick those. She always tried to put small vases of something in Michael and Claire and

Jackie's bedrooms, when they came for the weekend. It was a bonus to have some real flowers in winter.

Jackie always arrived before the others. One of her colleagues from the Leisure Centre gave her a lift on a Friday night. It saved Jackie having to wait for a bus, and meant she could get there a bit earlier. She looks a little bit peaky tonight, Nickii thought, as Jackie put her bag down by the hall table.

"You look tired!" she said, "Have you had a hard week?"

Nickii could not control the perpetual fear that something might jeopardise Jackie's fight for recovery. But Jackie tossed off her concern with a smile and a shake of her head.

"No, no, I'm fine," she said, " Michael and Claire are not here yet then; so I've got time for a quick bath before they arrive; that's good."

"Let's have some tea first!" Nickii suggested. "I bought some meringues in M&S for us to have with it. You will still have plenty of time for your bath."

Nickii lit the fire in the sitting room, which she had ready laid, and they sat beside it with their tea. Jackie showed her letters that she had had from the children that week. By the time she went off to have her bath, the colour had come back into her cheeks. I panicked again, Nickii thought, she is perfectly alright, just a little tired that's all.

"Hot chocolate, drinking chocolate," Claire muttered as they drove around the last bend.

"What was that?" Michael asked her.

It was the most positive thing she had said during the whole drive, and he didn't know what she meant.

"Oh nothing," she said, crossly again, "it's just that the sight of the pub, with its lights twinkling when we arrive, always reminds me of that advertisement for Drinking Chocolate."

Struggling in from the car, and up to the Laura Ashley bedroom, with their bags, Michael felt relieved to be there too; if only for the fact that a weekend with her mother might make Claire a bit more cheerful. She had been so crabby lately; he could hardly stand another day. He blamed that wretched book. If only she would just put it in a drawer and leave it alone.

They sat by the fire, drank some tea and he began to unwind.

"Have you done any more painting since we were last here?" he asked Nickii.

"Would anyone like more tea?" Claire said immediately.

"No thanks, not for me;" Nickii said, "we had one before you arrived; I'll be awash with tea if I have anymore."

She stood up then and turned to Michael.

"Yes," she said, "I think there is a portrait you haven't seen. Do you want to come and have a look?"

"Do you want another cup, Michael?" Claire asked as he and Nickii headed for the door.

"No thanks..." he said, over his shoulder, "...I'll be having a pint in the pub soon."

The chill hit them as soon as they walked into the studio, and Nickii gave a shiver as she lifted her painting on to the table in the middle of the room. The portrait was of a silver haired gentleman, with a rugged complexion and beetle brows. It had the feel of being a good likeness, even though Michael did not know the sitter.

"It's good," he said. "Who is he?"

"Oh, just one of the other members," Nickii said, "we can't always get a professional, so people sometimes have to volunteer; there's a horrible danger that I may have sit myself some day!"

Looking around at the rest of the paintings on the walls of her studio, Michael thought that portraits were definitely what Nickii did best. He said so to her, and they went on to discuss at some length how she went about it, and the different colours that she used to find the right skin tones.

"Have you brought your sketch books with you?" Nickii asked him, after a while. "Are there any I haven't seen?"

Michael had brought the books, but had left them in the car on purpose. Always embarrassed by having people look at his work, he also thought it presumptuous to think that they would be interested. But Nickii was pushy, so he went out to the car to get them. Spread over the kitchen table, Nickii devoured all the old sketches that she had already seen before even getting to the new ones. She was profuse with her praise as usual, which embarrassed him again.

"I've been daubing, as Claire calls it, some of them lately;" he said, to cover his confusion, "she says she likes them plain, but I enjoy putting a bit of colour to them. I would really like to get back to doing some real watercolours, but it's all a question of time and determination, I suppose."

Nickii suggested that an art holiday would be a way of getting him back into the habit of regular painting. She gave him an animated account of the one she had been on in Italy last year with a friend from one of her societies. She was just going off to get some of her magazines to demonstrate just how many there were available when Jackie came through from the sitting room.

"Are we going to the pub before they close, or what?" she said, "Claire and I are sitting in there with our stomachs rumbling!"

CHAPTER TWENTY-SIX

So an art holiday it was and, staring dejectedly out of the window, Claire watched white clouds, and some threateningly not so white, racing across the backdrop of a blue sky. She wished she could see more from her position there on the edge of the bed. If she had to sit staring out of the window, it would be nice to see more than the sky. But to do that she would have had to stand up and open the sloping roof window. From there she could look down into the courtyard, or across the lane and the fields to the church up by the main road. But she could not summon the energy. She was enveloped in inertia; rooted by the inactivity in her body, and over activity in her brain, to the insipid beige candlewick bedspread of an alien hotel room.

Sitting sideways, taut as a high wire, with legs crossed and curled ankle around ankle, she listened to the drone of the hoover, smoothing its lines on to the carpet in the next room. She had had to wait a while after breakfast, sit reading the paper downstairs in the bar, and then take a turn around the courtyard and the farmhouse, while young girls in overalls had worked the same magic in this room. They had also left fresh and fluffy, neatly folded, clean towels over the rail in the bathroom; washed the brown stains from their morning tea cups, and stuffed the little bowl on the tray with more tea bags, sugars and individual Nescafe packets in their dark brown wraps. There seemed to be more packets than usual. Claire was grateful for their kindness in noticing that she had used up yesterday's entire ration. She looked at the clean cups, stacked upside down on the clean saucers, and thought that she could have a coffee now. She could make coffee; she could get up and look out of the window; or something else, have a bath, paint her toenails, anything, rather than do what she actually came here to do.

All she had done since she got back into the room was to spread the neatly made bed with the whole of the contents of one of their overnight bags; just as she had done yesterday, and the day before that. Spread about her, over almost every inch of the candlewick were three folders, a thesaurus, the Collins English dictionary, a stack of three virgin, ruled, hole-punched A4 refill pads, her favourite pens, pencils that she had bought that may write more easily than pens, and a pile of miscellaneous papers that she might want.

"We've got the car! Why not just take everything you think you need." Michael had said. So she did.

She looked away from it all and back at the racing sky. Her mind raced with it, flitting backwards and forwards, as it might in a dream. How did she come to be here? Sitting alone, lonely, on a strange bed, watching the sky race over Anglesey, of all places. Anglesey, where it is cold and windy, and it rains for at least a part of every single day. Anglesey, where they came for a holiday; when, which year? It was the year, whichever year that was, that Claire had started her periods. She could remember feeling uncomfortable, gangly and awkward. There was a photograph in one of her mother's albums of her with burgeoning breasts, stuffed under a bright pink sun top; standing beside a donkey on the beach. Claire was sulky, confused, and difficult and, she remembered, feeling sorry for herself and misunderstood. Jackie was bright, chirpy, fun and lovable. She was wearing pale blue shorts and her thick brown hair was blown off her face. Her cheeky smile shone out of the picture. Even thinking about that photograph made Claire cringe. Why? Why, she asked herself, did that particular memory upset her? It should be a pleasant, warm and comfortable feeling to reminisce about being young, on holiday, and all together.

Her brain hurt. She delved into the very depths of it, while staring at a gap of beige candlewick left between the folders on the bed. She saw the photograph again; herself standing gangly and tall, holding the donkey's reins with a false and affected smile, probably where her father had said, "Say cheeeese...." and Jackie, much shorter and still with the rounded face of childhood, laughing genuinely, with the wind in her hair. And then Claire realised that it was that old enemy guilt again; the fact that she knew that there were times when the child in her had enjoyed Jackie's illness, because it turned Jackie into the sulky one, and Claire the one with some fun and laughter left.

Suddenly she found herself standing by the open window, looking down into the courtyard. There was nothing new in that. Why should this old acknowledgement of her own weakness come back now to haunt her? She had worked that out years ago; come to terms with it; forgiven herself. Slowly she came to the conclusion that the only reason for her depression was simply the same old self-deprecation that she still, still after all this time and two whole days of peace and quiet, was more or less at square one with her father's book. It was nearly four whole years now.

She gulped in the fresh air. Two grey-haired ladies ambled across the courtyard; setting off in search of subjects, loaded with bags, easels and folding chairs. Others were dotted around the landscape; small figures already encamped and nuzzled into nooks and crannies, ready for their morning's creativity. Claire experienced a surge of the greenest envy at their industrious attempts; their prospects of achieving something whilst she sat up there, confused, inept and inert. She couldn't see her mother anywhere, or Michael.

Looking back into the room, and the littered bed, common sense told her that she was going to get nowhere in this pent-up state. So, decisively, she took her old black car jacket from the back of the chair, and their room key from the dressing table. She would take just half an hour, get the wind and the sun on her skin and calm down; seek out Michael and her mother, say hello, and then come back, refreshed and able to concentrate.

The reception desk was deserted as she came downstairs. In the dining room, the girls that served their breakfast were busy re-laying the tables for the next meal, giggling over their private conversations. Claire could hear bottles chinking in the bar, presumably where somebody was restocking it, ready for the lunchtime session. The atmosphere reminded her of being in school at playtime when everyone was meant to be outside. As she pushed through the swing doors into the porch, two Yorkshire Terriers jumped up from their banished positions on the mat outside the door and scrambled around her feet. She bent down; stuffed the door key in her pocket, so that she could stroke them both at the same. Then, as she walked away, they settled dejectedly back down where they were, to await their next diversion. They reminded her of the Yorkshire terrier that Jackie had when she was a teenager after Claire had left home. There were photographs of her laughing with him too.

She found her mother nestled in behind a bush; perched uncomfortably on her aluminium chair, she was bending down to reach the paints on the ground beside her, and on the board on her lap she had already sketched out the small stream and the grasses in front of her, with the church on the hill in the background.

"You haven't wasted any time!" Claire said.

Startled, her mother turned round and said the painting wasn't going to be any good, but she couldn't find anything else to do. They always say that, Claire thought, and asked her if she knew where Michael was.

"He's hidden himself over in that field behind the hedge. He said he was going somewhere where 'teacher' couldn't find him! How are you getting on?"

Nickii said, still concentrating on the wash that she seemed to be smothering all over her sketch.

Claire muttered something about being fine herself, and for Nickii to keep up the good work. Then she said she would see her at lunchtime and wandered off towards the gate into the field. She had to strain her eyes, gazing around until she spotted him, well camouflaged against the hedge on the other side. Several black and white cows stared lazily at her as she began to walk across the damp grass; she could hear sheep bleating somewhere, and the hedges were alive with birdsong. She decided, then and there, that she could not spend the rest of the morning in that room. Reaching Michael, she said 'hello' and asked him if he was likely to want the car. When he asked her where she was thinking of going she told him 'just for a ride'.

"Anything to put off doing any work!" he teased.

But the words tingled like needles in her skin.

Back up in their room, she gathered all the folders, papers and paraphernalia from the dented candlewick, and stuffed them back into the bag; in her hurry to escape, the last pile collapsed all over the bed, and the floor. Claire tutted with irritation, and then, scrabbling them back together, she caught a glimpse of her father's handwriting on the dog-eared old envelope that had carried their homework backwards and forwards to each other all those years ago. That tingled too, but she laid it on top of the pile of stuff in the bag, and heaving that off the bed, left the empty room behind her.

With the bag full of papers on the passenger seat, she turned left out of the hotel, away from the main road and drove deeper into the country lanes, letting fate and intuition tell her where to go. The sun was shining. The lanes were empty, except for the odd farm vehicle or cyclist. She drove slowly, wound down the window to let in the air and the sounds, and she began to feel better. And then, suddenly, as she rounded a bend, there in front of her was a mass of tumbling yellow laburnum, glinting in the sunshine and dripping down over a crumbling old stone post. She stopped the car to admire it again; then pulled off the road and onto a small grassy clearing in front of the tree. She switched off the engine and drank in the peace and tranquillity.

After a while, she turned and took the old envelope from the top of the bag, turning it over and then over again, she fingered it, dreamt a little, and then looked away and studied the splendour of the laburnum. Eventually, she put the envelope down on her lap, took one of the virgin A4 pads and any old pen, the first that came to hand, from the bag. Resting the pad on the steering wheel, she began to write....

Dear Dee,
Since other people are still writing to you after all this time, I don't see why I shouldn't too. It used to upset Mummy, all the mail you got; at least one item in every post at the beginning. She used to write back to the senders, tell them of your whereabouts, and ask them to stop, but still the same old stuff kept coming. Then I think she tried some sarcasm, said there was no forwarding address where you'd gone. In the end I think it was just the passing of time that stemmed the flow, but even now there's still a steady trickle. Only the other day, when we went to pick her up, I saw a holiday brochure, and something from one of the Building Societies addressed to Mr J Tolley. As you have no need of holidays or investments now, we don't bother to forward them; it wouldn't be worth the postage!

Seriously though, it seems such a very long time since you left, and quite a lot has changed in that time. The landscape for one thing; the woods at Slindon still haven't recovered from the hurricane. It looks like the surface of the moon along that road. And it seems to me we have had many more strong winds since that one. I hate them. They feel like an omen of something horrid happening.

What else? Well, you should see the garden at the cottage, and what a difference four years makes. The clematis and rock plants have grown all around the pond that you had just finished building, and it looks as though it has been there for ever. There's a frog that has taken up residence; but he seems to live there all alone. I feel sorry for him and wonder why he doesn't find a mate; but perhaps the truth is that he likes to have it all to himself, and he fights off all intruders! I am sorry to have to report that the orgasmic fountain that made you giggle had to go. It kept getting bunged up, and poor old Em was for ever paddling in the green slime trying to make it work; she has got a more modest but reliable, one now. All the trees and hedges have matured, and Michael put in a new gate for Mummy to go into the field because the stile collapsed; yes, even in spite of all those nails. And speaking of nails; do you remember that little chest of drawers that you used to keep your screws and nails in in the shed? Well, Em has given it 'a do' and now it's resplendent indoors as a home for all the cutlery and fiddly kitchen bits.

Pippa's finished her course and she's living at home with us now and working in the local hospital, and David's got himself a good job and a really lovely girlfriend; you would like her. The recession's not so hot though; you would have hated that. Reading the financial pages every day would have been enough to put you back in the hospital I reckon. But you'll be pleased to know that Em has more or less kept her head above water financially, thanks to you leaving everything in such good order.

Things haven't been quite so good for us though. Michael's firm can't seem to get any work and people seemed to stop wanting to pay an outsider to do their secretarial work. Still, I was fed up with that anyway; but I had to get some money in from somewhere, so now I'm working as a doctors' receptionist. It's alright but I do seem to get rather a lot of headaches these days and I had to give up the writing classes. (Writing is really what I'm meant to be writing to you about, but I'll fill you in on all the gossip first!) We couldn't afford to run both cars anymore so we sold the Renault and the Celica and bought one ropey old Ford. The day the Celica went was really ghastly and I wondered whether you were watching and thought what a traitor I was! Em felt the same when your car went; she was really upset. How <u>did</u> you get all that mud on it by the way?

This is the first holiday we've been on in ages. Can you see us here in sunny Anglesey? Actually the sun really is shining at the moment, and I am sitting here in the ropey old Ford, under a truly beautiful laburnum tree. It's almost like heaven, or is it? Em and Michael are back there at the centre, beavering away over their paintings. Do you know, sometimes they drive me mad with their bloody art! Every weekend when we go down there, they're off immediately discussing their paintings and pouring over their magazines and books; they're like a couple of old hens clucking. And here we are in Anglesey (of all places) with a load of other old hens all busy achieving all day so they can all cluck over their achievements together in the evenings.

If that sounds a bit bitchy, it's because sometimes I feel a bit bitchy. Do you remember when I was little and I used to say that things were 'unjust', and then you used to say that the world isn't just, it was never meant to be just, and all that stuff about 'never promising you a rose garden'? Well, you were right, it is not just, because I've got nobody to cluck with. Of course I don't **really** mind Michael and Em hobnobbing about their art. It's been such fun for both of them and it's nice that they've got such a passionate interest in common. But what is so unjust' (don't smirk at me!) is that we can't hobnob about our writing anymore; we were just beginning to get going and then you buggered off!

Not only do I not hobnob about writing anymore, I don't actually write either, well not properly; I just seem to waste an awful lot of time thinking about it. I stopped doing the articles and stories a long time ago – (that reminds me though – you remember those competition leaflets you thrust on me after the Writers' Day at Worthing? Well I bunged in one of my old stories for one of those and won a small prize which was quite satisfying!) But anyway, I stopped doing the short pieces because what I have really wanted to do for the last three and some years was 'Creole'! Which brings me to the real purpose of this letter. You see I simply have to explain to you how I feel about it all, or I will burst. And please forgive me if the explanation seems a little incoherent because bursting is what my head's been doing for so long now that it hurts! Well anyway, here goes!

Let's go back to the very beginning; in those days when I was staying with Em at the cottage just after you'd first... well, gone! The first problem was that I couldn't work your computer and there was no one to tell me how. (And where you'd got it from I don't know because hunt as we might we couldn't find any manual!) Of course one of the differences that even only four years has made, is that the world is full of computers now, and so I am more computer literate. But anyway, then I wasn't, and in spite of the old 'if at first you don't succeed' philosophy, in the end I gave up with it. (And I think Em did too and gave it away, I'm afraid!) So I was left with only the hard copy you had, and I had to assume there was nothing more hidden in that impenetrable machine.

Then, when I began to study the difference between what you'd been working on in those last few weeks, and your original draft, I could see that you were making some very radical changes. I really needed to get inside your mind to see how you meant to carry on. I did try. Believe me, I really did try; but the harder I tried the more difficult it became and the more I was forced to realise the obvious – that my mind wasn't your mind, and even fathers and daughters don't think the same. (In fact perhaps it's even less likely with father's and daughters than two totally independent spirits; anyway rhubarb,

rhubarb...) You see, even from the beginning, when you first started to write the book, our visions of the story were fundamentally different; and then you left and the story went on living and it's changed a lot since then, and will go on changing I suppose. And there we have a good point that we could have hob-nobbed over! 'Where do you draw the line if the origin of your story is grounded in fact?' But I must get back to my garbled explanation....

...In your story the main character was Lytton, sorry 'Creole'! But it was Lytton who obsessed you because of all the pain he had given you over so many years and all the things he did to Jackie. But, although I hated the hurt he had caused you all, it didn't mean the same to me. There were, and still are, different passions from the same story that burn within my head. And, incidentally, the harder I tried to work on 'Creole' the more strange I found it that you'd actually given him quite an easy time. It was as though by writing about him for so many months, you came to understand him, almost like him, and then you couldn't give him the punishments you felt he really deserved. YOU SEE WE REALLY NEEDED TO TALK ABOUT ALL THIS!

(That was just me stamping my feet up and down and saying life's 'unjust'! But I'll calm down now and try to concentrate....)

For me Lytton is relatively insignificant. I don't feel he deserves all that attention. Let me tell you a little story that'll explain the way I feel about him.... David's new girlfriend is a real case; she's slim, attractive, blonde and witty. I'm really fond of her and I know you would like her a lot. Anyway she was always saying 'Oh Dily to that' or just 'dily' with a little smile and shake of her head and eventually we had to ask her what this 'dily' was. She was a bit coy about telling us then; but it came out in the end; and what it was was an acronym for 'Do I Look As If I Give a Fuck?" (A bit rude, I know, but you won't mind that!) Which comes to DILAIIGUF which, being a bit long, they shortened to Dilai (I assume although I'd heard it as 'Dily').

So, as far as I'm concerned, Dily to Lytton. What mattered to me was that Jackie was ill and even though her life with Lytton may have acted as the trigger, it was still her actual illness that loomed larger in my mind. She was ill and nobody seemed able to help her and, what's more, nobody seemed able to help you while you tried to cope with it. And I couldn't cope with it either and so many; many times I've wished I had done more to help you. But now the time has moved on.; and all the time I've been trying to work on Creole, the story has been changing, so that now another issue keeps popping up in my version of it. That is that the situation you left was so awful. Jackie was desperately ill. She was still married to the man you thought was the cause of all her problems; and she was living alone and lost in that ghastly house with no job, no prospects and no children. But what is so sad is that you can't see her now. If you could see her now you would do one of those little hop, skippedy, jigs, like you did that New Year's Eve on all the balloons. Perhaps you **can** see, perhaps you **have** done the hop, skippedy jig, but I can't know that can I? So I'll tell you about it anyway. She's got her flat. She's got her job – she's had it for well over two years I think – and only a few weeks ago she had all the children to stay with her for Easter. You should see them now too; they're really nice kids. Dane's got incredibly tall, Jodie seems really bright (I'm horribly afraid she's got the writing bug; she writes really good essays and letters). Flavvy's grown into an affectionate bubbly little kid. There's absolutely no doubt they know who their mum is! And Jackie's got her wit and sense of humour back. It would make you so happy to see.

But Lytton is history. He's an insignificant figure in the background of our lives. He's history but you're not. Which is funny considering he's alive and well and living ... I can hardly even remember where, except that I send birthday cards to the kids so I must have the address somewhere... and you're not alive, and living we don't know where. Do you remember once we had one of those 'afterlife' conversations, and you said that perhaps the quality of a spirit's afterlife was concomitant with the amount that they were remembered? Well, if that is the scheme of things, you must be bobbing around somewhere, because I can tell you that you are very much not history. I wonder sometimes whether you can see us turning the salad cream bottle upside down to get the very last dregs out in your name! And when Michael tossed an old black banana in the bin the other day and told you... yes even sceptical old Michael talks to you sometimes.... told you that he was sorry, he didn't care what you thought because the banana was beyond redemption and it had to go! We tease you in some way or another almost every day, fondly, of course!

Do you know my fingers have gone numb and my wrist is aching but I feel so much better. The bad news is that I have just looked at my watch and it's a quarter to three! I think I may be in trouble for not going back for lunch so I had better go soon. I think that what I have been trying to say is that I can't finish 'Creole' however much I want to fulfil my promise to you. I have come to realise that my book will have to be a different tale. If I ever get to write it I hope you will approve. Now I'm going to put all these pages of scribble into our old envelope. You didn't leave a forwarding address; so I'll have to put it back with all the other sheaves of paper! Then I think I will have to start right back at the very beginning, and do it my way!

I'm sorry! We miss you!

With all my love,

Claire.

P.S. If you've got anything at all to do with the robin at the end of the garden, please give me a wink to show you don't mind?